The Sycamore Tree

Christine Brooke-Rose

Forthcoming reprint titles:

A Grammar of Metaphor
Next
Dear Deceit
The Middlemen
Go When You See The Green Man Walking

by Christine Brooke-Rose

Forthcoming titles:

The Letters of Christine Brooke-Rose
Poems & Other Paraphernalia

edited by G. N. Forester & M. J. Nicholls

The Logαλφαgeis of kLeubʰ: /laːf/; /lʌv/

by Chretine Broke-Prose

other Verbivoracious titles @

www.verbivoraciouspress.org

The Sycamore Tree

Christine Brooke-Rose

Verbivoracious Press

Glentrees, 13 Mt Sinai Lane, Singapore

This edition published in Great Britain & Singapore

by Verbivoracious Press

www.verbivoraciouspress.org

Copyright © 2014 Verbivoracious Press

Text Copyright © 2014 The Estate of Christine Brooke-Rose

All rights reserved. No part of this publication may be re-produced, stored in an electronic or otherwise retrieval system, or transmitted in any form or by any means, electronic, mechanical, digital imaging, re-cording, otherwise, without the prior consent of the publisher.

The Estate has asserted the moral right of Christine Brooke-Rose to be identified as the author of this work.

ISBN: 978-981-07-9381-4

Printed and bound in Great Britain & Singapore

First published in Great Britain by Secker & Warburg 1958.

Chapter One

"**T**HIS is the opening sentence which I lost." Gael Jackson's protesting tone carried the unreality of his words as a harmonic progression sometimes lends conviction to some inane melody.

His publisher, who was inured to the oddity of authors, looked at him patiently, waiting for the explanatory development which usually follows incomprehensible statements in most printed texts; but Mr Quentin Yellowstone, Solicitor, expert on libel, did not like the inanity of the melody, and tapped the desk deliberately with his pencil, like a conductor stopping a rehearsal.

"What," he barked, "precisely—" he yapped "—do you mean by 'lost?'"

"Well———" Gael Jackson havered, then cleared his throat. He was a quiet man by disposition, and disliked having to give any account of himself or his working methods, especially to strangers and comparative strangers—for Mr Thomas Truelove, in spite of his name and unlike some publishers who like to cultivate an intimate acquaintance with the intricacies of their authors' literary plans, personal ambitions and private lives, Mr Truelove, of Truelove & Thorne, Ltd, was a comparative stranger.

"Well," Gael Jackson repeated, and decided there was nothing for it but to reveal the magic spells which set his inmost mind in motion. He spoke with a barely perceptible American accent, a slight nasalisation of vowels and blurring of consonants beneath the Oxford veneer.

"I can't start a novel unless I have the opening sentence and the last sentence. This particular opening sentence we're discussing, I suddenly thought of and carried in my head for a few weeks. I was very happy because it meant I could start the novel during the following summer vacation." He paused and looked anxiously around the oak-panelled room, as if the rings on the wood were recording the waves of sound in their mysterious grooves. "I had no idea what the novel would be about," he went on, "but I was content to let things simmer at the back of my mind, knowing that it would all come out once I wrote down the opening sentence and had the leisure to go on. Then suddenly," his voice dropped, on account of the spies in the secret panels, "I lost it. For weeks I carried on with my tutorials, all the time trying to remember what that sentence was. You see, I can only write during the summer vacation, so I had to find it before then."

"Well?" snapped Mr Quentin Yellowstone.

"Then I found it. I had just corrected the last B.A. Honours paper, and as I wrote 'beta-double-minus', the sentence came back into my mind, I jotted it down, and found myself writing a novel, although I was exhausted, and without allowing myself even a week's rest."

"Really, Mr Jackson," the solicitor said, "this is all very interesting, but it proves nothing whatsoever."

"I think Mr Jackson was trying to show pure coincidence," Mr Truelove intervened a little gruffly. "No malice, you know."

"That is entirely beside the point."

Mr Quentin Yellowstone tapped the large mahogany desk once more. He was facing Mr Truelove, in a high-backed Victorian plush chair, just outside the ring of light thrown by the desk lamp, and only the fact that his feet barely touched the floor revealed his small stature to Gael Jackson's observant eye, for his appearance was otherwise distinguished: thick silvery hair that gleamed in the flicker from a mountainous fire in the old-fashioned grate behind him, at the far end of the big room; flat, receding ears, an aquiline nose and sharp dark eyes set close together. Gael Jackson was sitting to the left of Mr Truelove's desk, not quite on his publisher's side, nor, indeed, on the solicitor's. He was, after all, the victim. Someone he had never heard—or part of someone—had apparently got into his story, and was threatening to sue him for libel. The novel, with its static title, *The Sycamore Tree*, and its dynamic dust-jacket, lay in a pool of light in front of Mr Truelove. Mr Quentin Yellowstone had another copy of it in his hand, open at page one. 'Why this fashion for mud backgrounds in jackets?' Gael thought. 'Mud, bile, and blood.' A nursery rhyme kept going round in his head:

'This is the book that Jackson wrote
This is the phrase that opened the book that Jackson wrote
This is the ego described in the phrase
That opened the book...'

He tried hard to concentrate on what the solicitor was saying.

"You don't have to prove malice for libel. It is sufficient for the plaintiff to show that several people have recognised him in a character, even if the name is fictitious, and that his reputation has suffered. Sometimes the mere coincidence of a name is enough. Mr Truelove, I am surprised at you. You are perfectly aware of the legal position. But—" he checked Mr Truelove's protest and raising his right hand, which was not holding the novel, like a witness swearing on the Bible "—you were naturally attempting to defend your author. I quite understand. This letter, however,"—his right hand came down with a thick forefinger upon a document lying before him on the desk—"does not complain of malice. Mr Howard Cutting, as you see, is protesting about a character who, though his name is different, is described in terms coincidental with certain features by which he says he is well known. Now, let me see, what are they?" He peered down the letter, "a reviewer of books, an expert on Carlyle, short of stature, a failed writer."

"That seems to have got him on the raw." Mr Truelove chuckled and stroked his five-o'clock shadow. It was only half-past three on a foggy November afternoon, but he was one of those dark, thick-set men who needed and did not get two shaves a day. His hair was also greying, but had thinned considerably more than that of Mr Quentin Yellowstone; his face, unlike the solicitor's, was rubicund, with gracious living and publishers' long luncheons.

"Quite so. Indeed—" Mr Yellowstone's shrewd eyes twinkled "—one of his conditions is that the character in question should be depicted as a success."

"But I can't do that!" Gael Jackson looked astounded. "The entire plot depends on his being a failure."

"Quite so, quite so, 'If the author takes out the reference to Carlyle,'" the solicitor read aloud, "'and changes *failed writer* into *successful writer* on page four, I shall be willing to overlook the opening sentence, which is of a more private nature, and to withdraw my proposed action.'"

> 'This is the author all forlorn
> That hit the ego described in the phrase
> That opened the book...'

"Who is this man, anyway?" asked Gael Jackson. "I've never heard of him."

Mr Truelove looked at him askance.

"You've not heard of Howard Cutting? My dear man, where do you live? And you a writer. Why, I believe he gave your last novel a very good review."

"Oh." There was a short pause while Gael Jackson felt very unworldly. "You see, I never read the papers. In fact," he added with embarrassment, "I never read my reviews."

Mr Truelove's eyes registered blank astonishment for a moment, followed quickly, as in a cash machine clicking up 'No Sale', with plain disbelief. Really, this author was getting on his nerves, with his innocent, staring blue eyes, his ivory face, ivory hair, ivory-tower complex and his damnable flaunted integrity. Gael Jackson's philosophic fantasies were politely received by the intelligentsia, enthusiastically analysed by a few cranks, and ignored by the greater part of the buying public. Mr Truelove liked to have him on his otherwise fairly middlebrow list, but he was hardly worth proceedings in court, even for the publicity involved. A libel case won might mean extra sales, but a libel case lost meant pulping the entire edition.

"We always send you the press-clippings," he said doubtfully.

"I know. My wife keeps them for me. She reads them and sums up the general impression in one word—'Good' or 'bad'—that's enough for me to carry on."

"Mrs Jackson no doubt," the solicitor put in maliciously, "always says 'good?'"

Gael Jackson smiled.

"Well, I've only written two novels, so far, apart from this one. And I did carry on. One learns nothing from the critics," he added, a shade smugly. "The public, yes, small though mine may be. A handful of letters from unknown readers—that's what counts. Then they may tell others, perhaps, and a few more letters may come. I write for individual people; not to please the reviewers."

"That's all very well, Jackson," said Mr Truelove, "but there's no point in annoying them either. They're the ones who advise the handful"—he stressed the word 'handful'—"to buy your book."

"I wonder now," Mr Yellowstone put in. "A friend of mine, who worked in a bookshop, used to ask customers why they bought certain books, which had been grossly —er—misrepresented—by the critics. The answer— especially from ladies—was invariably that they had had such marvellous reviews." He shook his head and smiled. "Space, space, that's all the public remembers, not contents."

"If you don't mind, Yellowstone, I think I know a little more about the value of reviews and publicity than you do. I repeat, there is no point whatsoever in gratuitously annoying reviewers."

"But I don't," Gael Jackson protested. "I merely avoid reading them. They can't know this and surely wouldn't care anyway. They don't write to please the authors, any more than we write to please reviewers. They write to show off their judgement, under pretence of informing the public. And as for this unfortunate coincidence, I tell you, I have never heard of this Howard—what did you say his name was?"

"Cutting."

For one alarming moment the name rang a very faint bell in Gael Jackson's mind. But no. It must have been the previous mention of him.

'This is the cur with the crumpled corn
That sued the author all forlorn

That hit the ego described in the phrase
That opened the book that Jackson wrote.'

He sighed and shook his head. Mr Quentin Yellowstone looked kindly at him and offered him a cigarette.

"No thanks, I don't."

Mr Truelove took one and the two lit up. The cigarettes were expensive, Turkish, and filled the panelled room with a luxurious aroma that rose to caress the book-lined wall behind the publisher's grey head, and up into the intricate cornices of the Victorian ceiling.

"Look, Jackson, we believe you," said Mr Truelove in a conciliating tone. "Coincidences do happen and it's all most unfortunate. This man Howard Cutting was unheard of two years ago. He wrote a pretentious little travel book about—er—Morocco, I believe, or South Africa—I didn't read it. Full of phoney politics, I gather. On the strength of it, and by dint of much pushing, he was given a job on *The Sunday Supplement*, which—in case you have never heard of that—was launched last year, by a banker with intellectual pretensions. The idea was to arbitrate between the two main Sunday papers, whose reviewers—those writers you never read—always flatly contradict each other on any one play, or film, or book. I won't bother you with names, but this banker got hold of all the newest upstarts he could get—mostly not so youngish chaps in their thirties who had somehow failed to make the grade as bright young men. He put them in as editors, literary editors, and columnists. It caught on like an epidemic! Nobody knows how they do it—some say they have spies on the other papers who steal the proofs. The fact remains, their articles do successfully and disarmingly arbitrate between those of the other two papers, even parodying them. It's quite uncanny, and their circulation shot up. Howard Cutting now influences quite a section of the intelligent reading public, and he has in a remarkably short time, become a fairly well lunched and cocktailed figure in publishing and literary circles. Rather inevitably he is known in the trade as Press Cutting. I met him once at some party. An insignificant little man, who seemed anxious to please. But his column—well, that's another matter."

Gael Jackson dug his heels in and out of the thickly piled red carpet as this little speech on world affairs proceeded. Howard Cutting. He searched his memory. He gazed at his shoes. A travel book. South Africa. Morocco. He had never been there. The publisher and solicitor seemed to be smoking their cigarettes in a silent rhythmic harmony, reaching for the large glass ashtray at the same time, and puffing out their fumes like two soloists conspiratorially doubling each other in the coolest kind of jazz. They would no doubt lay down their instruments together in due course.

"How does Carlyle come into this?" he asked at last.

"Well, he says here——" Mr Quentin Yellowstone read from the letter again. "'I am well-known in literary circles as an expert on Carlyle. A year ago I wrote to the *Times Literary Supplement*, asking for any biographical information or letters anyone might possess to be sent to me, as I was preparing a new study of him. And although I have not yet had much time to get very far with it, I have reviewed several books about him or his period.' It is strange," Mr Yellowstone commented, "how little can turn a man into an expert."

"Maybe he is really an expert," said Gael Jackson charitably. "Look, if that's the only identifying feature, I can remove it without affecting the plot. The character can be an expert on someone else. The other things could refer to anyone."

"But the book is printed!" Mr Truelove exclaimed. "Copies have gone out for review, that's how Cutting got hold of it. If he had seen a proof, yes, but we can't reprint the whole edition. If he persists, we either go to court, or withdraw the book. Going to court means taking a fifty-fifty chance on winning—and if we don't win we still have to withdraw the book, losing considerably more than we lose on you anyway."

Gael Jackson shouldered the snub with a carefully careless shrug, but he felt too stung to speak.

"Furthermore," said Mr Yellowstone, "there is this opening sentence which you lost," he added with a smile, "and found again. The one about the fish."

"It was a carp," Gael Jackson particularised wearily, "slowly baked in white wine, with a bayleaf."

"A carp, indeed it was." The lawyer read the sentence silently and there was a long pause as it caught his interest and led his eye further down the page, into the hinted intricacies of an intriguing situation, laid by the traps of words and phrases which are the materials of the storyteller's humble talent. "It seems that a lady dropped the head of a carp she was serving for dinner, on the floor before a gathering of distinguished guests . . . after a telephone call—dear me, was the telephone in the dining room?"

"Yes, it was, on a side table. It was a small flat, you see, and this was a dining alcove," Gael Jackson explained with fervour. Then he added politely: "You have a novelist's eye for detail."

"Thank you, thank you. I like things to be right. I see you make this clear further down. The telephone conversation, I take it, flustered the lady?"

"Yes. It was from her lover. She is the wife of this expert on—er—Carlyle—and they were entertaining some important people."

"I see. Well, Mr Howard Cutting says in his letter that a similar incident occurred at a dinner in his home—only it was a salmon, and his wife dropped the whole salmon. The telephone call was not, he says, from a lover, for as far as he knows his wife has no lover, but a great joke was made about the salmon jumping, and his friends would certainly remember the incident. Naturally, he feels that the opening of your novel must have been based on hearsay, and, together with the other—er—coincidences, reflect disadvantageously on both him and his wife."

Gael Jackson got up and paced the soft carpet. How on earth had all this happened? Telepathy? He winced at unpleasant memories of psychic disturbances. Nina laughingly called him a mystic, and she teased him about his premonitions and second sight, which were never quite proven. He had long ceased to speak about them, and even dismissed them from his mind as superstitions, so that when occasionally they came about, he had successfully forgotten the forebodings, and experienced no more than vague unease. It was the idea about the telephone that had produced the carp. A whole novel entirely in telephone conversations, that was the original conception. But he had dropped it as impracticable.

"You see," he blurted out unexpectedly, "people don't write letters any more. The art is lost. They ring up. Richardson could compose a novel out of letters. In the future we shall probably get books called *The Collected Telephone Conversations of So-and-So* instead of *The Collected Letters*, especially with all this telephone tapping."

His publisher looked at him as if he were a lunatic. Mr Quentin Yellowstone dismissed this apparent *non sequitur* with a forensic "hmmm" followed by an unforensic silence. They reached for the ashtray in unison and stubbed their cigarettes.

"What am I to do?" Gael Jackson asked wearily.

"Settle it out of court," said the lawyer.

"Make friends with him," said the publisher. "Ask him to dinner to talk it over. Make it grand, ply him with the best drinks. I'll advance you the money. As far as I know, Howard Cutting has never refused an invitation."

"And if that doesn't work?"

"We'll either have to withdraw the book or go to court. So make it snappy."

Mr Quentin Yellowstone was nodding his large head wisely. Gael Jackson bowed and walked to the oaken door, lifting with effort what felt like two heavy clay feet from the soft, springy crimson carpet.

Chapter Two

HOWARD CUTTING indeed never refused an invitation. Not that he received as many as Mr Truelove had implied, nor was he so well or so widely known. Messrs Truelove & Thorne, Ltd, tended to overrate the value of reviews. *The Sunday Supplement* was a novelty, and much talked of in the firm as a potential snark-hunter, a powerful dragnet trailed to catch the floating votes, but in fact, like the Liberal Party, it did little more than scatter the public's buying power, and confuse the literary issues among a vanguard minority, who liked to be told what to think in black and white. It had so far attracted little attention, it was poorly printed, a rag really, and was not doing well. Howard Cutting was invited to a few parties and lunches, mostly by small publishers who considered themselves *avant-garde*, for want of greater respectability and security; and by the rich, old-fashioned firm of Truelove & Thorne, who liked to keep in—for want of infallible literary judgement—touch.

Besides never refusing an invitation, Howard Cutting also never turned down an offer. He would write any article, for any paper or magazine he could get into, however insignificant and whatever its politics. His spell on *The Sunday Supplement* was by no means permanent, for the board's policy had been clearly laid down as one of constant change, to avoid editorial and reviewing ruts and to give every new name a sporting chance. He happened to be among the first chosen, and was shrewd enough to keep busy, consolidating his literary climbing elsewhere. And he would sign any contract with any publisher for any book on any subject, none of which ever got written. He was also occasionally invited to lecture at unknown literary clubs in remote coastal towns, whose inhabitants—usually ladies—felt left out of things during the long English winters. He always accepted, and would warm their lonely, elderly hearts with humorous accounts of the young literary movements, in which he liked to include himself, but with a great show of being Different, though Young.

"Why do you always go to these places?" his wife would ask him. "It doesn't really help you in any way, it's badly paid, and a nuisance."

"Any appearance, anywhere, is publicity," he would answer; "it all helps to get one's name around. Besides—" he was remarkably good-humoured, and would raise his eyebrows in mock innocence "—I enjoy it."

Elizabeth Cutting was a quiet woman, just on thirty, auburn-haired, thin without being slim, unaggressively proportioned. Fatigue often encircled her soft brown eyes, which gazed with puzzlement at the small structure of powerful ugliness she had married. It really was remarkably small. He was wiry and monkish, with sandy hair that crinkled round his head like a half-hearted tonsure, for the thin wispy matting on top was receding fast. His monkey-face was boyish still, but screwed up as if he were about to be pushed through a sewerage pipeline. It seemed to relax only when he talked of literary politics to a few well-chosen listeners, and then a knowing smile would illuminate his countenance like inner grace. What was it about him that captivated so many different kinds of people, including herself? Elizabeth thought on a dark November morning, as they sat face to face at the kitchen table, eating their breakfast and exchanging comments about their mail, and the batch of Friday weeklies. She was still in her blue dressing gown and looked tired and pale without makeup, but the electric light softened the little lines round her eyes. He wore a sports jacket of natty gent's suiting, in beige plaid, over brown trousers, pale green check shirt and an incongruous dark blue college tie. The jacket was just a little too tight, and buttoned at the waist, so that his bottom was emphasised, almost like a woman's.

"Hoo-hoo," he chortled. "Here's Larry lashing out at that book on child psychiatry I was so carefully lukewarm about last week. He's being positively psychotic. Just what the publishers want, silly ass," he went on, spreading marmalade lavishly over his toast. "Reminds me of that joke about the child psychiatrist who put a notice on his door saying 'Gone to lunch, back at fwee.'"

Elizabeth smiled dutifully and continued to glance through a long chapter from one of her students, about Árpád Szendrey, a Hungarian poet who had been deported to Russia during the war, and had never been heard of since. Elizabeth taught Hungarian at the Fidler Institute of Danubian Studies in Holborn, which was financed by a dead American millionaire of Hungarian origin. She had always had a flair for difficult languages, and had gone up to Girton College, Cambridge, on a German scholarship, but had insisted on switching to Russian when, in the middle of the war, our glorious Russian allies were beginning to behave suspiciously like an even more insidious enemy than the one we were fighting. Elizabeth was both sceptical and charitable by nature: as a girl she distrusted all propaganda, and passionately believed in the need to understand the enemy. Rapidly disillusioned, first with German literature, then with the neurotic Russian gloom, she had taken up Hungarian as a subsidiary subject—an even more difficult language which did not even belong to the Slavonic group—and she had romped home with a double first. She had once had romantic ideas about Secret Intelligence, and hoped to equip herself for the Third World War, which seemed so inevitably imminent as the Second drew to its ignoble end. But she had grown out of this adventurous notion when the Cold War settled down to its Siberian climate of opinion, and since the Foreign Office showed little interest in her unusual qualifications, she had drifted into an institution of ambivalent aims and dubious academic status.

At the age of twenty-three she had met Howard in some student club. He had just come down from Oxford, where he had—unaccountably he said—missed a Fellowship, but although he felt bitter about this, he was gay and full of spirit, and undaunted enough to embark upon a doctorate thesis in London, on the subject of Carlyle. Officially, he was still doing it.

"There's something very strange about Zoltan," Elizabeth said, looking up from the typewritten pages.

"Who? Oh, your Hungarian. Good lord, look at the colour!" The essay was typed in green with red titles and italics, on white halved quarto paper, so that it looked book-size. "Reminds me of those philosophical discussions on redness, which is green to the colour-blind."

"National colours." She smiled. "He seems to be carrying on a love-hate relationship with his country."

"That's not very strange, in the circumstances. Oh, good, they've printed my letter . . . I see Charles is weighing in on Bingy's side, damn him. Any more coffee?"

"Just a drop." He didn't thank her as she poured it out, but started opening his mail, which always took second place on Friday mornings, when the weeklies had to be glanced through for what went on in the reviewing world. "I didn't mean that," said Elizabeth. "He got his Fidler Scholarship to write a book on this poet Szendrey, who died in the war. I was appointed to help him but he seemed most reluctant. After months of research, he sends me a draft chapter which says nothing at all. Howard, you're not listening."

"I'm sorry, darling. Just look at this, from old Gael Jackson. Positively cringing."

He handed her a note.

"I can't see anything cringing about that," she said after reading it. "It's a courteously worded invitation, brief and pragmatic."

"Well——" He paused uncomfortably. Then the knowing look came into his eyes and uncreased his face like a revelation. "Let's say he's falling over backwards not to appear cringing. I know *this* one—" that was his favourite phrase "—dignified but wily. If he thinks he can pull the Old Oxonian on me and bribe me with a good dinner, he's mistaken. He's very much mistaken," he repeated hypnotically, and lapsed suddenly into a glum daydream, staring vacantly at the garish captions on the packet of Rice Crispies. *You can hear them popping—pop—crackle—pop.* And he thought, unaccountably, of his mother.

"Howard, you're not serious about this thing?" Elizabeth's voice was too low and gentle to pierce through the aura of abstraction which now enveloped her husband. "Howard, I'm talking to you."

"What, what?" He blinked his eyelids rapidly with a great show of surprise. She never really knew how far he pretended to be lost in thought, for when she dismissed what she had said with a "never mind", he usually answered a few seconds later, having heard it with at least part of his mind, from which it presumably re-echoed.

"Not serious, chum, no, not what you could call serious." He laughed. "It'll be amusing to watch their tactics. The next step, if I know anything about Tom Truelove, will be an invitation to lunch at Brent's, from the big white chief of Messrs Truelove & Thorne himself. After that——"

"But Howard, what's the point? You don't really want to take it to court."

"Well, I don't know. Not if I can help it, I suppose. But they haven't a legal leg to stand on and a little publicity never did anyone any harm. After all, Liz, I am the injured party."

"Are you?" Elizabeth sighed wearily and rose to clear away the breakfast things. The kitchen was small, so that she had to edge her way behind his chair to get to the draining board. "I really don't see why. What if this character is you, and everyone knows it? Who is everyone anyway? A few of our friends, who will surely take it as a joke."

"It's the aspersion on you I care about most . . . darling." The hesitation had ushered in a gentle tone, so that the nonce-word of marital conversations suddenly reacquired its meaning. He turned in his chair and caught her waist as she passed, putting on his pussy-cat face.

"I know, honey." She knew nothing of the kind, but always fell victim to his momentary tendernesses. She ruffled the frizzy wisps on top of his head and bent over him to pick up the butter-dish.

"Ooh," he exclaimed, and nuzzled her breasts. Then he smacked her bottom and let her go.

"Don't do that, you know I hate it." Elizabeth stepped across to the refrigerator and put the butter away.

"La, ma'am."

She slammed the door shut and stood leaning against the fridge, stiffly in touch with its cool vibrant hum.

"But I don't mind in the least. Who was here, after all, at that dinner party? Brandon and his wife, Furnivall, Sonya Dandridge, who else?

Nobody I care twopence about. What they think, I mean."

"No, but I care."

"That's what I thought. It's not really me you're worrying for."

"I care because you're my wife, and the story as he tells it, makes me look ridiculous as your husband, and I don't like looking ridiculous to these people in particular."

"Oh, Howard. You know perfectly well they wouldn't take it like that— if indeed they remember it at all. Aren't you being a bit paranoiac about the whole thing?"

"Paranoiac my arse." Elizabeth flinched but he took no notice. "Here is this cretinous author describing a scene which happened in my own house, in front of some of my most influential friends, making it even more grotesque than it was, and implying, into the bargain, that I am a cuckold. I don't mind people thinking you have a lover—they'd hardly believe it, anyway—it's the absurdity of the scene itself I object to."

"The scene *was* absurd." She smiled as she walked back to the table and cleared away the last remnants. "Besides, everyone knew it was only my student who rang up. You announced it yourself when you took the telephone and said it was for me."

"Your Hungarian, yes."

"Zoltan isn't 'my Hungarian.' Oh do be sensible, darling."

Howard slumped in his chair and put his elbows on the table.

"And he said I was a failed writer."

"Who said?"

"This moron, Gael Jackson. Don't you see that if I am identified as an expert on Carlyle, it does me a lot of harm to be described as a failure."

"So that's what it is, really." She wiped the table with a cloth, knocking his elbows off.

"No, that's not what it is really." He got up angrily and stalked to the door, then returned to collect the papers and correspondence.

"I'm sorry, darling," said Elizabeth, turning towards the sink. "But I do think you're exaggerating the importance of this recognition. I've only read Gael Jackson's first novel, but if this one is similar it probably leaves reality altogether after the first chapter."

"Of course it does, you mutt." Some of the papers fell to the floor, followed by Gael Jackson's note, which fluttered down as innocently as a butterfly. Howard cursed and crouched to pick them up. "But if he thinks he can get away with libel merely by using his immortal poetic soul as a mask, he's very much mistaken. Very much mistaken," Howard repeated, still crouching and gazing blankly at the leg of the table.

Elizabeth recognised the momentary coma, switched on the light over the sink and turned on the hot tap. The Ascot plopped and the detergent foamed up in the basin as the water steamed into it. The gushing noise roused him and he got up slowly, gaping at her stupidly. She turned the tap off.

"Don't you think you may be drawing attention to the identification?" she said slowly, her auburn head haloed in the steamy light like a winter dawn. "To do nothing is always more dignified."

This was a sore point between them, but she took the risk. He never could resist the temptation to write letters to the press, airing his views on any minor controversy, and rushing in where more cautious authors fear to tread.

"Oh, dignity!" he exclaimed. "Everyone's so damned sensitive about their dignity. Diplomacy's only another word for cowardice." He flung out of the room. But Elizabeth had seen his eyes narrow cunningly for a moment as she had spoken. The seed had been sown and might germinate. 'Tomorrow,' she thought, 'he will have forgotten I said it, and will produce it as his own idea.' She turned back to the sink and rinsed clean the crockery of their morning conversation.

Chapter Three

DIGNITY, as well as sensitivity, were two words which came readily into people's minds when they met Nina Jackson. She was not just elegant—for many women are that—she had that rare sense of harmony in clothes, down to the last detail of earring, purse or footwear, and the surest commingling of delicacy and daring which enabled her to carry off the most unusual juxtapositions of colours. "Nothing ever clashes," she would say, "if the clothes are so good that the mixture is obviously meant." Indeed, she worked for a glossy fashion monthly, but rarely, in fact, obeyed its rulings, preferring to trust her own flair within the general trend. Half Irish, half Italian—her full name was Giovannina—she was dark and minute and lively, and only the unexpected blue of her eyes, and the alarming white clarity of her skin, gave her an air of unreality which would sometimes take complete possession, overshadowing her gaiety and apparent confidence.

Yet both dignity and sensitivity were the wrong words. Poise and delicacy, rather, she certainly had these, but there was something else, a streak of—no, not vulgarity, not even exhibitionism, but of pride in her femininity mingled with a deep uncertainty which men were quick to sense. She was one of those women who make sweet, devoted wives to sweet, devoted husbands, but to whom most men find it impossible to talk without making some crude reference to her physical attractions. Something in the way she walked—the short, nervous steps that nevertheless managed to suggest loitering with intent to steal a few lecherous looks or lewd accostings—evoked more wolf-whistles from workers than many girls younger than her twenty-six years could boast. On a cold November day she walked down the King's Road, Chelsea, in soft velvet trousers the colour of crushed strawberries, a thick-knit and loose fitting pink pullover with a fisherman's high hood, and luminous pink socks vanishing into purple leather shoes that looked like tiny gondolas, with gold embroidery and turned-up Oriental toes. Her gloves, too, were purple. The men who were pulling up the street outside the Post Office stopped their infernal drilling in a unison of silent gaping.

Nina walked on, smiling to herself, and loudly singing some Blues as soon as the drilling started up again. She liked the feeling, that the song could not be heard under the louder noise of work and traffic, ceased to exist, in fact, except in her own consciousness of vocal chords tensed to produce a sound she could not hear even in her own head. She didn't feel particularly attractive today, hugging a large bundle of dirty washing stuffed into a cellophane bag. A straight black fringe and a white face, with startling and darkly made up blue eyes, peered out of the knitted pink hood, and her chin rested on the bundle she was carrying as she crooned through pale pink lipstick into the dirty linen.

"Ain't gat nobahdy
Ain't gat nobahdy to care for mee."

This wasn't true in the least, nor would she have sung it if it had been. The river fog which London had been wearing like a powdered wig for three days had lifted, and the wintry sun was filtering through the brisk frosty day, warming the white, grey and yellow houses of Chelsea with pale gold. A lady in a mink coat tripped in front of her, in high Italian stiletto heels which picked up damp autumn leaves and scraps of paper like a litter-collector's pike. A grey poodle trotted beside her on a lead, with the remnants of a summer shave, in the shape of a cross, on its back. The cross looked like a runway for flies to land on, except that there were no flies at this time of year. Nina stepped aside and went into the bank. She dumped her laundry on the floor by the counter, and wrote out a slip for paying in the cheque she had just received from *Elegance*, the fashion magazine for which she wrote. Then she drew out almost the same amount, smiled coquettishly at the goofy-eyed clerk who counted out the notes for her, stuffed the money in her bag without reckoning it, and picked up her cellophane bundle.

"Bye, Mr Fawcett. See you soo-oon."

"I hope so, Mrs Jackson. Goodbye."

When she reached the launderette, she was alarmed to see a high-heeled lady in a mink coat emerge, carrying a large pigskin travelling bag full of laundry, and trailing a snow-white fluffy poodle on a lead. Had she popped him in the machine? The lady walked to her car, flung the bag on the back seat, shooed in the poodle, sat down elegantly at the wheel and slammed the door. Nina went in, giggling as she placed her laundry on the scales.

"Too many high-heeled ladies in mink coats," she said brightly to the attendant.

"Pardon, dear? Hot wash, did you say?"

"Hot wash, thank you. Eight pounds of washing and a dirty poodle."

"Any bleach or blue?" The woman looked at her in alarm.

"Blue, please."

"Lovely day, isn't it? You're in number thirteen."

"Oh dear. I'm superstitious."

"I can't help that, we're very busy this morning. Don't forget your blue, dear."

"*I gat the bad luck thirteen blues,*" Nina improvised to the click and hum of the machines as she stuffed in her washing. "*I gat the wash-day blues, and the bleak bleach and blue blues.*"

She sat down with a year-old copy of *Elegance* and read herself with a smile. Why did the editor like her inanities? She was paid twelve guineas a month for turning out the silliest light verses on fashion trends.

"*Tweed the colour of old stone this year,*
Matching your complexion, madam.
Drab olive silk for evening wear
To set off the reflection, madam,
Of the drab highlights in your hair . . ."

"Your light's on, dear," said her neighbour.

"Oh thank you."

She rose to put in the first soap. A row of women in drab olive, old stone, red, blue and purple winter coats, fur coats, dirty white sweaters and bright slacks, representing the proletarian, the rich, and the artistic female population of Chelsea, sat gazing glumly at the round windows of their machines, behind which their washing jumped and bubbled anonymously up and down like sickly, palpitating entrails. The women looked so hypnotised they might have been watching television.

When Nina got back to their small house in Paultons Square, Gael was hard at work by the drawing room fire, correcting essays.

"*Caro mio!*" She had been brought up in England from the age of seven, but liked occasionally to use her native language for terms of endearment. "Is it warm enough for you?" She dumped the cellophane bundle on the sofa, snatching the essay from him and threw herself on his lap, covering his neck with kisses.

"Hey, you little minx!" He put his arm round her and reached for the essay with his other hand, but she held it aloof. So he pushed back her hood and ruffled her fringe. Her black hair was cropped like a boy's at the back, but sleek and carefully groomed.

"What are your ignorant students saying about the nature of reality this week?" She laughed and stopped his mouth with more kisses.

"Oh, the usual stuff"—kiss—"nothing exists"—kiss—"except as a system"—kiss—"of collective representations"—kiss—"arising from the combination"—kiss—"of unrepresented atoms"—kiss—"electrons"—kiss—"etcetera"—kiss—"and our sense perceptions."

"Let's see if the essay exists when we don't look at it!" she exclaimed and threw it away as she put her hand on his eyes. "No, it simply isn't there."

"But you're there, honey. I can feel you. It's all in our senses."

"No, it isn't." She disentangled herself and rose to pick the essay from the blue carpet. The decoration of the room echoed her complexion, her blue eyes, her black hair and the clothes she was wearing: the walls were white and a royal blue ceiling reflected the carpet. The armchairs were upholstered in a soft red velvet and all the bookshelves, small tables, and other wooden furniture, were black as ebony. "We have an extrasensory perception between us—you know, like primitive people who identify themselves with the object. You're me and I'm you." She laughed and glanced through the essay as she pranced her red velvet legs around the room. "Ah! famous quotation!" And Nina jived, in exaggerated rhythm as she crooned out the limerick like a love song, fluttering her long black, lashes and wavering her small hands suggestively down her body.

"There was a young man who said God
oo-di-doo-di-dum
Must think it excessively odd
oo-di-doo-di-dum
That the sycamore tree (she yelled)
Continoos to bee
When there's no one (her voice dropped)
No, there's no one
di-doo-doo-doo-doo-di-doo
No, there's no one around in the quad."

In trousers and with her cropped hair, Nina could look very boyish indeed. 'Got me a nice boy-girl,' Gael would say teasingly. She dropped the paper on the floor and stalked the room like a teddy-girl aping a film gangster. She put on a deep male voice and a fierce frown.

"Dear Sirr, yer astahnishment's ahd
Doo-doo-doom-di-dumb
Ah's always around in de quad
Doo-doo-doom-di-dumb
So de sycamore tree
'll continoo to bee
Since observed by yrrs faithfully
Yes sirr—faithfully—
Observed by yrrs faithfully . . . de Lord Gahd."

She picked up the essay, flung it back at him, then danced out of the room, singing "*Doo-di-doo-doo-yrrs faithfully—yes sirr—observed by yrrs faithfully—Gahd—didoo-doo-di-doo-doo-di-doo.*"

"Frau Yackson is frivolous today morning?" said Frieda, when Nina reached the kitchen. "Fantastisch, familiar and freundly, yes?" Frieda was studying English by working through the dictionary, learning every day a page by heart. Although she had been with the Jacksons for six months, she still spoke German to the children, having so far reached only the letter F. Nina was always terrified of what she might bring out in front of guests.

"*Kraft durch Freude.*" She smiled. "Have the children been good?"

"Ya, ya, yes. Nicht fermenting. Zey fornicate."

"Frieda, what are you talking about?"

"Zey form ze fornix wit bricks in ze Feast-Zimmer."

Nina rippled with laughter. Frieda looked hurt and said primly: "Forthwith I will to the forum fare."

"The market, Frieda, like *Markt* in German. Not forum."

"Ze market."

"That's right. Here's the shopping list, I have to change. I am going out for lunch, you understand? Everything is ready for Mr Jackson in the oven. It is on very low, so don't touch the regulator. You understand?"

"Ya, ya."

Frieda had learnt her first English from the Americans, and was adamantly convinced—in the face of all verbal evidence—that the English, with their wilful orthographic inconsistency, pronounced as *yea* what they wrote down as *yes*. The fact that Gael was American hardly helped, for in spite of his carefully nurtured Oxford accent, he lapsed easily on small words.

"You give the children their lunch at twelve, and put them to bed as usual. I'll be back at three to take them to the park. You understand?"

"Ya, ya."

"You have the afternoon off. Tonight we have a guest to dinner, so you will serve, you understand?"

"Ya, ya."

When she had changed, Nina looked in to the drawing room. She was loosely tailored in smoky blue, with white cashmere just showing at the neck, and wore a pudding basin hat of blue straw, absurd for the time of year, whose broad descending brim completely covered not only her fringe but her eyes. Her nylons had a blue tinge and her shoes, gloves and bag were of a soft blue-grey suède.

The Jacksons were comfortably but not well off: Gael's literary earnings hardly supplemented his lecturer's salary and Nina's own small effort at writing produced mere pin-money. What they had, however, went on their children and their home, for they both laid great stress on beautiful surroundings combined with enough leisure to enjoy them, as one of the prerequisites of happiness. Nevertheless, Nina always managed to look expensively dressed. She made all her own clothes, as well as her children's, and she had the Italian knack of being able to copy any model just by looking at it in a window and taking a few notes. She deplored the English habit of buying off the peg—all women seemed to look exactly alike, and unfitted. Even when they were smartly dressed they usually went to pieces at the feet, and this she could not bear. What money she had left she spent on good materials and expensive accessories, especially shoes, which she had made to measure.

"Bye, darling."

"Nina! Where are you going?" Gael looked up in surprise. "How smart you look!"

"But I told you! Furnivall asked me to lunch."

"Oh, yes," he said vaguely, "who's Furnivall?"

"Oh, darling. He's the literary editor of *The Sunday Supplement*. I've never met him and I can't think why he wrote and asked me, unless it's to get me to produce my nonsense for his paper."

"Oh, yes. *The Sunday Supplement*."

"Darling, I would never have accepted if I'd known you were going to be here."

"Of course, honey. Anyway, if it wasn't for *The Sunday Supplement* I wouldn't be here. Nuisance, this dinner, I had to change three tutorials."

"I know, darling, never mind. It has to be done and you can be back in Oxford by ten tomorrow. I'll try and get something out of Furnivall about this character. Frieda will give you your lunch, it's all prepared. Must rush now. Bye."

He blew her a kiss and returned to his students' essays on the nature of reality.

"Tell me about this man Cutting," said Nina to Jocelyn Furnivall, as they sat over their last course in a small Italian restaurant of enormous menu cards and enormous prices. The food had not been particularly good. The *agneau en chasseur*—translated for the benefit of the ignorant, as 'huntsmanlike lamb'—had not been huntsmanlike at all. Nor were the surroundings more than passably unshabby, and Nina was always shocked by the figures charged for dishes she could have produced at a tenth of the cost. She never understood why smart people in England thought so highly of Soho as to do most of their business there, expensively, watched by rival editors, publishers and writers, instead of discussing it for ten minutes over an office desk. She had a feeling she was being bought for a meal and was at the same time annoyed by the low estimate of her value, evident in the lunch itself and the dinginess, if not in the presented bill. Jocelyn hadn't been particularly interesting either, and she was determined at least to get some information out of the transaction.

"My dear," he miaowed, "what do you want to know? I'm not in the habit of gossiping about my staff. Can't afford to, my dear, not in my position." He spoke very fast in a high-pitched voice. His greying blond hair swept back carefully from an almost unlined brow that topped a characterless face, the face of an outsize baby—indeed, his chin was so smooth that he was rumoured to have had his first beard electronically plucked by a process apparently guaranteed to give a man eternal youth. But Jocelyn must have been nearing forty. His lips were soft and sulky, and he had small colourless eyes, like a pig's. The features, however, were regular and the bones nobly set so that the general impression was that of a handsome man—a pretty boy, some would say—and he looked remarkably stupid.

"But I don't want gossip," Nina replied in a hurt tone. "I just want to know what kind of man he is. Gael has asked him to dinner tonight."

"Has he, indeed?" Jocelyn's interest perked up as he looked at her quizzically and pursed his lips to the coffee cup.

"Oh dear, is this wretched story all round town already?"

"What story, my dear?" He lifted his well-groomed eyebrows innocently. "Nobody ever tells me anything." His voice varied from mewing to quacking, according to the degree of aggression. Now he was nearer to quacking. "All I know is that I sent him your husband's book with the last batch. Two days later he rang up to say he couldn't do it, but then he changed his mind—on my persuasion, my dear."

"He didn't say why?"

"Of course riot." Jocelyn's eyes shifted as they met the direct blue gaze from under that blue straw rim.

"*Caffe nero, signorina?*" The waiter bent over her, either recognising a countrywoman or flattering English linguistic capacities.

"Yes, black, thank you."

Unlike those who did not speak a language well, Nina avoided showing off her native fluency, especially to waiters. For native fluency always led to native friendliness, and in matters of class distinction, she wanted to be unmistakably English. But she couldn't help smiling at him in the most alluring way. The waiter's eyes narrowed as he flicked the crumbs from the tablecloth with his napkin, brushing her hand as if by mistake.

"*Scusi—signora.*" He noticed her ring and bowed himself away, smiling. She frowned at the lack of respect.

"My dear, not to worry." Jocelyn seemed to purr suddenly. "Howard Cutting is a delightful person, one of my liveliest contributors, and quite incorruptible—even if it's he who likes to say so," he added smoothly. "I rather like having him on the paper, you know, it protects me. Whenever a queer edits anything, or reviews books, he is inevitably accused of giving undue prominence to the boys, and of course he does. Howard is married to some perfectly ghastly academic type who makes him feel just too inferior for words, though actually, he's madly learned himself—philosophy, you know."

"Really?" Nina's eyes opened wide. "That's Gael's subject," she added enthusiastically.

"So it is, my dear, so it is. I believe Howard was up at Oxford, too. But his wife's never forgiven him for washing his hands of the academic racket."

"Oh dear, I didn't know he was married, perhaps we should have asked his wife," Nina said, ignoring the cliché description of her husband's world.

"Don't worry, my dear, she never goes to literary parties."

"We're not a literary party, I hope. But it's rather rude not to ask her."

"Oh, he's often around on his own. Or with the latest author in the news." Jocelyn went on, suddenly absorbed in his own talent for brief biographical sketches, and not noticing Nina frown. "He had an affair two years ago—or was it three?—with Kitty Lippman. You know, that Jewish girl who writes those sentimental novels. She helped him quite a bit with contacts and—but my dear, it's common knowledge!" he protested as Nina put her hands to her ears.

"Perhaps I'm not common enough," she said wryly, "and anyway, I didn't ask for that kind of information. Let's change the subject, shall we?" But in order not to make him feel uncomfortable she wasted a coquettish smile on him, intended as a sign of false complicity in his indiscretion, and talked of other things.

"So there you are, Mr Furnivall. I'm afraid it's no use putting me up to your editor for a fashion column. My contract with *Elegance* forbids me to write for any other paper."

"Shameless, my dear, shameless."

"Besides, you know, I'm not really a fashion expert. I just use the news to air my views. Silly views, too. I'm only a housewife." She carefully posed herself into a hand lotion advertisement and told him about the poodle and the washing machine.

Chapter Four

ALL evening her hands floated incessantly before his eyes. They were so small, so white, they reflected in the ebony table like silver fish in a pool, together with the candle flames; they fluttered among the silver spoons, doves' wings descending on flashing waves, they sailed and tacked away into their conversation and swept back over a wine glass in blasphemous blessing. She was herself the wine, aromatic in a pale silk dress that seemed to be fluently contained within the white transparence of her skin. All evening her hands floated before his eyes, steering their phrases along into the candlelight, offering up her laughter as carriers to their wit.

Pale gold the wine, and his host's hair round a pale face, and ivory the candles and pale gold the plates, on a dark table, dark as the girl's shorn head, and the room so dark beyond the table, and her wrists so frail, so white.

Howard Cutting blinked himself out of his intoxicated whimsy and rose unsteadily as Nina Jackson suggested adjourning for coffee. Coffee would bring him to his senses.

He had come in an uncertain mood, conciliatory but determined not to lose face, on the defensive but anxious to impress. Gael Jackson was distant at first, angry at the inconvenience, the waste of time and money on a reviewer he had no desire to meet. But Nina had carried it off admirably, breaking the ice and putting them both at their ease at once. So far, they had talked of everything except libel. Gael was surprised to find he had quite a lot in common with this little man, in spite of his knowingness, while Howard, who could certainly switch on the charm and, indeed, could be a pleasing enough man when relaxed—was delighted with Gael Jackson.

And, of course, with his wife. Always in the corner of his eye—when he forced his eye away—she shimmered gold in the firelight and her white face hovered above the talk. She gave him his coffee in a wafer-thin Worcester cup, and her hands were small and well-manicured with a pale nail varnish. He looked up at her and saw her small rounded breasts as she bent over and dared not meet her eyes. Howard drank his coffee quickly and asked for more, with the raised eyebrows, spaniel eyes and ingratiating smile which he not altogether incorrectly assumed was his most sociable expression. He wanted to sober down. He wanted, also, to see those white hands again as she returned the cup.

He took out his cigarettes and offered them. Gael didn't smoke. She did, with a long ivory holder. Howard rose and walked across to the red velvet sofa where she blossomed like a yellow rose and struck his lighter. It wouldn't work, and she laughed, bending forward to reach the heavy silver lighter on the coffee table. He glimpsed her breasts again, and took the lighter from her hands, just touching a fingertip. But suddenly her hands were far away from the cigarette, beyond the ivory lighter, her small fingers holding it like a pencil. And all the time, Howard was talking to Gael about Oxford, and his college, and his philosophy tutor, and his London University thesis.

"Yes, we must have been up together," he said quickly as he sat down again, concentrating hard on Gael. "I was at Beverley, your present college. Quite a generation, that post-war lot. Most of us have done something or other." He never liked to be left out of things. "Boy, those were the days." He gave a mock-sigh and stopped, suddenly aware that it was he, not Gael Jackson, who was pulling the Old Oxonian line. And still her white hand, fingering the ivory holder, flowered in the corner of his eye like a damned arum lily.

"And then, I turned writer." He puffed at his cigarette and fixed Gael with a conspiratorial look. "Like you, dear boy, except that I have to live on it. And I haven't written a novel yet, but I will, I will. We all do, in due course."

Gael smiled at him pleasantly. Nothing had been said about his own novel, or the expert on Carlyle, or the carp baked in white wine and dropped on the floor after a flustering telephone call.

"Yes, you must!" Nina exclaimed enthusiastically. "It's all a matter of getting down to it regularly. Gael writes during the summer vacation, don't you, darling?"

"After exams are over. Couldn't do it any other time."

So this was the man who had got the Fellowship at Beverley, Howard thought. His own college, and they had given it to a Balliol man. He remembered how bitter he had felt when he heard, not only that he had failed, but who had succeeded. Gael Jackson was known in Howard's generation chiefly because he kept so aloof. Of course, he was a graduate student, but even so he might have taken part in some of the University activities. Only once he had read a paper on the nature of reality to the Philosophical Society. Anger surged again within him. So this was the man. An American, an expatriate, almost denationalised, one would think, he was so English in his speech and manner. Must be from Boston or Philadelphia. City of love, he reflected tipsily, Philia, brotherly love. Howard couldn't help liking him, and damned him in the same thought. He remembered his bitterness and his face clouded. 'If you think you're going to turn that boy into a ruddy intellectual, you're very much mistaken,' his father shouted down the narrow stairs of their brick house in Berkshire. His mother's pale, reproachful face floated out the fireplace—only there it was tiled in green round a gas contraption. 'What was good enough for me's good enough for him.' His mother had been a fairly successful small-part actress. She had met enough interesting people to get big ideas, but not enough to marry into show business, and she had given up her stage career for a local horticulturist. Bulbs, flowers, manure. And the inevitable jokes about cuttings at school. The smell of flowers pervaded his memory like the smell of death, white lilies on his father's coffin, and his cold lack of grief. He was an only son, and she worked him through his scholarships, spending all her savings to see him comfortable and unashamed in Oxford. Then, in spite of an excellent first, he had failed in the final step towards academic respectability.

"What, what?" he was startled into clumsiness by the softly ascending note of a query. And then, politely: "I'm sorry, what did you say?"

She laughed.

"You obviously don't want to get down to it if you don't hear a practical suggestion. I said, why don't you start now, a little every day?"

"Start, what?" He blinked nervously.

"Your novel. That's what we were talking about, wasn't it?"

"Oh, that. My dear girl, I intend to." He didn't notice Gael flinching at his familiar tone, and went on—"as soon as I can manipulate three weeks off to get started."

"Oh, no!" Nina exclaimed. "That's what they all say. One day I'll write a novel, next year, next month, next week. Any time, but not now. It's so much easier to write books about books, isn't it?"

"Nina, don't bully him," Gael said playfully, "we all have to work out our own methods, in our own time."

"Yes, and how would you have worked out yours, if I hadn't bullied you?" she teased him. "Why, I had to scratch your head for you to make you think!" She stretched out towards him on the sofa and ruffled his hair. He seized her by the waist, drew her up to him and gripped her sleek boy's head by the back hair, tugging it down to plant a kiss on her throat. Howard shut his eyes.

"You bundle of wickedness. You caused more interruptions than anything else. Without you I'd have written The Great American Novel by now."

"Instead of a little yanky-panky?" She nestled near him and slipped her legs under her wide skirt on the sofa, showing a certain amount of frilled petticoat as she moved them. "Did you like his last novel?" she asked Howard suddenly, fixing him with her disarming blue eyes from the security of Gael's shoulder.

"Yes, very much." The opening gambit at last. He had expected it, all evening, and was entirely prepared to show the impartiality of his literary judgment. "I admired the way you make reality shift around, and even disappear altogether, according to the percipient faculties of your characters. The God's eye view, as it were."

Gael smiled wryly.

"The only snag is, if I may say so, old boy, that you expect your reader to see all, too, you expect your reader to be God—you know, always around in the quad."

"Well, I deal all day with the theory of knowledge, you know," Gael smiled affably.

"Oh, that!" Howard exclaimed, suddenly aggressive again. "I know that one! Present-day philosophers are simply screwy with it, but screwy. Whenever anyone mentions the theory of knowledge to me I feel like kicking them in the—in the teeth. It's done for, dear boy, finished, it's trickled down from the experts to the masses—you know, like Freud. When that happens one just can't go on. There's nothing more one can *do* with it."

"I thought you said you liked my novel?"

"I did, dear boy, I did. I was talking about the modern schools of philosophy. In a novel, of course you're entitled to use any notion, however outdated or popular."

Gael laughed. "I wish my novels *were* popular. No one seems to understand them."

"That's what I mean, old boy. You expect the reader to see the sycamore tree even when your characters can't."

"Or can't see the quad for the trees?"

Howard liked the crack and suddenly relaxed, chortling loudly to ease away his previous clumsiness.

"So the sycamore tree will continue to be," Nina crooned gently. She suddenly wriggled free and sat up, stretching her legs again. "Oh, darling, isn't he clever! You've found your one and only reader—male reader I mean. Women understand these things by instinct."

"Oh, since when?" Howard asked, his face set consciously into a mischievous look.

"Since preserved by yours faithfully, God—their instinct, I mean." She had a curious way of propping the tip of her nose with her fourth finger when she laughed, as though she were afraid it might fall off. She leant forward to pick another cigarette from the ebony box on the low table; threw one at Howard and lit hers quickly, sliding the silver lighter to his side. Then she placed the cigarette in her holder—it was odd of her to light it first, he thought, and knew she had wanted to avoid his gallantry —and flung herself down at the other end of the red sofa, carefully poised with her white arm stretched along its back.

"Nina is more of a philosopher than you think," said Gael. "She read Greats up at Oxford."

"That's where we met," Nina put in, making it clear that this was much more important to her. She somehow never referred to her own classical education, having discarded it as readily as most women change the blue for the silk stocking when a man comes into their lives. She had borne Gael's first child during her last term in Oxford and had nauseated herself into a rather bad degree. But after a few years of wearing the intelligent-modern-mother personality, she had tossed that aside like an outmoded dress, carefully grooming herself into a frivolous dumb sweet thing.

Howard blinked with unconcealed surprise, in fact, he was so used to playing the expected reactions that he exaggerated the surprise, prolonging it as soon as he had registered it. Nothing in social intercourse struck very deep with him and he always had to overact the response. "La, ma'am," he cooed, "let me raise my metaphoric hat to you. I hope you will take it as a compliment if I say you don't look it."

She was used to this particular brand of compliment and accepted it formally with a minuettish gesture of her hand, and it seemed to wave at him like a scented lace handkerchief, guiding him through a complicated pattern of steps in a perpetual dance that would always end in a farewell curtsy, a curtsy so low that he would see her breasts as he bowed over her to the last long supertonic trill that would finally come to rest on the home chord.

"Shall we have some Mozart?" She broke into his thoughts as if by celestial divination and the little room suddenly seemed the centre of all the spheres, widening into each other as their music swelled out, further and further away into an expanding universe. Ancient and modern scientific notions of reality mingled in his mind as he smiled at her, nodding his assent. "I hope you like Mozart?" she went on, crouching suddenly near him to open the cupboard under the record player on his side of the fireplace. "Or do you prefer bop?" She turned and faced him, and he noticed for the first time how her eyebrows disappeared into her fringe when she asked a question.

"I like Bach too," he said softly, and remembered the days when he had devoted so much time to getting well up in classical music, and how little he listened now.

"Bach! Oh honey, did you hear that?" Nina turned to Gael, still crouching and holding on to Howard's armchair as she rocked with laughter. "Bop confused with Bach: how's that for inverted snobbery?"

"He's not so far out, either," said Gael, smiling across at them. Off she went again, and her laughter didn't belong to her, it was like a child's, spontaneous and ungraceful, a cackle almost, and with an alien ring of vulgarity. Her hands were on the red velvet still, like strange regalia, and her throat seemed to beg for kisses as she laughed, with her head thrown back. Howard dug his fists into the armchair's sides, and focused resolutely on Gael, almost screwing up a smile, and winking to show he appreciated the joke. Suddenly the hands were gone, and there was her back, in golden silk, and the sleek boy-cut of her black hair. She chattered as she chose some records, the pick-up clicked, and thin discordances of debilitated rhythm came out of the ebony case. Faint cymbals clashed offbeat, and notes like those of a harsh oboe climbed up and down across the clipped counterpoint of a nervous piano. Seemed to be bop, after all. "Bird," she murmured enigmatically, and her hands seemed to flutter over him. But suddenly she wasn't there, only a whiff of scent, and she was far away, sitting on the floor opposite, her head on the sofa, her arm towards her husband, but bent inwards, not reaching him, her thin wrist drooping down the red velvet.

At last there was an excuse to close his eyes. Her hands were so very small. They floated across to press his eyelids down, coolly, and he was dead. She bent over him and kissed him lightly on the lips, and he lived, and raised his fingers to her throat, travelling gently down into her small breasts. No. He mustn't think of it. Impossible. Besides, she would never think of it either. He was short and ugly. Elizabeth. He concentrated hard on Elizabeth. How impressive she had been, quiet and thoughtful and so unexpectedly passionate. And romantic. Then the stormy scenes, the reproaches, and the gradual building ups of their *modus vivendi*. She had withdrawn, he couldn't reach her any more, that was it, he couldn't reach her any more. Liz: auburn hair, soft brown eyes, puzzled, hurt, suddenly grateful, affectionate, proud of him. No, no one could be proud of him. Not even his mother. Blue eyes. Music. Nina. Mozart, Bach, Bop. Nina.

Somehow or other, nothing more was said about libel that evening. Gael hadn't tried to explain it, or apologise for it, he hadn't even mentioned it. That damn little bitch had turned Howard's upper hand into a begging hand, no, not a begging hand—for what could he beg without rebuff—a hand placed over his eyes so that he wouldn't see. He couldn't reach her, he couldn't reach Gael, he couldn't reach anyone. Nobody cared what he did.

When he left, she waved goodbye at him from the nursery door, about to look in on her children. "Gael will see you out," she whispered, and waved. She had not shaken hands with him when he arrived, either. He would never touch her small white hands.

Chapter Five

"I JUST can't reach him any more," Elizabeth said to Zoltan Torday as they sat in the empty basement of an espresso bar near Holborn Tube Station. "But then, neither can he hurt me. It has its advantages."

They always spoke English together, for though she knew Hungarian well, she preferred to keep foreign students at the proper distance by talking English. Then, as their relationship had grown more delicate and special, they had kept to English, partly out of affection for the language in which they had met, partly in order to preserve the precarious balance of their quiet love.

Zoltan's black eyes laughed behind a serious facial expression. He himself knew English well enough to recognise the slightly false earnestness of her phraseology, but he also understood her basic sincerity and the unhappiness out of which she built a separate world for herself, centred on her work at the Institute, on him, and on their shared Hungarian interests. He was grateful, but also sometimes frightened by her intensity. It was too strained, not real enough, yet close enough to his own to engulf him. Not that she had no sense of humour, but it needed bringing out, and his own special East Hungarian brand of light, quick-fire wit had been lost, somewhere in Germany and elsewhere, during the horrors of the Second World War. It emerged at times, but with a bitter tinge.

"Perhaps he is too busy to hurt you. It is not the literature that takes the time, it is the literary life."

Elizabeth laughed and looked at him almost with adoration. He gave her the extra dimension that made her feel superior and by which she could somehow bear her life with Howard. His mild, pinpointing attacks on her husband even moved her to defend him, partly out of stereotyped loyalty, partly to make Zoltan jealous.

"Well, he does work hard, you know, and he's quite a success."

Zoltan gave an impish smile.

"Any man can find a circle in which he is congratulated," he announced oracularly. "That is good, until perhaps he pushes accidentally into a circle where he is a joke."

Elizabeth masked her slight umbrage with an uncertain grin.

"But I think he does hurt you, Erzsébet," he went on gently, "because if he did not, you would not turn to me. I think you only love me out of despair." He took her fingers in his big peasant hands and stroked them. She caught her breath.

"And you, Zoltan?"

"I love you out of despair, also. But that is different, that is how it must be, for me, but not for you."

"Why not? I made a mistake, so did you."

"I did not make a mistake," he corrected her carefully. "I loved Ilona very much. It is she who has divorced me, to marry this AVO man. I was not even there."

"All right, all right." Elizabeth was inexperienced enough to resent hearing about his great love for Ilona. Then she laughed at herself as her eyes met his amused but infinitely tender gaze. "You know—" she reverted to her own marriage "—I remember how impressed I was when I first met Howard. He wasn't always like this, he was much more uncertain and he needed me. In fact, I congratulated myself on cornering him. I remember saying to myself happily: 'I think that by now I can safely say he can't do without me.' And do you know, even today I don't think he can."

"Any person can do without any person if he has to." Zoltan smiled and raised her hand to his lips. "Perhaps it is you who cannot do without him?" His eyes peered wistfully over her wrist, like a child's over the rim of a cup.

"Zoltan, you know that's not true."

"Why do you not leave him, then?" He was suddenly sombre. "Nobody is indispensable. You are like those people who refuse to take a holiday because they are completely certain that their office will collapse if they are not there."

"We'd better go, it's late." Elizabeth's chair scraped the floor as she got up, taking the bill from the table. "You have the complex of the broomstick," Zoltan said amicably. "Always you go off when a difficulty happens. You plunge down to the basement of a café in the middle of a question, you go straight up to the top of a bus. You wish always to be very up or very down. They would have burnt you as a witch in the Middle Ages."

The frown of annoyance at not being indispensable left Elizabeth's brow. Zoltan always managed to say something which made her feel interesting and unusual, and being burnt as a witch in the past subjunctive was rather nice. Howard made her feel stupid and ordinary, which she knew she probably was.

They walked upstairs, arm in arm and friendly. Her shoes were unexpectedly protected by transparent plastic bags, like two gay gifts wrapped in cellophane. She paid the bill at the door and they went out into the drizzly November morning, up Kingsway and across Red Lion Square, where the bombed seventeenth- and eighteenth-century houses had now been replaced by tall modern blocs, which gave it a somewhat anachronistic appearance. She wore a thick winter coat of grey Harris tweed, cut straight, and a matching hat which fitted snugly over her auburn hair.

"Maybe I do run away," she said, pleased for a moment at the idea of unattainability, "but I'm not a witch, and I'm pretty helpless." Her voice dropped to the loud echo of his steps. "You're probably right, I do need Howard. But I need you more." She looked up at him and smiled shyly. "You said yourself I always go round on someone else's push."

He had teased her once at the way she went through the swing door in the British Museum, always just after someone else, without pushing it herself. She remembered everything he ever said about her, and loved to remind him of it.

"Erzsébet! Marry me." Zoltan stopped in the middle of the street and the frost condensed his words into visible vapour. 'That was how Creation happened,' Elizabeth thought irrationally, '*fiat*, and the Word became a vapour of planets, whirling with atoms and crawling with ants, men and dinosaurs. Marry me, and so it is done.'

"Oh, Zoltan, you know I can't. Don't let's talk about it. I can't marry you and won't live with you, we both accepted that. Let's be grateful for what we have."

Although Elizabeth had early given up her notions about being a beautiful spy, other romantic longings, so quickly knocked out of her by Howard's crudeness, lingered on and found a welcome outlet in Zoltan, who was subtle enough to humour them, recognising but allowing the novelettish bravery of her words and manner. For he himself, forced to wear the mask of exile, fell only too easily into one or other of the many modes expected from the violent, the passionate, the enigmatic foreigner.

She looked up at him quickly and away ahead of her as she walked on. "As long as you're at the Institute we have to see each other, and it would be intolerable to make our relationship purely formal now. If you ever have to go away, we'll think again. Meantime, please, no dramatics."

"No, no dramatics."

His hands were pushed into the pockets of an American flying jacket, whose fur collar made him look very Russian. He glared at the trees as if they were ranting actors shedding false tears on a dusty stage, and then frowned at their calm and indifferent rustling. Nothing ever moved in England and no one was ever dramatic.

Zoltan looked taller than his actual height, for he was broad-shouldered without being stocky, and his head was reminiscent of a young Beethoven, with a portentous brow and thick straight black hair that shot back without a parting. Piercing black eyes and high cheekbones gave his face a fierce Mongol appearance, and altogether the impact he made was more impressive than his stature. Only his smile transformed him, for it was at once childlike and compassionate, gentle, yet uncertain and disturbing.

They walked up the stone stairs of a graceful eighteenth-century house in Bedford Row, which wasted its dignity around the Fidler Institute of

Danubian Studies.

"I'm afraid this just won't do, Zoltan." A complete change came over Elizabeth's manner as she sat down at her desk. Gone were the diffident looks, the moments of gratitude or uncertainty. She was now his supervisor, and he too, seemed to alter his bearing as the tutor-student relationship dropped over them like actor's costumes. She handed him the white, red, and green booksize typescript and he took it gingerly, as if it were a revolutionary or heretical and very secret document. He said nothing, waiting for her to speak.

"Zoltan, what is the matter with you?" she asked gently. "You were asked to write a book on Szendrey, and after all these months you produce nearly fifty pages on Alexander Petöfi. Oh, I know Petöfi disappeared too, but that's just about the only parallel. Besides, there's no mystery about Szendrey's disappearance, he was simply deported, and after years of enquiry the Russians have reported him dead."

"In 1954," Zoltan murmured. "Petöfi was officially declared dead in 1854."

"Of course, it's an interesting coincidence. But Petofi was killed, or probably killed, in battle in 1849. Szendrey was deported in 1944. Petöfi was a Revolutionary and a Romantic, Szendrey was extreme Right Wing."

"There is sometimes little difference. They both loved their country."

"Zoltan, my dear, all this is known, it is an obvious parallel. You can't spin it out into fifty pages of mere facts. You're supposed to be a critic."

"Creeteek! Creeteek!" Zoltan suddenly lapsed into a strong foreign accent on a screech like a scraping chair. He leapt up and paced the room, gesticulating wildly with square thick hands. He seemed like a gorilla in a cage of books. "Creeteeks are parasites, they feed and get fat on the great. They live on them, they make their reputations and swell their . . . their *amour-propre* on them, what-would-they-do-with-out-ZEM!" He banged his fist on the table with each word and faced her suddenly, holding out both his hands. She noticed for the first time that only one of his hands was square and thick. The left one was noticeably slimmer, longer, more delicate. On the wall behind him was a large coloured picture of the Holy

Crown of St Stephen, with its bent cross, the whole hanging, it seemed, just above his head. By turns he could be a wild Tartar, a king, a cautious peasant, an angelic nincompoop.

"Zoltan, what is it?" she asked again patiently. "You know very well that you *are* a critic, that's why when you applied for a scholarship, you were asked to do a critical study of Szendrey. You yourself had all these ideas about him not being a Surrealist at all, as he's always been labelled. I agreed with you."

"Soo-re-a-leest!" Zoltan squeaked again as if his whole machinery of speech needed oiling. "He is not."

"I know, Zoltan. Why didn't you write about that?"

Zoltan sat down with a gesture of despair and a long, long sigh. Elizabeth knew him too well to laugh. They both humoured each other's moods. After a silence which made her question definitely rhetorical, she said softly: "You never really wanted to work on Szendrey, did you?"

"No." He opened his hands out like a priest in adoration or a fisherman exaggerating his catch, then dropped them to express the uselessness of words and gestures. Suddenly he got up and walked over to a map of the old Austro-Hungarian empire.

"He was my friend," he said with his back to her and his hands in his pockets. "He came from my village, here, just where the mountains start in Transylvania. Sometimes we belong to Romania, sometimes to Hungary." He took out his right hand—the square one—from his pocket and fingered the map sensuously, staring blankly at it, as if it were braille and he were blind. "But we are Hungarians. He came with me to Budapest in 1935. We belonged to Romania then, since Versailles. Until 1940. He was, how to say, a mystical nationalist. Árpád Szendrey. Árpád Szendrey," he repeated in a trance, "my friend, Árpád Szendrey."

"Were you—with him—when he was—taken?"

Zoltan's thick finger followed the map from Budapest out of the Hungarian plain and back to the mountain ridge of Transylvania, around it, into Romania, Bucharest, and suddenly zigzagged vaguely upwards towards Odessa.

"I saw him ... taken ..." After a long silence: "I got away." His finger moved up to Kherson. Then he dropped his hand and turned round. "It is ... difficult for me to write about ... Árpád Szendrey."

"Zoltan, *drágám*!" She used the Hungarian term of endearment. And suddenly she was an ordinary woman again for a moment, a woman in love, uncertain, aware of the pointlessness, the precariousness, and the carefully built-up pretence of their relationship. All this reading of Hungarian poetry together, in his room, and all this romance of culture! Yet there was half a continent between them, a whole country behind him, a whole life of which she knew nothing, in which she could never share, however many books she might read. She added lamely: "Why didn't you tell me all this at the time?" He didn't answer. "It would be difficult to change the subject of your book at this stage," she went on, "but I suppose I could——"

"I wanted to write it!" he exclaimed, walking back to her desk and gesticulating again. He grasped the edge with both hands and bent towards her, his voice dropping to a loud stage whisper. "I wanted . . . I still want. . . I will . . . I shall. Erzsébet! Give me more chance. I will write my pen into him, but she will have to go round the long way, covering much mountains and plains of paper, of history, of poetry, but she will reach him. Then I cut, I cut all what is unnecessary. I reach his heart again through many Siberias. Erzsébet. I have been so confused. I love you." He suddenly placed both his hands on hers across the narrow desk. There was a knock on the door and he removed them quickly, standing, rather absurdly, to attention.

"Come in," Elizabeth's voice sounded from across the Carpathians, very small.

"Oh, I'm so sorry." A blonde girl came in, carrying a pile of books under her arm. "Am I early? I'll wait outside." Her tone suggested that she wasn't early at all, and had no intention of waiting outside, and a glance at the clock, which stood at three minutes past twelve, emphasised her thoughts.

"No, Miss Forsyte, we have just overstepped the hour," Elizabeth said primly, "but you should wait till the previous class is over, you know. Mr Jones isn't here yet, is he?"

"He's just coming up the stairs." She stared at them blandly, mockingly.

"Well, we have finished now. Mr Torday, I do understand your difficulties. Just keep on at it, do it your own way, please. She measured her words carefully, and looked Zoltan straight in the eyes, black unflinching eyes, blazing with fury still, then suddenly impassive as she smiled, formally. "And send me anything you write, anything at all, you understand?"

"Yes, Mrs Cutting. Goodbye." He didn't quite click his heels but straightened his legs even more rigidly than before to suggest it, and swung round in an about-turn which marched him to the door mechanically, like a large puppet-soldier; with a curt bow of the head to the girl. She was smiling and unexpectedly he smiled back at her as he went out. And he smiled at Mr Jones, too, a skimpy young man in rimless pale blue spectacles. One could not, after all, be unfriendly to the few, the very few natives who were crazy enough, cranky enough, courteous enough to learn one's wild, remote, and difficult language, could one?

Zoltan clanked down the stone stairs in his heavy boots and the elegant house seemed to shake. He walked out into Bedford Row and through the small gate of Jockeys Fields, sniffing at the November frost critically, as if he were comparing smells, or trying to remember other Novembers, walks and arguments in the streets of Budapest with Árpád Szendrey the poet, walks and arguments in the woods with Árpád Szendrey the son of the local—what would they call it in England?—squire, yes, squire. He smiled to himself. Such funny words, the English had. When he had first arrived in London, in 1946, he had thought that *Esq* on the envelopes meant "excuse me", for the English were so polite. And he had addressed a man in the street, to ask his way, as 'gentleman'. He remembered the first lecture he attended, at a British Council course for foreigners, in Cambridge, that summer. The man talked incessantly about Ovid, though the lecture was, apparently, on Lord Byron. Then a knowledgeable Swede had explained to him, amid great guffaws, that he had taken down "Ovid" for "of it" every time. He was twenty-seven that year. He had come a long way since then. A degree in English, then a scholarship from this American's fund. The Fidler Institute. Erzsébet. So gentle. So unhappy with that vulgar little husband. No, that was not being the good cricket, was it? Howard was really very kind, she said. He meant well and in his own way he loved her. In her own way—what a self-deceptive phrase—she loved him. The English seemed to be able to reconcile every uncomfortable fact with their consciences by living in different departments. Of course they wanted the Poles, the Czechs, the Hungarians, the Yugoslavs, the Chinese, the Indians, the Cypriots, the Negroes to be free, but it was all so difficult, they were not ready, there was one kind of freedom for the English, and one kind for the Negroes, and another for the Cypriots, and yet another for the Poles, the Hungarians, the Chinese. There was one kind of love for the husband, and another for the lover, and never the twain—yes, they used old words and proverbs and catchphrases and slogans when they did not wish to face reality—shall meet, because if the twain, or the thrain, or the quain, or the multain complications of life, and love, and brotherhood and freedom met and clashed, then it was all so very inconvenient. They lived on an island, they lived each on their own island, and each of their emotions lived on its own tiny, very desert island, a precious stone set in a safe and silver sea, never to be reached by the invading tanks of ungentlemanly, un-English, unpublic school passions, not even by the mighty aerial armies of raining insults, or by the channel tunnels of guilt and shame.

Zoltan walked on in anger and despair, through the streets of Holborn, past Gray's Inn and the old wine shop of Henekey's, past the Elizabethan houses which bulged forward with their darkly striped bosoms. St Paul's loomed in the distance across the bomb sites of the city. Yes, the English suffered all right, but then they accepted the *fait accompli*, the wounds and the defeats, turning them miraculously into perfectly natural victories, about which no one spoke, and without even troubling to mend the damage. There it lay, seventeen years later, derelict and unashamed, proclaiming hypocritically to the world that they too had known the foreign yoke, and had had their finest hour. Clerks and shorthand typists were hurrying by unconcerned, on their way to the cheapest sandwich bars, messenger boys tinkled past on their bicycles, the tall red buses lumbered along towards the Holborn Viaduct, waiting without one hoot of impatience in the traffic jams.

He turned left into Ely Place, a small cul-de-sac of eighteenth century houses beyond a quaint old gateway.

"When I was last in Holborn, I saw good strawberries in your garden there: I do beseech you send for some of them," Richard III had said to John Morton, Bishop of Ely, to get rid of him, and this was where these Shakespearian strawberries had grown. Here had died John of Gaunt at Ely House, talking of precious stones and moats and blessed plots. Beyond the wall at the end of the cul-de-sac lay Little Dorrit's Bleeding Heart Yard. Now the plaques of solicitors, city consultants and, oddly enough, a firm of distillers, adorned the houses.

Zoltan loved London. He had learnt it from Dickens and Defoe, from Shakespeare and Decker and other stray books in the library of the village schoolmaster, who was an addict to English literature. In the beginning he had been delighted by London, then terrified, hating its size, its loneliness, its inhospitality. Then he had visited every street and every church, like a tourist at first, and had gradually come to know it and love it better than any Londoner. *Maybe it's because I'm a foreigner*, he had hummed to himself in lighter moods, *that I love London so.*

In the middle of the Ely Place cul-de-sac, on the left, were some stone steps which led down into a tiny crypt. Two churches stood one on top of the other, set well back from other houses, one somewhat restored and to be climbed into, one very old, down below—St Etheldreda's. He went into the crypt. It was very dark. Only very narrow windows in one wall, giving out on brick, and a few candles round the statues in small side niches cut into the other wall on the left, gave any light at all. Zoltan fumbled for the stoup, dipped his fingers, and crossed himself. He sat down in a back pew and peered into the darkness, accustoming his eyes, waiting for the familiar figures to grow into his sight. The low flat wooden ceiling was supported by thick wooden beams sprouting out of short stone pillars down the centre of the crypt, like the Y-shaped crosses of early times, right up to the North wall, dividing it so that there were two altars. The walls were of very rough-hewn stone. A Roman-British church originally, then Saxon, then Norman. Saint Etheldreda, Queen of Northumbria. The English had known conquest and occupation, after all. They had absorbed it, proudly turning it to riches. A long time ago, though, like the Magyars and the Turks, the Groats, the Austrians. A woman with a scarf on her head was kneeling in the front row. Zoltan got up and walked round. On the right, in one of the window niches stood the tiny black figure of Saint Etheldreda, a crowned nun with ermine on her robes. She reminded him somehow of Saint Elizabeth of Hungary, and he often came here to look at her. But he couldn't pray. His own language seemed far away and today she looked alien and insular and xenophobe, uncomprehending. *Maybe it's because she's a foreigner*—the tune hummed silently through his mind—Northumbrian and coldly lost in the coldly busy metropolis.

Chapter Six

"MAYBE it's because she's a foreigner." Mr Quentin Yellowstone looked kindly at Gael Jackson and offered him a cigarette. He shook his head, "your wife is, I believe, Italian?"

"Half. Oh, what does it matter? We're all foreigners. I'm a foreigner, you're a foreigner!" Mr Yellowstone waved his wrist to put out the match and seemed to be silently denying the accusation while letting it pass. The light went out, together with the flicker of anger in his eyes.

"Mr Jackson, please do not misunderstand me. I advised your publisher to settle the matter out of court. He advised you to get the man—er—intoxicated and—er—to show goodwill. You come to me now and tell me the operation was successful. Only he was intoxicated by your wife, who showed him a great deal of—er—goodwill. I cannot see what you have to complain about. On the continent, I believe, women in certain circles are trained in the arts of—er—diplomacy, and are frequently selected by ambitious husbands for their proficiency in the art of—er—charming away potential enemies and—er—other barriers to advancement."

"Goddam-son-of-a—" Gael breathed inaudibly and stopped. He did not like the Americanisms which emerged from beneath his carefully anglicised self when made angry. He got up and walked to the window of Yellowstone's office.

The walls on the right of it were lined with heavy books, Jarman on Wills, Hart on Banking Laws, Chitty on Contract, Eversley on Domestic Relations, Latey on Divorce, the whole collection of Halsbury, in fact, the entire history and theory of human relationships codified, summarised, commented, handed down from Ethelbert's Laws to the latest pronouncement on Obscene Libel, was here on Mr Yellowstone's shelves, and Gael looked at the familiar titles sceptically. He had 'concentrated' at Harvard

Law School after taking his A.B. in philosophy, but, once in Oxford, had returned as quickly as possible to his first love. All these books about quarrels! And wedged shamefacedly between Fry on Specific Performance and somebody on Tort was a strange little set called The Nutshell edition. So England had its potted culture too. As Mr Yellowstone continued his monologue, Gael picked one out idly and gave a wry smile: *Carriage of Goods by Sea in a Nutshell*. The ancient maritime nation of King Alfred still had its sense of humour.

He gazed out of the window, where the old English peace of Ely Place reigned unmolested and unbelievable in the quiet cul-de-sac. A church stood opposite, receding from the street, with one flight of steps leading down into a dark doorway almost underground, another turning up to the left into the church itself, which seemed to have been built later, over the dark doorway. A man with a large Mongol head and straight black hair swept back, walked up the narrow street, nodding to himself. He wore an American flying jacket. After staring at the houses, and, it seemed, up at the very window in which Gael stood, he turned suddenly, stumbled down the steps and disappeared into the dark doorway.

"What is that church?" Gael asked morosely.

"Church? Oh, that is St. Etheldreda's. Two churches, one on top of the other, most unusual." The solicitor was glad of a more amicable opening, and toddled to the window, looking very short of stature next to Gael. "The lower one is very old, a crypt really. The top part is fine Gothic, but it was bombed and restored after the war."

"It looks Catholic from the inscriptions."

"Yes, the Catholics bought it back, after 300 years, in, I believe, 1874, or thereabouts. It's been everything—American, Welsh, Episcopalian, Spanish Catholic, a hostel for poor children, Elizabethan offices, butteries, even a drinking house. Quiet little street, Ely Place. Do you know, Mr Jackson, it's the only street in London where a nightwatchman still calls out the hours at night—ten o'clock and all is well—but of course, there is nobody around to hear him. All these houses are offices now, solicitors, mostly." He puffed on to the glass, fogging out the November light on the view. "The police are not allowed in here, you know. Strange, because Ely Place was once converted into a prison, in 1642. London is full of such relics, Mr Jackson."

"But how extraordinary! Do you mean it was a Sanctuary?"

"Possibly. I do not know the origin of the custom."

"But supposing a murderer hid here?"

Mr Yellowstone smiled.

"He would certainly not be at a loss for a lawyer to defend him. Maybe that is why we are here."

"We?"

"Solicitors, I mean. You are here to discuss Mr—er—Howard Cutting. What do you think his next move will be, Mr Jackson?"

"Oh, yes." Gael sighed and returned to his chair. Mr Quentin Yellowstone padded across the carpet and sat down, suddenly dignified again as soon as his short legs were hidden behind the desk and happy that the proper relationship was restored between his client and himself.

"But that's just what I came to ask you, Mr Yellowstone. I can't make him out. He sends this angry letter, with the tone of a vulgar little upstart anxious for publicity and then he turns out to be really quite cultured—an Oxford man—even a little on the nervous side. No doubt that's what makes him aggressive. But he doesn't say a word about it! My wife wound him round her little finger, and I—well, I just couldn't bring myself to mention the subject. I have nothing to be ashamed of, how can I apologise for something I can't even explain!" He was getting heated again.

"Gently, Mr Jackson, gently. You must understand my position. On the face of it, Mr—er—Cutting certainly has grounds for complaint. But I was called in to advise Mr Truelove, not you personally. Mr Truelove now sends you here, to discuss the next step. Nevertheless, I am your publisher's legal adviser and have to look at it with a view to helping him, not you. Now, let me see, you say he is an Oxford man."

"Yes, he was up five years ago—when I was doing my doctorate thesis."

"Very interesting, could he conceivably have met you then?"

"I don't think so. I told you, I had never heard of him till the other day. And yet—" Gael drew his hand over his forehead and back into his fair hair "—the name rang a very faint bell."

"Did it indeed? You see, Mr Jackson, sometimes one makes more of an impression on other people than they on you. He may have met you, or heard of you, in his University days, and held a grudge against you ever since."

"But how? I was a postgraduate when he was up, and mixed very little."

"Did he tell you what he was reading?"

"Modern Greats."

"Philosophy. Hmm." Mr Yellowstone tapped his nose gently with a thick forefinger, "could he conceivably have applied for the job which you now hold?"

"At Beverley! His college!" Gael looked thunderstruck. "Mr Yellowstone, you may have something there. I know there were two other applicants, one from Beverley. I may even have been told the name and then forgotten it. I could find out. Funny, though, he never said anything about it."

"For a novelist, Mr Jackson, you seem remarkably er—unworldly. Perhaps you will allow me to enlighten you, out of my wide experience of litigation psychology. More often than not there is a secondary, and invariably unmentioned, even unconscious motive. A man who fails to get a Fellowship is likely to remember the name of the man who succeeded, whereas the latter will hardly remember those of his rivals—if indeed he ever knew them. Secondly, Mr—er—Cutting may not be fully aware of the reason—if this is the reason—for his antagonism, but he would be just sufficiently aware of it—without admitting it, least of all to himself—not to mention the fact to you, as a fact—if indeed it is a fact and not a supposition." Mr Yellowstone cleared his throat loudly after delivering this syntactically confused little lecture on elementary psychology, but the noise expressed a colon into further enlightenment rather than a full stop. "From what you tell me of your dinner party, it seems to me distinctly within the bounds of possibility that Mr—er—Cutting may have been so delighted with his evening, with your kindness and culture and hospitality and with the—er—charming—er—atmosphere which surrounds you in your home, that he may quietly drop the whole unfortunate business. And here you should not feel angered, Mr Jackson, by the—er—contribution which your beautiful wife so naturally and—er—loyally made. Such advantages are a blessing, Mr Jackson, in certain circumstances which life so unfortunately thrusts upon us. One cannot always be aloof and uncompromising, Mr Jackson."

"But———"

"On the other hand," Mr Yellowstone interrupted him with his favourite oath-taking gesture, as if concretely to exemplify the very other hand he was speaking of, "on the other hand, we cannot dismiss the possibility of a psychological reaction in favour of aggression. Mr—er—Cutting may have, been—er—intoxicated and bewildered into passivity and—er—timidity, yes, such people are often timid, Mr Jackson. Aggressive in print or rash in letter-writing, but suddenly anxious to please and fearful of antagonising when faced with live, human personalities—especially, Mr Jackson, unexpected personalities. He may have been thrown off his balance, he may—if my wide experience of litigation psychology can be trusted—later feel ashamed and angered at having been so thrown, and attempt to recover his self-esteem by proceeding with the case. In which—" Mr Quentin Yellowstone nearly said 'in which case', but his training in forensic oratory saved him "—contingency—"

"He was scouting the ground, I tell you!" Gael thumped his fist on the desk. "He was finding out what kind of a sucker I would be."

"That is very succinctly put, Mr Jackson." He smiled. "Indeed I was attempting to say very much the same thing, but I would hardly have expressed it in such—er—unprofessional terms."

"What do I do?"

"Wait, Mr Jackson. You have tried one method, suggested to you by Mr Truelove. A wise man, Mr Truelove, and greatly experienced in the occupational hazards of his profession. It may well have succeeded, and we cannot at this stage precipitate the outcome. If it did not succeed, we may still be able to settle out of court in a more formal and of course more—er—expensive way. Otherwise we fight it out. We have a case, Mr Jackson, a —shall we say—*fairly* strong case."

"Lawyers always have a case. How would they live otherwise?"

"Very well put, Mr Jackson, very well put." Mr Quentin Yellowstone chuckled and rubbed his hands, determined to humour his client and mentally invoking his entire 'experience of litigation psychology' in order to do so. "We live on the quarrels of other people. It is difficult for us sincerely to hope for heaven on earth, Mr Jackson, for if everyone loved their neighbours as themselves, there would be no necessity for our existence, no necessity at all. However, heaven is not of this world," he chattered on amiably, mixing up his New Testament quotations, "and Christ came not to destroy the law, for where no law is there is no transgression."

Gael Jackson walked down the rickety wooden steps in a state of bewilderment. They reminded him of his college in Oxford. It was all very well for England to be quaint and ye olde, he thought, but couldn't it sometimes be practical? Or was gentlemanliness a well-tried ancient formula for being practical, like an Anglo-Saxon charm against the stings of bees?

Gael was American enough to be profoundly mistrustful of old-world customs and old-world politics, and yet to fall so in love with the old-world enchantment of Oxford as to leave his country for it. And Nina. He loved her so jealously he could think himself into her, he felt he knew what she was doing at any moment; there had been times when it seemed he shared her dreams. He smiled as he remembered how often it happened, so often he had stopped telling her. The first time she had been quite alarmed. He was recounting a dream at breakfast, how he found himself going up on a moving stairway, and knew that she was in an elevator with a strange man, very dark and tall, going down, going down, and he couldn't reach her. Nina had stared at him in terror, for she had dreamt that she was in—as she put it—a lift with a dreadful dark man, and called out to him, but he was going away from her on an escalator, and she could see him through the lift doors and transparent walls as the lift went down, very fast. He had had the same dream again recently with the same dark man in the elevator, taking her away, down, down. But he hadn't told her.

Yes, he loved her jealously yet unpossessively. He hated even the brief separation of his weekdays at Oxford, but she had insisted on living in London. She would die, she had said, as a don's wife in a house at Iffley or in the Banbury Road. He had a room in college and it was much better for married couples not to be together day in and day out. At first they want nothing but that, she had said, but it's most unwise because later they can't understand how they could ever have wanted that and they then try to invent explanations as to why they don't any more. Much better to stick to the later system from the beginning, because then the short separations, which seem so hard at first, go on being hard and reminding each one all the time how much they miss the other, and the reunions go on being absolutely wonderful. Think of my happiness when you come home after five long days! she had exclaimed. Besides, there'll be so much more to talk about, I can't be bright all the time, you see. And indeed, the joy in her eyes when he walked in and the fling of her arms round his neck, the scream of delight as he lifted her off the floor, the hugs and the kisses, even now after six years, were worth every day away from her, and had evidently proved her right. All he wanted was to be left alone to enjoy his life with her, his work and his writing. Yes, in spite of his voluntary exile, Gael was American enough to fiercely resent intrusion, criticism, or the expectation that he should play an unwanted role. He was American enough to feel impatient to the point of hysteria when such an intrusion was made, rousing him from his basic emotional isolationism, his easy-going, unproblematic, lethargic goodwill towards men.

He stood irresolutely in the street, unable to shake off the familiar sense of unreality which had descended on him and surrounded him like a cloak of invisibility. Perhaps it was his prolonged study and teaching of theories of perception which made him slip so easily into a feeling that nothing around him existed, or alternatively that he did not exist in anything around him. He found himself in the doorway of the old crypt and went in. It was so dark he couldn't see anything and bumped into a man coming out.

"I'm sorry."

"It is quite all right. Very dark in here." The man's black eyes narrowed as they faced the pale sunlight. Black hair. The dark man in the elevator...

"Here, tell me, who are you? What is this place?" Gael caught the man's sleeve as he walked on up the steps. The man looked round in alarm.

"Why should I tell you my name? This is a Catoleek church. I come out of it, you go in, we are both Catoleeks, that is enough?"

"I'm sorry," Gael said again. "I could have sworn I had seen you before —please don't think I'm crazy, but I thought I saw you in a dream."

"A dream?"

"Yes."

The man looked at him carefully and decided that there was no cause for alarm. English eccentricity never ceased to surprise him, but a refugee had to be careful, nevertheless, about whom he talked to.

"My name is Zoltan Torday," he said slowly, then bowed and put his hand forward. "I am Hungarian."

"Gael. Gael Jackson. American. Glad to know you, Mr Torday."

"American! Ah, you are used to foreign names over there."

"We have quite a few," Gael looked at him with the sudden friendliness which comes so naturally even to the quietest of Americans. "Were you in the Rising?"

"No. I have been here since the war."

"Look, I'm sorry I frightened you. I remember now where I've seen you. I was standing at that window up there, a solicitor's office, and you walked by and into the church. I'd completely forgotten it. The truth is, Mr Torday, I was in a sort of trance down those steps, and—well——"

"I understand, Mr Jackson. Please, it is quite all right."

"That's very kind of you. Would you care to have a cup of coffee with me?" They were walking towards the gateway of the cul-de-sac.

"Thank you. I should like to very much."

"You know, you needn't have been frightened that I was from the secret police. I learnt today—from that solicitor, curiously enough, that this is the only street in London into which the police aren't allowed. Sort of sanctuary, I guess, from old times. Isn't that strange?"

"The English are very peculiar people, Mr Jackson." Zoltan smiled sadly. "But such traditions would hardly stop a foreign spy from our secret police, I fear." He looked at Gael sideways and added quickly, "I was not frightened of that, you know. I am not important enough to be a wanted man, or kidnapped."

"No, no, of course not. You were just surprised by my rudeness. Say, is there a coffee bar round here? I don't know this part of London."

"Mr Jackson, please, if you will come to my place, it is not far, I will make you coffee and we talk, yes?"

"Sure. But I invited you."

"We are both foreigners here, Mr Jackson, nobody is host."

And so they chattered their way back into High Holborn and up a narrow street called Leather Lane, where Zoltan had his room. They had to cross Greville Street, into which debouched the back of the hideous Prudential Building, which generated its own electricity with a noise like constant hot water, garrulously assuring passersby that the holy light of financial security would continue in all emergency. "That house makes such clamour at night," said Zoltan. "It must be a factory."

His room was above a tobacconist in a small brick house dating back to Queen Anne but in a sad state of disrepair and leaning slightly forward. The green front door was incongruously modern and so was the narrow hall, paper-embossed in a slimy dung colour up to eye level, and plastered in dirty margarine, peeling off, above. Zoltan led the way up a flight of weary-looking stairs that seemed to exude a smell of over-boiled cabbage.

His room, however, was quite different. He had painted the walls white, and the ceiling red. On the floor, which sloped violently, giving the room a surrealist aspect, a cheap green carpet completed the Hungarian flag, and the curtains were red and green. On one wall were pinned some pre-war travel posters of the Elizabeth Bridge in Budapest, of Debrecen, of a mountain view with forests. The latter's caption, 'Come to Romania', could just be read under the green paint which crossed it out. Above the gas fire, which Zoltan lit at once, some press cuttings and photographs had been pasted on a large black sheet of paper, and on the chimney ledge stood a photograph of a woman with sad dark eyes. The other walls were lined with homemade bookshelves. In a corner, a divan was spread with black, and no cushions; a table near the window was covered with books and papers, neatly sorted and stacked, and an old portable typewriter; two clumsy brown leather armchairs, a low table, a very expensive wireless which looked as if it could get any station on the moon or Mars, or the latest earth satellite; a small cupboard with a gas ring was near the fireplace.

Gael studied the press cuttings on the wall while Zoltan started grinding coffee in a strange tube of orientally carved brass. The pictures were of the Budapest Rising, out of a German illustrated paper; the texts were mostly from English newspapers, a few were in Hungarian.

"Why you have to see a solicitor?" Zoltan asked politely. "If I am not indiscreet, you are in trouble?"

"Oh, no, not really." Gael sank into one of the leather armchairs. "Just some goddam critic who thinks I've lampooned him in my last book."

"Lampoon? What is lampoon?"

Gael smiled. "Mocked. Well, that's not quite correct. I described an incident which apparently happened to him, and hit on one or two other features by which he says he's known. I'd never heard of him before—he literally got into my novel without my knowing him. Do you ever have—er—psychic experiences, Mr Torday?"

Zoltan looked at Gael thoughtfully, then bent over the gas ring, mixing the coffee in the Turkish copper flask with a small wooden stick. He added sugar and a pinch of dried thyme, and watched it in silence.

"I have," he said after a while. "But from the past, Mr Jackson, from the past, not the future." He poured the coffee into two small cups without handles and brought them to Gael on a round tray of beech wood which he placed on the low table. Then he sat in the other armchair and said: "Explain to me more."

Gael was weary enough of the whole unpleasant business to talk dispassionately, as if it were all over long ago. Yet he wanted to give this dispassionate account fully but with no names, to a complete stranger, a foreigner even, who would not only have no stake in the matter one way or the other, but who would probably be totally incapable of giving advice. He was a mere dictaphone into which Gael could clear his thoughts, but which would not play them back at him. As he talked, Zoltan looked startled at one point, then let it pass. He put his face in his hands, forgetting his coffee, and rousing himself only when Gael had finished. Then he took his cup and sipped slowly from it.

"This lover, who telephoned the woman in your novel..."

"Yes?"

"It was I."

Gael stared at him. Zoltan finished his coffee at one gulp and thumped the cup back on the tray. 'He's mad,' Gael thought.

"Except that I am not her lover. I know the man. Howard Cutting." It was Gael's turn to start. "I heard about the fish, his wife told me afterwards, she dropped the fish, it was a salmon, I think. They joked. But Erzsebét—that is Elizabeth, his wife, I call her in Hungarian Erzsebét, there she is in that photograph—she was angry with me, because I confused her. You see, one evening I was very sad and very desperate, and I telephoned. I thought she would simply put down the receiver and say it was a wrong number. We have this arrangement for urgent messages. That day was not urgent, except for me. He answered the telephone and I am so desperate. I do not just push the button B, I ask for her." Tension made Zoltan forget tenses and he was pressing his palms one against the other, producing gasping noises with them. "I think she will invent something for my call. I say I love her and I adore her and I cut off. She said afterwards she goes scarlet in the face and drops the fish, but it was joked, and while she pick it up she thinks of what to say, that I telephone because I cannot finish the chapter I am to show her next day. The chapter on Árpád Szendrey. Mr Jackson, you do not have Árpád Szendrey in your novel also? No. You do not know Árpád Szendrey. Mr Jackson, I, too, am in great trouble. In great trouble, Mr Jackson."

Chapter Seven

"HE calls her in Hungarian, er, Erzsebét, m'lord," said Mr Austin Barnacle, QC, shifting the stress from the first to the second syllable.

"Did you say sherbet, Mr Barnacle?"

"I did, m'lord."

"How very confusing. I thought that was some kind of Eastern drink." A titter went through the court.

"It is, m'lord. But the Hungarian for Elizabeth apparently sounds similar. It is—er—Erzsebét." Counsel for the defendant looked down again at his brief.

"I see. Novelists certainly choose the most disconcerting names for their heroines. Am I to understand that the lady in the first defendant's novel is called—Sherbet?"

"No, m'lord. The witness."

"Then why are you wasting the Court's time with all these irrelevancies, Mr Barnacle?"

"I apologise, m'lord. Your lordship asked what the witness was saying and I merely repeated it to your lordship."

"All right, proceed, Mr Barnacle."

Howard Cutting straightened his face again for the rest of Mr Barnacle's cross-examination. He had found it difficult not to chortle visibly during this brief altercation. He was enjoying himself. He glanced at the public gallery, which was pretty full. Journalists were sitting in the wooden rows behind counsel. And Nina Jackson in a lovat-green spring outfit with a deep lilac silk scarf and lilac gloves, and a pale blue pudding basin straw hat whose low brim hid her fringe, and almost her eyes. She was flirting with the junior barrister, answering his questions in confidential whispers accompanied by much eyelash labour. And Elizabeth, at the other end, frowning.

"Now, Mr Cutting, can you tell the court who your guests were at the dinner in question?"

"Certainly. My publisher, Mr Geoffrey Brandon, and his wife. Mr Jocelyn Furnivall, literary editor of *The Sunday Supplement*, and Mrs Sonya Dandridge, editor of *Elegance*, to which paper I have contributed the odd cultural piece."

"I see. And you claim that if these people were to believe that the incident of the fish, as described by Mr Jackson in *The Sycamore Tree*, were true in every detail, your professional reputation would suffer?"

"That's about it."

"Would you say that you invited these people because they are important to your career, Mr Cutting?"

"Not at all. They are my friends, who happen also to be professional colleagues."

"They are all what one might call literary people?"

"If you like the term, yes."

"Is it not a fact, Mr Cutting, that literary people are particularly carefree about such things as other men's private lives?"

"If you mean they don't gossip, the answer is decidedly no."

The public gallery tittered.

"I was not referring to gossip, Mr Cutting, but to moral disapproval strong enough to affect a man's advancement. I put it to you that even supposing your literary friends saw any connection between the incident in your flat and that described in my client's novel—and I hope to show this is far from being the case—they would not care whether the telephone call was from your wife's lover or not, and that if they thought your wife had a lover, the fact would in no way affect their attitude to either of you."

"It's not a question of moral approval, merely of ridicule. The real incident was quite normal, but the incident in the book was close enough, and described in terms which make me look ridiculous."

"Yet there was no real similarity between the two, since you have declared that your wife was not flustered by the call, and that the call was not from a lover, but from a student. This was said at the time. I put it to you, Mr Cutting, that you are taking it a little too personally, and merely attracting attention to yourself."

"My lord, I object to my learned friend's manner of putting the question." Counsel for the plaintiff leapt up to Howard's rescue.

"I see nothing wrong with Mr Barnacle's cross-examination, Mr Fell, apart from its lack of brevity. Proceed, Mr Barnacle, and try to cover your ground a little more speedily."

"Thank you, m'lord. As I was saying, Mr Cutting, don't you think you are taking it a little too personally?"

"No, sir," Howard answered with exaggerated politeness. He had been given ample time to think and was glad to be allowed a word in between the bobbing wigs. "I have told you before, I am not complaining about this scene in itself but about this scene in conjunction with other features in the book. No doubt you will be cross-examining my dinner guests on the scene in isolation?" Howard had inherited some of his mother's talent. As a student, he had acted in the OUDS, and now he spoke clearly, with a crude stage irony.

"If you don't mind, Mr Cutting, I am doing the questioning."

"I beg your pardon."

The case ambled on, never quite falling into farce, nor indeed rising to drama. Howard was relaxed, wearing that knowing look so familiar to his wife. Now and again he glanced at her and felt inspired to a better and better performance by her dismal, sorrowing disapproval. In the corner of his eye Nina's lilac gloved hands wrote something down for a journalist, lay on the panelled ledge, moved to support her cheek, to touch the tip of her nose, to arrange her hat, disappeared—for all he knew to hold hands with the reporter—moved up again to her lapel, lay on the panelled ledge . . . For five months he hadn't seen her, not since that first time. He had put her out of mind: he had proceeded with the case, almost, if he cared to admit it to himself, not to invite them back, not to be allowed to collude with the opposing party. Almost, if he cared to admit more to himself, as a revenge on Gael Jackson for having so much that he himself wanted, a Fellowship, a creative imagination—for Howard was a good enough critic to be dimly aware of what that was—and Nina. But Howard never admitted anything, least of all to himself: he had put her out of mind and that was that.

The second defendant was called. Mr Truelove made a good impression as a successful and obviously respectable publisher. The defendants were denying that they had published the words of the plaintiff or that the words were capable of bearing any meaning defamatory to the plaintiff. Alternatively they claimed that they had published the words innocently and had made offers of amends in accordance with Section 4 of the Defamation Act 1952, as soon as practicable. They seemed in fact to be trying three lines of defence at the same time. Howard felt very confident indeed now, in spite of the fact that his counsel, Mr Fell, behind whom he was now sitting, was only a junior, whereas Messrs Truelove & Thorne had engaged Austin Barnacle, QC. Mr Austin Barnacle, QC, was obviously getting on his lordship's nerves. Mr Fell, on the other hand, was doing very nicely.

"You did not, then, really offer to withdraw the book, Mr Truelove?"

"We offered, through our solicitor, to publish a statement in the personal columns of *The Times*, to the effect that the novel was fictitious, and that if anyone had misidentified the plaintiff with the character described as an expert on Thomas Carlyle they bore no relationship to each other."

"Of course, it is very nice for a publisher to have an advertisement of his books in *The Times*, but would such an advertisement not send readers in great haste to the bookshops and libraries, to find out just what was said about this character?"

"It might indeed." Mr Truelove smiled with pleasure at the idea. "But we should be exonerated from malice."

"You are surely aware, Mr Truelove, that it does not matter in law whether or not the defendant intended a passage to refer to the plaintiff, but whether people reading think it does?"

"Yes, of course."

"And yet you did not offer to withdraw the book?"

"That was understood in our suggestion, that is, if the plaintiff was not satisfied with an advertisement in *The Times*. But he ignored our letter and started proceedings."

"In what way was it understood?"

"It is surely perfectly clear that after such an advertisement no bookshop would dare to sell the book and no library would lend it, since they would no longer be able to rely on their own innocence. In practice that would have meant withdrawing the book."

Howard looked across at Gael Jackson, who was sitting behind Mr Barnacle, staring at the judge. He seemed in a complete daze, but would suddenly listen with great attention and jot down something in a small black book. 'Copy, no doubt,' Howard thought sourly. 'His next novel will be a philosophic fantasy in wigs and robes. The witnesses will change sides mysteriously and counsel for the plaintiff will start cross-examining the judge. Then the court will suddenly not be there at all, like the sycamore tree, because everyone has gone to sleep. Oh, I know that one.' He blinked as his favourite phrase of literary discussions jolted his own fantasy. The court was certainly unreal—'I'll give him that.' The wigs reminded him of Mozart and Mozart reminded him of Nina Jackson, and her small white hand minuetting at him like a lace handkerchief and the minuet somehow turning into bop, and her hand into wings as she murmured 'Bird.' She was behind him now and he couldn't turn to see her. The whole court, smelling of dust and gowns, was dancing a drab minuet in very slow motion, to a low, timeless, patternless noise like an old record endlessly turning on an unwound gramophone. Then things livened up towards the end of the session.

The dinner guests were called, Jocelyn Furnivall giving quite a coquettish performance and smoothly assuring his lordship that he had recognised Mr Cutting from the carp scene taken in conjunction with the references to Carlyle and reviewing. Mr Cutting was one of his very best contributors, he said, and not a failed writer at all. Mr Geoffrey Brandon, Howard's publisher, was rather more cautious. His was a small, struggling new firm and he did not enjoy finding himself on the wrong side of Messrs Truelove & Thorne. Sonya Dandridge, editress of *Elegance*, for which glossy fashion magazine Howard had once written a short but sentimental piece on Oxford, was also in a difficult position, since Nina Jackson was one of her regular contributors, and she hovered accordingly. Two famous novelists testified that Gael Jackson was a most promising young writer of great integrity who would do nothing out of malice. Phineas Antrobus, a Cambridge English don known for his curious ideas about Shakespeare, came forward to say that he had known Dr Jackson for several years and had corresponded with him on the subject of psychic phenomena, in which he was deeply interested. He was convinced that this unfortunate coincidence was due to the author's unusual and perhaps unconscious powers of telepathy, even with unknown people. No one from Oxford appeared. The judge seemed to wake up when Phineas Antrobus suggested that counsel for both sides had misunderstood the book, which was an allegory based on telephone communications, taking a comic incident as a mere point of departure for a higher plane.

"Did you say comic?"

"I did, my lord."

"You think then, that it is worth my while reading this novel?"

"It is indeed, my lord."

"Can you promise me that I shall have an entertaining evening?"

"Your lordship will be unable to put it down."

"Thank you. Thank you. I haven't read any good books lately."

The court adjourned.

"How dared you drag me into your answers?" said Elizabeth as they walked past St Clement Danes on their way to Henekey's wine bar, in the Strand. "And Zoltan, too."

"Oh, come off it."

They were followed by Geoffrey Brandon and his wife and Jocelyn Furnivall, who were joining them for a drink but kept at a tactful distance. Howard looked nervously over his shoulder.

"If you want to make a scene, wait till we get home, it'll be all the more boiling by then."

"Hypocrite. Why do you suppose they're walking ten paces behind if it's not to let me blow up? If you're so fearful of what they'll think of you why did you drag them all to court? They don't think much now, I can tell you. Brandon was the most cagey witness there."

"You slay me . . ."

The bend of Aldwych was a one-way thoroughfare and traffic came from the left instead of the right as Elizabeth stepped forward to cross. He caught her arm and drew her back. "Careful, darling! Ooh, nearly lost you for ever then."

Like most men, Howard couldn't bear recriminations, especially from women, least of all women who knew him well. He would enclose himself against the familiar accusations in a thick skin of indifferent silence, retaliating in crude repartee, or rudeness, or flippancy, only when that skin, less thick than it seemed, was punctured by the sharp mockery some women were so clever at using as their only means of defence against men of his kind. But with Elizabeth he had learnt that unruffled geniality often worked better than rudeness, and he was determined to avoid even apparent tension in front of his friends.

"Fat lot you'd care. Or I for that matter. My God, how I hated you today. I particularly asked you not to mention Zoltan."

"Ah, your Hungarian. Perhaps I mentioned him simply to test your reactions, hmm?"

"You know perfectly well he's in a difficult position politically and can't afford to have attention drawn to himself."

"No, as a matter, of fact, I didn't." Howard was genuinely concerned for a moment, then flippant again, dismissing her statement as dramatisation. "You're so damn mysterious about him you never tell me anything."

"You never listen. And if you do it goes out the other ear, because it doesn't concern you or your literary prospects. Oh, yes, you got worked up enough at the time of the Budapest Rising, everybody did. You attended every meeting of all the literary clubs, who were sending useless telegrams of hope and cheer about the brotherhood of writers, and you posted letters to every paper to show how indignant you were. You even talked of joining a secret group of armed volunteers—for forty-eight hours. Yet you pranced around supporting all the papers who with one unanimous and self-righteous outcry were confusing the issue as best they could. Even Zoltan saw that, and he in agony over his own country. You make me sick."

"You're echoing his views very eloquently, darling. Have you finished? Because we're here."

But she wouldn't stop. "If the Hungarians knew how many beautiful friendships were ruined and how many marriages were split down the middle by the short-sighted self-revealing passions their Rising caused among the unpassionate English, they would be most flattered no doubt, but hardly encouraged." They walked into the carriage yard and up the old wooden stairs into the beamed and panelled wine bar. A waiter ushered them to a table by the window, overlooking the Strand, and moved off tactfully as he saw the grim faces of marital love in mid-argument.

"You know, I rather like you when you're being as unpleasant as you know how." She glared at him and sat down. "I didn't notice your Hungarian being particularly heroic at the time. He kept remarkably quiet."

Elizabeth gazed blankly at the wine list. The others were coming up the stairs, joking noisily. "Zoltan went to Hungary," she said in a low voice. "Officially he is still there, writing for an underground newspaper to which he sends the stuff by special channels. Naturally they can't find him to arrest him. Now, do you understand what you've done?"

"I—oh, there you are!"

He turned to the others and the uneasy expression on his face changed as if by a switch to one of jocular amiability. The waiter hovered round as they shambled into their seats, Howard carefully placing himself on the other side from Elizabeth, next to Mrs Brandon. "What'll it be? Shall we get a bottle of wine?" Howard studied the list with the carefully casual air of a connoisseur and ordered *Liebfraumilch*.

"Howard, my dear," said Jocelyn, "you did very well."

"You didn't do so badly yourself." Howard suddenly put on the grateful spaniel face which he usually wore when he didn't know how to thank people. "Bless you," he added with a wistful smile. His unexpected meekness was always charming and at least partially sincere.

Gael's party went, rather more quietly, in Mr Truelove's Jaguar, back to his house in Onslow Square, where they were all invited to dinner. Gael and Nina, Mr Truelove, Mr Yellowstone, Phineas Antrobus and Sonya Dandridge all piled easily into the enormous luxury car. Sonya Dandridge, having finished giving her evidence for the opposite party, had approached the group outside the Law Courts and asked Mr Yellowstone if it would be in order for her to talk to the Jacksons now.

"Sonya, hello!" Nina settled it for him. "You were wonderfully ambiguous."

"Well, darling, the truth and nothing but can be ambiguous, can't it?" She had already explained by telephone how she had been, as she put it, hauled in against her will.

"Mr Truelove, can she come too? This is Mrs Dandridge, my editress on *Elegance*."

"How do you do. You're very welcome."

After the suitable protests about not crashing in to their dinner party, she came.

"You have more *savoir-faire* than Mr Cutting," said Quentin Yellowstone to Sonya in the car. "Do you know he tried to come and see me last winter? Out of charity I assumed he was ignorant of the fact that I was acting for Truelove & Thorne, but after his performance today I really begin to wonder."

Everyone was a little subdued at dinner, and the case was hardly discussed. Both Gael and Mr Truelove had made a good impression in the box, Mr Yellowstone said, but he would not commit himself as to the outcome. Nina looked depressed and Gael was quiet. Only Phineas Antrobus talked freely, mostly about Shakespeare's undoubted knowledge of Greek.

He was explaining his critical experiment, called New Subjectivism, to Mr Truelove, whose firm had long ago turned down his first book, thereby missing an author who had lately become quite a vogue.

"I send questionnaires, together with a poem I wish to evaluate, to a cross-section of the reading public, to find out what the poem means to them. In the last analysis, a poem is the sum of all the meanings read into it by everyone. All those meanings are there, whatever the poet may have consciously intended. Don't you agree, Mr Truelove?"

"That would certainly explain why there is such an abundance of critics these days."

"Indeed." Phineas went on, ignoring the irony. "New Subjectivism led me to my most startling discovery, as you no doubt know, I sent a Shakespeare sonnet round, and one of the replies—from a garage mechanic in Aberdeen—said that it sounded like Greek to him. Just a phrase, of course, but even flippancy has its element of truth. After all, this young man might equally have said 'nonsense' or 'double Dutch.' But he didn't, he had unconscious telepathic insight. His very individual reaction gave me the idea for a most interesting hypothesis. I worked on it—I had considerable experience in cryptography during the war, you know—and lo and behold, the sonnet turned out to be a most ingenious pun when transcribed phonetically into Greek. Little did Ben Jonson know when he said that Shakespeare had little Latin and less Greek. I am working on the other sonnets, now, some of them are coming out very nicely indeed."

Sonya Dandridge asked Nina if they were going away in the summer. Nina said it was most unlikely, what with the children, and the probable expenses of the case—looking archly at Mr Yellowstone. Sonya, anxious to appear impartial, was making vague offers.

"Cordelia Tullis is leaving next month to have a baby. I was wondering if you'd like to take over her Talking Points."

"But doesn't that mean going to all the press shows and reading all the best books?"

"Not all, darling. We're an elegant monthly for the highly fashionable women. The weeklies sort things out for you and you can pick and choose the books which seem to be most talked about. As for first nights and film shows, it's usually fairly clear from advance propaganda and gossip, and if you do miss anything that's hit the headlines you can always go later, on expenses."

"Well—I'll have to think. It's very sweet of you." Nina was not at all her usual self tonight. "I'll ask Gael."

"You do that thing, darling," said Sonya smoothly, thinking that Nina needed more sophistication and independence than she appeared to. "Did you see Elizabeth Cutting? I wonder why she wore that appalling readymade suit?"

Gael was gazing dreamily at his cranky friend, Phineas Antrobus, of whom he was unaccountably fond.

"Indeed," Antrobus was saying to Mr Truelove, who looked bewildered, and to Mr Yellowstone, who looked incredulous. "I hope to publish my next book about the subject soon, on which I shall definitely make my—er —name."

Gael smiled at the hesitation. Phineas Antrobus was already fairly well-known among poets and critics, but he was also sensitive about his surname, which he had long believed, in spite of all evidence to the contrary, went back to Greek *anthropus*. His father had called him Phineas, under the same delusion.

"I was most interested, Mrs Dandridge, in what you said earlier on about truth," Phineas went on suavely. "There is, of course, no such thing as absolute truth, or absolute meaning. We live by the sums of multitudinous viewpoints, do we not, and all the possible meanings are inherent in the value of any statement. This, of course, produces the ambiguity you spoke of. Not just one, but many. Truth is not ambiguous, Mrs Dandridge, it is, if I may coin a phrase, polyguous."

The next day they lost the case and were ordered to withdraw the book. His lordship exonerated the defendants from all malice and deplored the unfortunate coincidence. He awarded costs and forty shillings' damages to the plaintiff, Mr Howard Cutting.

Chapter Eight

"NO one is interested in Truth *per se*," said Howard Cutting forcefully, "the honorific capital doesn't make it any truer."

"Nor does the lower case make it any less true," Sonya Dandridge replied with a smile as swift as a zip fastener, "people often seem to think they can make God smaller by spelling Him with a small g and putting Him in the plural."

Religion was rather fashionable these days and Sonya was nothing if not that. She had kept her figure and always managed to look the latest thing, even in jeans and a sloppy jo, which she was wearing now, and which somehow did not look ridiculous in spite of her greying hair. Indeed, grey hair was so much in vogue just then that girls of eighteen would step out of hairdressers with startling powder-blue heads over their lineless young faces, further uncharacterised by pale lips, dead white makeup and a mauve doe-eyed look. Sonya emphasised the grey with carefully whitened streaks, as if it were all intended, not by nature as it was, but by art. She had the reputation of a wit, but her religious repartee was somewhat misplaced on this bright Sunday morning, since she could hardly have gone to church dressed as she was. Indeed, she was accompanied by two hideous pedigree bulldogs—gallantly escorted one might say, had they not been bull bitches—over which she constantly petted and fretted. They were called, in a weird Freudian way, Dump and Hump.

"Oh, Hump darling, don't do that."

Hump was sniffing at her legs.

Sonya's eyes looked upside down, with the upper rim less curved than the lower, instead of the other way round, and this somehow accentuated their glassy look. She spoke in a fashionably low voice, and Howard, who liked to think he was attractive to, instead of attracted by, older women, stood very near her, almost touching her hand as they both held their glasses of bitter in front of them. He was wearing his tight jacket of beige check suiting, brown corduroy trousers, and a green check shirt with a dark blue and yellow college tie. She looked down at him, amused and he put on his spaniel look.

"Oh? Since when have you turned religious?"

"Since talking to you, you old monster."

"I trust I'm not monstrous enough to send you scurrying to the cloister? I don't see you as a holy nun."

"No, but if ever I spat on you, the sprinkling might be just not unholy enough to redeem you." She smiled at him with mock allure in her experienced eyes.

"I can't think of anything nicer," he almost whimpered, "except perhaps you licking me, all over."

"Ice-cream?"

"You scream, I scream."

"Oh, Howard! Elizabeth, can't you house-train your husband? He's just made the most ghastly pun."

"Well, we are out of doors, you know," Elizabeth smiled indulgently.

They were standing in the Chelsea Embankment Gardens, which every spring or summer Sunday was turned into a mockery of a smart cocktail party, and that was mockery enough. It took quite twenty minutes to struggle for a drink in the crowded pub, and everyone stood outside in the narrow street, or overflowed into the gardens, uncomfortably from one foot to another as they exchanged their well-rehearsed views on the Sunday morning papers. Indeed, it was quite a ritual, and for that reason vital to read every article and every review with extreme care from nine till twelve, when the pub opened. Important people—that is, writers, reviewers, critics, BBC talks producers, anyone, in fact, either on the make or anxious to show that they were no longer on the make, but had made it —came from all over London to meet other Important people on the Chelsea Embankment of a Sunday. It saved them, for one thing, from having to invite each other. "What did you think of Willy's piece?" someone would say, and out it would come, wittily worded and voluble, until someone else's cue came up.

There were, in fact, two rival pubs in Chelsea, and Howard, who came all the way from High Street, Kensington, sometimes walked casually past the other—which had a front garden with tables and chairs and was much more comfortable, though quieter—to see if anyone important was there. If not, he would walk on in a preoccupied way, or wave absentmindedly to anyone he knew who had spotted him, as if nothing were further from his mind than a drink on a Sunday morning. Today, however, Elizabeth was with him, and he had arranged to meet Jocelyn Furnivall and his new boyfriend on the Embankment, so he had no idea who was at the other pub, and this rather worried him, since no one Important had yet turned up here.

Howard was about to whine playfully at Sonya's teasing but his face changed as he saw two well-known critics approaching the group. Elizabeth watched him, ironical yet fascinated.

"As I was saying, no one is interested in truth *per se*. They're interested in particulars from which they generalise, and the generalisation is always false, for the simple reason that it's impossible to see all the complexities. The sum of all those particulars is probably nearer to the truth than any one of them, but nobody can see it at any one time. Charles, dear boy, how are you? Hello, Martin. Nice to see you."

"Ah, you must be airing your views on Bernard's shameless little performance this morning," said Charles Fortescue, who had reviewed the same book in the opposite paper. It was a feature of all these discussions that somebody's review or view of a book was far more important than the book itself.

"Now, *you* talked more sense, if I may say so, dear boy," said Howard, pointing his finger at Charles' middle button, "and I *know* about this truth business, it's the one thing I can flatter myself I know something about. Really, the book is nothing more than a philosopher's power-fantasy. The man's screwball——" He was talking of a popular television philosopher, a brains trustee, who had written a first novel. "Why, look at the hero—or hero-apparent—with his tallest tower in the world—I don't know what Freud would have to say about that—and all the sub-Dean Inge-ism, and the sentimentality underneath it all, cold mush under the hair-shirt, going back to Voltaire and his garden, digging and all's right with the world—it makes me want to throw up. The trouble is," he went on, blissfully unrestrained in his enjoyment of a listening audience, "I fear everyone's going to be taken in, like old Bernard. Except you and I, Charles, except you and I."

"Hmm. Can I get you another?"

"Bless you, dear boy."

"Sonya? Jocelyn? How about you?" He smiled affably at Elizabeth to disguise the fact that he had forgotten her name.

"Well, thank you."

"I'll come and help you fight through and carry," said Sonya, a little too visibly anxious to get Charles to herself.

"What about mystics?" Jocelyn asked suddenly when they were gone.

"Eh?" Howard blinked with exaggerated incomprehension.

"You said, my dear, that nobody can see the sum of all the particulars at once. Don't you think mystics can?"

Jocelyn was wearing jeans of yellow sailcloth and a sky blue pullover, which made his question sound a little incongruous, but he too was showing off his seriousness of purpose for the benefit of his youthful attendant, a pale boy with long lashes and lacquered hair, who was rather formally dressed.

"Possibly," Howard replied with surprising deference. His accesses of politeness after a bout of floor-holding were always a little too deliberate, and yet, if one analysed them, not altogether insincere, as if he were dimly aware that he had gone too far. "But mysticism," he went on carefully, "*ipso facto* goes beyond expression. As soon as it is expressed it has to fall back on relativistic terms, concentrating on one or a few particulars, or abstraction and—er—general-i-sa-tion," he tailed off as he noticed that Jocelyn wasn't listening, but waving at somebody behind him. He turned round and saw no one he knew, just a haphazard group of people walking down Cheyne Row beyond the crowd of drinkers on the pavement.

"There's Nina Jackson," said Jocelyn, and suddenly Howard saw her, minute and smiling as she waved back at Jocelyn, hesitating, then walking towards them. She was wearing a jersey dress of soft tan, with, somewhat unusually, the same lilac silk scarf and lilac leather gloves she had worn at the trial, but her head was bare, black-fringed and boyish at the back. As she approached he noticed she was carrying a black lace mantilla and a missal.

"Hello, Jocelyn." She nodded politely at Howard, not quite certain how friendly she should be. "I didn't know you came here. Oh, look, and Sonya, too." Charles and Sonya tottered from the pub, carrying four drinks each.

"Nina, darling," Sonya gushed, "how very unusual and how nice." She introduced her to Charles and Martin. "How extraordinary! We couldn't remember whether it was seven or eight drinks, so Charles got eight. He said someone would be bound to turn up, and here you are!" She talked fast and amiably, to tide over any awkwardnesses between Nina and Howard Cutting. But she needn't have worried, for Nina had decided to show no ill will, at least in public, and was busy showing none.

"You know, I used to walk past this place with my eyes shut on my way out from Mass. I didn't know all my friends came here." She laughed delightedly, pushing up the tip of her nose with her fourth finger. She had removed her gloves. Everyone laughed too. She smiled at Charles as she took a cigarette and a light from him, and he gazed at her with admiring concentration. "If all those horrid people weren't here it would be so pretty. Look at the sun on the river, and the bridge through the trees. It's quite as beautiful as Paris, no, more beautiful, because it's ours." Everyone turned to look, and suddenly felt poetic. They were always so busy talking about who had reviewed what, and where, they seemed to see Chelsea for the first time. She was so very tiny, and kittenish, that in anyone else her manner would have been *fée*, but in her it was like a breath of fresh air, as if they had all been enclosed in the beery, smoky, crowded four walls of the pub, and suddenly come out into a magical spring morning on the banks of the Seine. "It's still a little chilly, though." She shivered and pouted up at the sky. A strong wind was shuddering the fresh green leaves in the trees. "The wind's changed since this morning," she said, sniffing the air, "it's North West now. Isn't the North West wind supposed to bring snow? It used to, when I was little."

"Darling Nina, not snow in May!" Sonya exclaimed. Charles put his drink down on the kerb by the bushes and took his jacket off. He placed it gently on her shoulders and she looked lost in it, but gave him a dazzling smile, not questioning his motives or his own risk of cold, since he was wearing a blue jumper underneath. Howard growled inwardly, and the corner of his mouth dropped into the sulky, discontented look which was his natural expression when he was not watched, not acting. His face wrinkled like a squeezed washing-up mop.

"All the men seem to be wearing sky blue jumpers today," Nina observed, and indeed, when one looked around at the crowd, after that remark, they leapt to the eye. "Look, even the publican," she whispered with a giggle. He was coming round the gardens to collect empty glasses, rather grumpily. "Beware, Jocelyn, if the publican is wearing a sky blue jumper, it *must* be out of fashion."

"You should know. What do you think, Sonya?"

"Darling, you look good enough to eat in those yellow pants. Doesn't he?" She turned mischievously to his youthful attendant, who hadn't spoken all morning, blushed furiously, and spoke even less thereafter.

Nina was the centre of attraction, and was thoroughly aware of it, enjoying it with such diabolical poise and charm that not even Sonya—who was in any case a wise old bird, and rather fond of her—could feel envious. But through all her chatter she watched people carefully, especially Elizabeth, who stood quietly next to Howard, thin and ordinary, yet oddly haunting with her puzzled brown eyes and her auburn hair that reflected the sun. Nina's professional eye took her in at a glance and she suddenly wanted to take her away and dress her. 'That girl could be quite beautiful,' she thought, 'if she took a little trouble and was happily married. My

God, how tense she looks.'

"You're Elizabeth Cutting, aren't you?" She edged her way round, and the group she had been surrounded with seemed to shrink away, politely, regretfully, as if at departing royalty. Elizabeth smiled.

"Yes. I was so sorry about your husband's book."

Howard shifted uncomfortably.

"That's very nice of you. I should have asked you to dinner that evening, in November. I apologise, but you see I didn't know about you till later."

"I'm sorry too, Nina," Howard said miserably. "I didn't mean the book to be withdrawn. I just——"

"Never mind." She smiled sweetly. "You know, it has its funny side, for an expert on the nature of reality. You write a book called *The Sycamore Tree*, and suddenly, it isn't there anymore, like the tree in the quad. Do you know, Gael was approached by a shady character from the Honeycomb Press, who had managed to get hold of an unreturned review copy, and who offered him £500 down and royalties for permission to reprint it, with those bits left out or rewritten."

"Well, why not? I wouldn't mind."

Nina looked astonished.

"Oh, well," she said carefully after the briefest pause, "he can't do that, you know. He's under contract to Truelove & Thorne, and if it were permissible surely they would have made the same offer. Besides, he's superstitious about it now, he feels it's brought him bad luck and he mustn't touch it. He'll be writing another this summer. He'll soon be rather like that statue of Carlyle, look!" She skipped, absurdly in Charles's jacket, towards the other group, who were standing at the foot of the statue, and turned to Howard and Elizabeth with a laugh. "Poor old Carlyle!"

Howard winced. Was she getting at him? The others all looked up as if they had never seen it before, a dark figure thinking in a sitting position, with a pile of black bronze books under the clumsy square-backed chair.

"I wonder how soon anyone would notice, if one added a real book to the pile?"

"Let's try it and see," said Charles amiably, and tried to grab her missal. "No! Not that one!"

He frowned at his mistake and went to the kerb where he had placed his things, returning with a book.

"I've already reviewed this. I'm only reading it now," he quipped, but by then the joke had worn off and nobody really wanted to add to Carlyle's studious reserves. She took it from him and looked at the title.

"Oh, I'm reviewing this too. Tell me what to say." She eyed him flirtatiously and Howard's face tensed but smoothed itself out again as he took in what she had just said.

"I didn't know you did any reviewing. Where?"

"Darling, Nina's quite revolutionised my paper, haven't you, angel-child? She's only done one *Talking Points*, but she ignored everything that everyone's raving about, and picked the oddest things. The fashionable ladies who read her after you and you and all the others are marvellously confused, and those who don't are none the wiser."

"You mean in *Elegance*?" Howard sounded disappointed, for the women's glossies hardly counted.

"But of course!" Sonya exclaimed. "The drawing room and the hairdresser's salon are just as important for culture, you know. And Nina's column delighted me. It was fresh and unusual. She's quite a gal."

"I know." Howard looked at her with undisguised lechery, but she was gazing thoughtfully at Elizabeth.

"After all," Sonya went on, "you all echo each other. Look at the fuss over Sammy's novel, Nina's more sensible. I can't see why everybody got so steamed up about it."

"*Succés de* steam?" Nina put in, with a twinkle in her eyes.

They all laughed, and Howard felt snubbed. One was allowed to make ghastly puns, it seemed, if one was delightful and attractive. Steam indeed! A ship's horn sounded far down the river and a train rumbled distantly over Victoria Bridge. Trains puffing over his father's beastly tulip fields in Berkshire, curses, visions of bulbs and the smell of manure . . . mingled with the odour of death, flowers, lilies on a coffin, and he looked away at the river beyond the trees, and the graceful lines of the mid-Victorian bridge, which they wanted to pull down, and a sudden depression clouded over him as the wind swept through the leaves above. Yet it was she who had made him look at these things anew, they hadn't been there before, or not so strangely beautiful. He had never really noticed them. He gazed at the bridge, lost in reverie, then suddenly blinked, pulled himself up and turned to her, talking rapidly and volubly again, of books.

"Oh, but I thought it rather charming," she said naively, after a long diatribe of his against a film she was going to write about. "At least in contrast to the pretentious woolly nonsense of that American play." He had rather liked that one.

"It was the wettest thing I've seen in years," he replied, determined to put her in her place. "Don't you ever read what people say, chum? Everyone slashed it."

"No, I don't. I pick what I like. Perhaps charm and sincerity would seem wet to you."

"La, ma'am, hoity-toity, aren't we?"

This was Nina's only flash of resentment that morning and he knew he had deserved it, taken all in all, and a good deal more. He knew also, if only for a moment, in a sudden glimpse of the future which vanished as he tried to grasp it, just how angry she could be made to be. And as the moment of intuition, so rare in him, sank away into the deep layers of feeling beneath his many masks of crudeness, many skins of self-defence, so did the knowledge that he loved her, wanted her, wanted to look after her, protect her and hurt her.

She had turned away and was giving Charles back his coat, with a smile that made his day. The pub's first bell went, announcing two o'clock, and she gasped, exclaiming something about lunch and her children. She turned to Elizabeth and took her hand, saying suddenly very earnestly: "Please come and see me." Then with a wave at everyone she skipped beyond the trees and ran up Cheyne Row, her high heels clapping on the hard macadam. Not quite as silently as an elf, but as effectively, she was gone.

Chapter Nine

GAEL heard her high heels clapping on the pavement, scattering his angry thoughts. He was so rarely home, at weekends only, and she had to be late for Sunday lunch. Of course, Frieda was looking after the meal, but that wasn't the point. She had brought the children home after Mass and told him that Nina had decided to go for a walk—"Frau Yackson will be loitering a little" was her phrase—but it was now after two o'clock and the midday Mass ended before one.

The front door slammed and he heard her singing as she crossed the hall, one of the many popular songs she liked to distort into mockery:

"*I love Paris in the springtime,*
I love Menelaus in the fall,
I love Paris in the springtime,
And in the meantime
I love 'em all . . ."

She must have stopped for a moment in front of the mirror. Then the kitchen door slammed too and voices spattered the echo. Gael laid his book, aside with a sigh and went downstairs slowly.

"*Carissimo!* I'm sorry, sorry, sorry," she exclaimed with a belying look of pure delight as he entered the kitchen. "I met some friends on the Embankment, outside the pub . . . I forgot the time. You will forgive me, won't you, *caro mio*, lunch is absolutely about to be served *prontis-sissississisissimo*."

She was crouching down at the oven door, giving the joint a last basting before taking it out, Nina was English enough to fall back on the traditional Sunday joint, but she refused to make puddings and apple pies.

"Of course," said Gael, a little stiffly, but melting nevertheless. "Nice friends?"

"Very nice . . . Frieda, you always forget the parsley on the carrots, it's all chopped and ready, there. Did you sugar and butter them? Sugar, Zucker, I keep telling you, just half a teaspoonful . . . Let me see, there was Jocelyn Furnivall and Sonya Dandridge, and I met Charles Fortescue, you know, the critic . . . Frieda, call the children, will you? *Die Kinder* . . . Oh, and guess who else."

She had hesitated, uncertain of his reaction, and the very hesitation made his reaction certain. "Your archenemy, Howard Cutting . . . His wife's very charming," she added, a little too casually.

Like most attractive women, Nina always knew when a man responded to her physically, even if he didn't show it. The trouble was, Gael knew it too, almost as if he were in her place. When he wasn't there, she basked in the crude admiration and the obvious though easily restrained desire of men like Charles Fortescue. She dealt with such encounters by frankly flirting back, and the very frankness of her flirtation somehow obviated the next step. Between this and the next step she was, moreover, protected by her married status, which at least formally disqualified her from men's usual pursuits. She knew by instinct and hearsay—modern society being what it is—that this protective disqualification no longer operated beyond the next step. Nevertheless it enabled her to play a half-conscious dual role: with Gael or when speaking of she was the adoring and loyal wife, with others she was the innocent teaser. Sometimes the two roles overlapped, and she either found herself flirting in Gael's presence, or had to make a quick switch. Gael seemed to understand all this and was on the whole tolerant in the modern style, but his own intransigence often intervened. As far as Howard Cutting was concerned, Nina herself wasn't too sure what her behaviour towards him ought to have been in the circumstances. Gael, she knew, would quite unhesitatingly have produced his frozen politeness, almost natural to him with strangers and even more natural with people he didn't like. And Howard had, after all, caused him a good deal of trouble. Nina's own instinct was to forget and be friends, but she felt vaguely guilty at having, as it were, let the side down by not adhering to what Gael's behaviour would have been.

And Gael's behaviour was in fact as she expected, all the more irritating for being so. His face hardened and seemed to fall to pieces, into separate triangles and squares, like an abstract painting. She could never quite focus on the illusion, because it vanished a moment later, but his eyes retained a surrealist quality, as if they had been brought in from another picture, fish-eyes on a guitar-faced dish. This was his jealous look, his suspicious look, which she couldn't bear, which came over him in spite of himself when she reported the most harmless appointments and activities. It was enough—the thought would flash through her at such moments, without being even formulated—it was enough to drive her into another man's arms. After all, if she had to undergo this suspicion she might as well get some joy for it. But she knew only too well his suspicions were half justified.

"Cutting?" His pitch queered on the query, then adjusted itself. "How is he? Boisterous as ever?"

"Yes, positively chummy."

"Hmm. I must say I've always found that kind of chumminess offensive."

"I suppose it is, really, but I don't think he can help it. As somebody or other said, we're all so uncertain underneath. Underneath what?" Nina was still feeling flippant and echoed Howard's way of talking. "Well may you ask! Here, can you take this in, darling, and start carving?" She handed him the joint in a long dish and turned to the stove to make the gravy and serve the vegetables.

The children were waiting in the dining room, noisy and restless. Frieda had tied napkins round their necks and was trying to control them. Sunday lunch with Mummy and Daddy was a special treat, and they had become hungry and impatient. The twins, Michael and Marisa, were four years old and very like Nina, both dark-fringed. Josephine, who was nearly six, was more like Gael, blonde and pale, and wore her long hair in a ponytail. She was banging her plate with a spoon and shouting a snatch of song she had curiously misheard from the wireless. The change she made was not, like Nina's, intentional, but it was no less apt:

"Mummy is the root of all evil
Mummy is the root of all evil
Take it away, take it away, take it away..."

"Josephine, be quiet." Nina came in with a tray.
"Oh, Frieda; I forgot the children's orange juice, could you get it?"
"I'm hungry," Marisa announced.
"Frieda says Mummy's late," said Michael, as if repeating a lesson just learned.
"*John, John, said to his mother,*" Josephine chanted in lisping tones, "*Mother, he said, said he, you must never go down to the end of the town without consuck-ting me.*"
"I met some friends at the pub," said Nina, in a needlessly defensive tone. "Now keep quiet and eat."
"Mummy's been drinking gin atomic," Josephine informed the twins solemnly, proud of some overheard piece of adult knowledge.
"Lie low," said Frieda authoritatively, out of the *l*-pages of her dictionary. She was cutting Marisa's meat.
"Well, I had a drink too," Gael announced with slightly forced exuberance, when the children had settled down to their food. "With a Hungarian."
"A beautiful spy, I hope, dancing a chardash down Piccadilly?"
"No, a man." Gael smiled sheepishly, half amused, half annoyed at not being able to say it was a woman. "Zoltan Torday, that fellow I told you about. He rang me up, after you'd gone to Mass."
"I wish you would go to Mass with us," Nina said suddenly, showing no interest in a man she hadn't actually met. Then she frowned at her mistake. Anxious somehow to put him in the wrong—or perhaps to imply that if he had been with her they wouldn't have stopped at the pub, or if they had she would have known how to behave with Howard—she was treading on an old agreement to differ and moreover breaking all the rules of civilised conversation. "Sorry, honey."

Gael grinned and wrinkled his nose at her, always a sign that he didn't want to discuss something but forgave her for bringing it up. Theirs was more or less a 'mixed' marriage, the Church's hope being always that the Catholic partner would bring the non-Catholic one in. Or, in Gael's case, back. For he came from Irish-American stock and had been reared a Catholic. But something had happened, she never quite knew what. His voluntary exile was connected with it and she had never probed too deep. Gael once told her how, as a young man at Harvard, he had had, or fancied he had, a call to the cloister. He couldn't explain just how it had come, but it was quite unmistakable. Horrified, he had run, physically run all the way from the spot to his rooms. Why him? No, it just couldn't be. He was young, smart, popular with the girls, he had a brilliant future before him, he wanted to do things. He had smiled wryly as he told her, calling it his Hound-of-Heaven period. At that age, he explained, the idea that one is chosen is attractive, even the idea of suffering, of a tumultuous struggle within the soul. He had turned from philosophy to law in the hope of becoming more worldly, he had womanised and whored and hated it, returned to philosophy, withdrawn more and more. It all sounded so simple and obvious when told like that, in retrospect, in the light of a happy marriage, but she knew that something more had happened. And moreover, that he was still on the run, that the call had been real and he was still pushing it away, even though he had moved out physically, to the Old World, and to her. She understood his carefully, generously tolerant, yet fiercely jealous love for her. But she resented it too, without realising it, for the burden of it was too great. He was, as he once said himself when they were discussing religion, a man with no illusions left, but happy to have none, happy to recognise the essential unhappiness of man's lot, and to live with it—happier, in fact, than most people are with their self-deceptions. But this also meant that something had died inside him, so that he lived too much by her love.

Nina looked at her husband with deep affection, and wondered how much two people could know about each other, still excluding so much; how little could one know within the vast extent of knowledge accumulated by love, both in and out of time? He seemed sometimes to know everything about her, without ever mentioning any specific fact—for he believed that naming things brought them into existence with an uncontrollable life of their own. But did he know the worst of her, and still love her?

"Tommy says the Virgin Mary had a *sizzarion*," Josephine was telling Frieda. Tommy was a boy of nine who lived down the road and sometimes allowed her to join in his games. She worshipped him.

"What's a *zarion*, Mummy?" asked Michael.

Nina yelped with delight, throwing back her head as she laughed, and her daughter looked pleased at the effect she had unwittingly produced on the grownups.

"Josephine, have you any idea what you're talking about?"

"I have, I have. Tommy says Jesus wasn't born like other babies so she must've had a *sizzarion* to bring him."

She obviously didn't really understand, and rather than prove this to her and then have to explain, Nina just smiled and said: "Yes, I expect she had. But you'd better finish your potatoes or you won't get any fruit."

"Daddy, why Mummy won't *scuss* anything? You *scuss* things. I want to *scuss* the Virgin Mary."

"You'd soon get tired if we did, Josephine. She's kept people busy discussing her for two thousand years."

"And I'll scuss her for more two thousand years." Josephine had just started catechism classes and was going through the sweetly unnerving 'holy' stage, the Children-of-Mary stage which usually precedes the lavatorial stage of dirty jokes. She adored going to Mass—the longer the better—and insisted on being taken to Benediction in the evening as well.

Frieda got up to clear away the meat course.

"I met a scatty woman on the bus this morning," said Gael conversationally. "She recognised me from a photograph during the trial, and started talking. She said she'd written six novels and a dozen plays, and wondered how to get them published. I'm afraid I was very wicked and put her on to an agent. Then she asked me, 'How much do you have to *pay* your publishers to print your books?' I was so astonished I replied in a grand manner, not my own at all: 'My dear lady, *they* pay *me*'—as if I made a fortune out of it."

"Darling, you will. You never know, the fuss over *The Sycamore Tree* may turn out to help you in the end. Why don't you rewrite it?"

"Couldn't, honey, just couldn't touch it."

"Are you still . . . *very* angry about it? I mean, with Howard Cutting? I was going to ask you, after all, we may meet socially, like this morning, and I wasn't too sure how you'd want me to behave."

"Darling, I don't *want* you to behave in any way but the way you feel is right. I don't impose my own standards on you."

The last sentence seemed to have about five edges, 'Don't you, don't you,' she thought, knowing his were the standards she wanted and needed, yet hating the backhanded way in which he did, after all, impose them.

"I know, but . . . Oh, Frieda, how often have I told you to wash the fruit before laying it out. That's how one gets polio. Wash . . . *waschen das Obst*. No, I'll do it." Suddenly she wanted to get out of the family circle.

Gael joined her in the kitchen, however, bringing in Josephine's plate, cleaned up at last. He planted a kiss on her fringe.

"Sorry, honey, I worded that phrase badly. I only meant that you don't have to do what I do, any more than you have to keep aloof because I do. I don't defend aloofness as such, it's just grown in me because of, well, several betrayals."

"What sort of betrayals?" Nina asked quickly as she turned the tap over the red and green apples, the tawny pears and the pale muscat grapes.

"It's difficult to explain, I know it's a big word." Gael piled up the plates on the draining board, separating the cutlery. "All spontaneous friendly relationships, anything involving love of any kind for a fellow being, from true friendship to passion, means a kind of generosity, a naivety of emotion, an essential trust. That naivety, that trust, is quickly twisted or abused by the more sophisticated, at least, I've found it so every time. So, I prefer not to give my trust and friendship too easily, that's all."

Nina was silent for a moment.

"Why do all the apples float and the pears sink?" she asked suddenly, to mask her nervousness. "Look."

They were drying the fruit together, sharing the same clean dishcloth. Gael laughed.

"The apple is the treacherous fruit. It wouldn't save you if you clutched at it but it pretends to swim. The pear doesn't even pretend."

In the drawing room, over coffee, he changed the subject and talked shop.

"There's one American girl who just hasn't got a clue. She actually has a degree in philosophy from some provincial university in the States, and so got into Somerville. Do you know, last week I asked her in a tutorial how she could be sure that her room was still there when she left it, and she looked at me as if I were nuts."

"I used to be frightened as a child," said Nina quietly. "I used to think all my toys would have gone from the nursery, even the room itself would disappear if I were taken away for a moment. Even now when we have nice guests, and it's fun, I always come back as quickly as possible if I have to go out, as if they might all have vanished in the meantime."

Gael frowned at the background of emotional insecurity. He had once discovered some old letters and papers among a pile of family photographs and other oddments in a trunk. They were marked. "To Be Burnt" in an old-fashioned hand. There was a newspaper cutting about Nina's father, a barrister, who had disgraced himself. It was difficult to gather just how, because the article was very much *post-factum* and assumed public knowledge. It was really a portrait, and cruel as only the press can be, just this side of libel, to a fallen man. His Italian wife, the article implied, had stepped up from a most disreputable London milieu. Gael never asked whether Nina knew, but he had quietly destroyed the cutting.

Cutting. She would come back to him.

"He was very sorry, you know, about your book being withdrawn. Quite abject, in fact. Don't you think we should let bygones be bygones? After all, the verdict did make him look rather silly. And we're bound to come across him at parties and so on."

"We didn't before."

She puffed at her cigarette.

"Because you never go to parties. But now that I'm a critic (ha-ha)—well, Sonya's already asked me to hers, for instance, and I like parties. I'm bound to meet him, even if you don't. It would be easier if we were all officially friends."

"It's up to him to invite us, if that's what he wants. Darling, you must do whatever you feel. I'm not a monster, dictating your behaviour. If we meet, well, I'll just see how I feel then. At the moment, I just can't like him, or make the first move." He got carried away and said more than he meant. "I only want you to be careful. I know when a man lusts after you and—well, you do lap it up."

Anger deadened Nina's eyes for a moment. But then hers met his and melted into their teasing smile.

"You beast," she muttered with a mock-wicked look. "You know very well who I want." His arms stretched out towards her and she flung herself on him. They made love on the red velvet sofa.

Chapter Ten

ANGER deadened Zoltan's black eyes as he faced his hosts. Since the trial, Howard Cutting had gone suspiciously out of his way to be genial with him, inviting him for drinks, for little triangular dinners of false amiability and over-deliberate blindness. He had taken an unwarranted interest in his book on Árpád Szendrey, every quotation from whom he suggested should be translated; in the nineteenth-century mystery over Alexander Petöfi's disappearance; in Hungarian history, literary feuds, revolutions, lost and regained territories, origins and ethnography. Zoltan almost suspected that Howard was picking his brains and brain-child in order to set himself up as an expert on Hungarian affairs for *The Sunday Supplement*.

But Howard's concern was genuine enough. Like most Westerners, he had been deeply disturbed by the Hungarian Revolution, and maddened by the general feeling of helplessness. His tactlessness at the trial had gnawed at his conscience and he was trying to make up for it—and for the general damage he had caused all round—by helping Zoltan to feel more secure in exile, among friends, and to become better known in English literary circles so that any small fame he might acquire would protect him from reprisals such as quiet kidnapping, murder or blackmail.

But Zoltan was a little uncooperative. He refused to join any literary clubs—even those which had special branches and meetings for émigré writers of all nations. He would look at the lists of the latter members and laugh at the credulity of the English who really imagined that these people were respected in their own country or could represent it in any way. He refused to write on Hungarian affairs for any of the intellectual periodicals, who, he said, were all in their own fumbling way collaborating with whatever governments happened to be in power in the various

Soviet satellites. They didn't mean to, he said, it was the natural consequence of the diplomatic necessity of recognising these governments as legal, but he would have no part in their friendly advances, their exchange of cultural visits, their credulous interpretations, and, moreover, they had an understandable distrust of any opinion from an exile of ten years' standing, who would be unduly prejudiced, necessarily ignorant of present-day conditions, and, probably, blinded by bitterness to their vital attempts at bridging the cultural and political chasm. They preferred—and his tone of resignation was ironical—to trust one-time collaborators who had been virtuously disillusioned by lack of advancement, threatened disfavour or sudden danger of arrest, ex-communists, half-hearted part-time communists, never-really communists, sad communists, muffled communists, genuine Marxists, Leninists, Trotskyites, Titoists shocked by the Soviet betrayal of the old ideals, once-communists-always-communists, who would escape, usually by stepping quietly into a foreign embassy, and arrive with dramatic tales of torture and imprisonment and dangerous frontier-crossing, to sell their interpretations of the Problems facing the Intellectual in a Captive Society. After a while, they too, were out of date, and had nothing more to sell except reiterations, reinterpretations, rearranged confessions of the Alienated Soul, the Soul Alienated by their own self-seeking stupidity.

"How's the book getting along?" Howard had asked affably during dinner. "Should be nearly finished by now."

"Yes, it is finished. But I do not want the Institute to print it."

"But Zoltan, why?" Elizabeth looked dismayed. "You can't do that, they gave you the money."

"If they insist, I will repay the money, somehow. I am leaving the Institute."

Elizabeth stared at him, unable to disguise her sudden terror. He was tired of her! No, he couldn't be, not in the usual sense. He was tired of not being tired of her, he was tired of the tension. She should have given in to him and lived with him, let him make love to her on that black couch in his flag-like room. She very nearly had, after the trial, when he said everyone would think it anyway. She closed her eyes, remembering his passion: how she had wanted him, and then suddenly as he was about to take her, how she had gone cold and limp, and not wanted him at all, and ran away. He had accused her later in fury, of hypocrisy, puritanism, romanticising, mockery, cruelty, selfishness. She wanted only the flattery and emotional insurance of a love-relationship without giving herself, she wanted the adoration and the desire, the petting and the sensuality, without the sin—but whoever looks on another with adulterous thoughts has already committed adultery, Christ said, there is no difference at all. She was using him, he was a mere romantic projection of her desires. She had said nothing, nothing at all, except that it was all true, but she couldn't help it, and nevertheless loved him. And he had gone down on his knees—yes, on his knees, pandering to her romanticism, and she couldn't bear it and wept. Things had been smoother since, but there had still been a feeling of strain beneath the kinder understanding. And now this.

"Why, Zoltan?" she asked again as calmly as she could. "What's wrong?"

"Everything is wrong. The Institute is—what is your word—phoney."

"Oh?" Howard pricked up his ears, always eager for any hint of intrigue.

"The Fidler Institute of Danubian Studies! Have you ever heard a more rid-ee-culous name? Founded by some pseudo-Hungarian who made millions of money in America and had a guilty conscience after the Yalta Agreement. Who runs it now? Who are the trustees of this fund for cultural freedom? The people who run the Institute are perhaps innocent enough, ignorant enough, oh yes, but they are being used. Behind them and behind those who are behind them, are Trotskyites and ex-Trotskyites, anxious to undermine the present regime, oh yes, but with the wrong ideas, the wrong reinterpretations, and they have no scruples about using the ex-well-meaning-pinks of the thirties, these who are also anxious, but stupidly anxious, to understand, to ease their consciences, to stretch a helping hand. It makes me—" Zoltan stopped, about to thump his hand on the table, and said hopelessly: "Oh, what is the use? You all think European politics are too complicated, that we make too much fuss, that we make—dramatics—" he used the word bitterly "—out of nothing. If only we would compromise, you say, who have built up your power and your prestige upon that word, and lost it too, upon that word."

"Not at all, dear boy, not at all," said Howard amicably, eager to pacify, to show his lack of insularity, of prejudice, of xenophobia—in brief, to compromise. "Tell us more about it. This is fascinating." He liked the feeling that he was on to something.

"Shall we adjourn? I'll go and make some coffee," said Elizabeth. She didn't really want to go through all this again.

"You know, old chap, you mustn't get so worked up," he said to Zoltan when they were alone in the living room—for so he called it, and indeed, it could hardly be called a drawing room. They had tried to be contemporary with different wallpapers and indoor vegetation, but everything was somehow wrong. A fluffy canary yellow carpet was so dirty it no longer matched the one canary yellow trellised wall, though the grey patches on it recalled the pseudo-bricks papered over the chimneypiece. The wooden furniture was 'Special Plan (add-another-when-you-can),' in light walnut. It was really his workroom—here he had his big desk and typewriter and swivel chair, his correspondence files and his indexes. He treated journalism like an office job, except that he was at it all day and all evening—when he was not at a literary club meeting or a literary party —turning out articles, essays, reviews, draft chapters of books on books, translations, abortive novels and first acts of unfinished plays, stopping only for food, or entertainment necessary to the earning of advancement. He sat now in his swivel chair with his back to his desk, like a business executive ordering the next plan of overall production. The desk faced the window which gave out on a magnificent view of a blank wall and someone else's backyard. Beyond it, in someone else's garden behind the houses in the next street, was a solitary chestnut tree, now with its candle flowers alight in the setting sun of late May. Zoltan was sitting miserably in one of the armchairs, which was upholstered in a nobbly grey and leaf-green furnishing fabric from a popular store.

"You must keep quiet about it at the moment," Howard went on with a smile which he made as sympathetic as he could. "And about this book—" he leant forward confidentially in his chair with his elbows on his knees and his fingers joined at the tips "—don't worry about the Institute. My dear boy, I know every publisher in London and I'll get someone interested without any difficulty. I'm always being asked to be on the lookout for unusual manuscripts. Everybody's talent scout, that's me. I've put quite a few publishers in the way of new authors and they're grateful to me. I'll try Jeff Brandon first. If he's interested, they'll want to see you. You'll meet a smooth operator called Sam Ginsburg who'll try to persuade you to popularise it. He won't be interested in the book but he'll want to sum you up to see whether you'll insist on saving your immortal academic soul. You'll agree with everything he says, and you'll take no notice. Jeff's the one who'll prepare the thing for publication. I'll get you a good advance, and that'll help if you have to repay the Institute, now, won't it? And that's a big if." The knowing look came over his face. "Don't forget they may not be anxious to have complications, if you make it clear why you're leaving."

"If, if. Your English publishers will not look at a book on Árpád Szendrey."

"Oh, I don't know. Hungary's quite in fashion these days. You've covered the most significant political period, and dealt with a disappearance which may make things a bit awkward for some people."

"Yes, Hungary is in fashion," Zoltan said bitterly. "So much in fashion that everyone is accepting official invitations. Deputations of workers and miners and journalists go there to talk to carefully selected workers and miners and journalists, to investigate the riots and the conditions, at the mercy of interpreters, and they come back and write articles, having swallowed all they were told and shown, and hold meetings, pass motions, give votes of thanks, all to the effect that—praise be to the gods of peace and compromise—things are not so bad as they had feared, much better than they were, though not yet so good as they obviously will be if everybody just keeps quiet."

Zoltan's English had improved considerably as he wrote his book, and passion could now unleash his tongue to an astonishing fluency and ease, even with subordinate clauses and parenthetical statements. Only fatigue and despair would still at times' cause him to lapse into broken, ungrammatical sentences, to say left for right and he for she, to forget the simplest words and generally to become incomprehensible. Elizabeth came in with the coffee and looked alarmed at his new outburst. Had Howard annoyed him further? She sat down on the green sofa and poured, handing the men their cups in silence.

"Zoltan, please don't be so angry with us. We're only trying to help."

"I know. I am sorry." He was full of mistrust, he hated this new friendliness on the part of her husband, and yet, perhaps Howard meant well, perhaps he should give him the book and it might help him to have it published. He put down his cup, got up suddenly, and went out. They looked at each other in puzzlement, then he returned with a briefcase.

"Here you are. Take it," he said to Howard, handing over the book-sized manuscript with a mixture of defiance and childlike trust in his eyes. They seemed to say, 'there, I dare you, I bet you my next Saturday's sweets you won't find a publisher for it.'

"Bless you, dear boy. I'll get to work on it, you leave it to Uncle Howard, and not to worry."

Elizabeth winced, and changed—or so she thought—the subject by mentioning the Petöfi Centenary celebrations in Budapest the following November, to which both she and Howard had been differently invited—she as representative of the Fidler Institute, he as a writer who had expressed himself so volubly in print on the Hungarian cause at the time of the Rising. Zoltan listened to her, appalled and speechless.

"You are not going?" he asked at last in a weak voice.

"Why not? I've always wanted to see Hungary. It's my first love, you know. We can't afford a holiday this summer so it'll be rather nice. It sounds very well organised, a visit to the mines, a journey down the Danube, a tour of Transylvania and the Carpathian mountains in the

North."

"A tour of Budapest—from newspaper offices to nightlife," Howard put in.

"Budapest nightlife! Tour of Transylvania!" Zoltan could hardly believe his ears. He got up and walked about the room, quietly at first, then quickening his pace until he looked more like a wild beast in an alien jungle than a man. "Do you know what these celebrations are? Erzsebét! You! You should know better. Alexander Petöfi died in 1849, he was officially declared dead in 1854. They did not bother to have a proper centenary in 1954 with international congresses! It was not at all convenient. But now they want all the intellectuals of the West to come and shake hands with them, to show the people how easily they are betrayed. With telegrams of good wishes from those who are unable to attend. So they have a Centenary. But the real anniversary is the defeat of the Rising. Do you think you are being asked for the love of your innocent Western blue eyes, or out of respect for all the splendid things you have written, or for the sincere interest you take in our affairs? You are being used, used as tools in a propaganda campaign, to destroy the morale and the last hopes of the Hungarian people. The more right-wing and the more Catholic writers they can get, the better. You see, they will say in effect, even the Catholics, even the reactionaries, counter-revolutionaries and the bourgeois fascist decadents of the West, in whom you placed your trust are shaking hands with your rulers."

"Look here, old boy, this won't do, you know. You're going too far. It's very important to exchange information, to talk to these new leaders, to ask awkward questions and to spread our own views and our sympathy, among as many people as we can meet. I can see why you can't have any official dealings with them, but it's different for us."

"Yes, it is different for you. For one thing you will not understand a word of what is going on." Zoltan turned on him and opened his large uneven hands, which trembled as if he were about to strangle some imaginary concept that stood between them. Elizabeth noticed again how much finer and delicate his left hand was than the square-fingered, thick right hand, which was that of a peasant. "How do you suppose your awkward questions and your useful information and your sympathy with the Hungarian people will be translated? Someone will ask about the Cardinal, and they will say that he has just praised the Hungarian system of transportation. Someone else will ask about the writers in prison, and the conspiracy of silence from other writers. Yes, there is a strike of writers, isn't that funny? They are digging out the very old ones, and promoting unknown nincompoops, because the writers who matter will not write for them. And that question will be translated as an expression of admiration for the splendid rebuilding of the great streets of Budapest, destroyed in the Fascist Counter-Revolution. You will be allowed to meet nobody, except the officially chosen, and to see nothing. You will interrogate miners and workers through an interpreter—oh, my God, my God, what is the use?"

"Don't be an idiot, Zoltan. I speak Hungarian, I won't let them fool me."

"You? You are already stamped as a representative of the Fidler Institute. Do you think our underground doesn't know all about it, and you? They will not trust a word you say or speak frankly to *you*."

She was hurt and silenced, uncomprehending, anxious for their love.

"There's no need to be rude, you know," Howard said in his best let's-be-gentlemen-about-this voice.

"There is no need to be hypocritically polite either." Zoltan walked back to his armchair and sat down, tense and glaring, ruffling his fingers nervously through his black hair. "Unlike you, I cannot be angry and polite at the same time."

"My dear boy, I sympathise. I understand perfectly. But this is a wonderful chance for Liz, you know, and of tremendous interest to me."

"Tremendous interest? Then go as tourists, go as private persons. If you can get in. Do not go by official invitation. What do you know of Alexander Petöfi, apart from what you have read in my book? What will any of the other Western writers know? It will be a farce, all these people listening politely to tributes and speeches about a poet they have never read and would probably find a national provincial bore, if they could read him. You will no doubt return and write amusing articles about train-stoppages, bad hotels, funny linguistic misunderstandings, taking great care to show that you talked to ordinary people, railway porters, waiters and such, off the official route, and that you were not taken in. In the meantime the emotional damage of your mere presence will have been done."

"Oh, don't exaggerate. It's a free trip, after all, we can't afford——"

"A free trip! Oh, yes. But it is a small step, my friend, for the man who can say 'it is a free trip', in such circumstances, to saying 'oh, well it is a free living' when he is asked to write or otherwise collaborate under an occupation. Especially to write. What else can a writer do, except keep silent, and that is the most difficult thing of all for him. One must live, he says to himself. Your country has never been occupied, Meester Cutting, but you would continue to write, for any paper that asked you. You have the makings of a potential collaborator."

Howard got up, went to the door and opened it.

"Get out."

"Howard, wait. I want to speak to Zoltan."

"You can run after him in the street. Get out, both of you."

Zoltan stood irresolute for a moment, shut his eyes, trembling with rage, then suddenly became very calm, as if in answer to prayer. He walked up to the door and bowed.

"I apologise for that last remark, Mr Cutting. I was angry, I take it back. But please think again. There is plenty of time. At least find out who else is going. They may not be such respectable people as you think."

Howard breathed deeply and couldn't answer. He suddenly felt horribly small, so near to Zoltan with his almost Mongol wildness. He nodded curtly, tight-lipped, and let him pass. Then he shut the door and walked back, with deliberate steps, to his desk, flopped into the chair and swivelled towards the window, turning his back on Elizabeth. He hardly heard the door open and shut as she let herself out, or her footsteps as she raced through the flat and down the stairs. The front door banged, distantly, with a muffled sound that seemed to him like the dropping of the Iron Curtain over the frontiers of human understanding. In front of him on the table lay Zoltan's curiously small, book-sized typescript, which he had forgotten to take. Howard opened it idly in the middle, staring stupidly at the green and red characters on the white paper. A sentence caught his eyes and he read it over and over again to himself without understanding it: "Who shall shrive, what we choose not to do? the poet is asking." The poet is asking, the poet is asking, the poet is asking. Howard's mind had stuck on a cracked groove as it revolved, then suddenly something lifted the stylus and he read on. The author was explaining a difficult poem by Szendrey and a strange feeling of complete fusion of the critic's mind with the poet's came over Howard, without his having to read Szendrey's poem. In all his critical experience he had never got inside someone's skin like that, he was always putting himself across. Yet this was not even particularly well written:

> The action we do not commit exists in God's mind, and out of time, and we may yet commit it in time, at some other place, in different circumstances. The child unborn because of the chemistry of wombs and the revolution of the moon and stars, lives yet, like the child born elsewhere, like all the actions that are other people's, and not ours. And the poet ends by looking at his own hand and calling it the world, and says 'All the world's wrinkles on the map are mine.' We are all responsible, all of the time, for everything.

Howard closed the manuscript and gaped out of the window like a drunkard in a coma. Dusk had fallen and the night breeze was rustling through the lonely chestnut tree, causing the small white petals of its candle flowers to flutter down, like wax, like tears, covering even the backyard on his side of the wall with gentle snow. 'Phallic symbols,' he thought stupidly. The tree in his quad was just a common chestnut with big trumpet flowers, that would bloom over and over again, spring after damned returning spring, like his father's bulbous tulips, and would flutter away into nothing, like the tree in the quad, like reality that shifted and vanished and returned again in different guise. 'Nothing is real, save in our own perceptions, and even our perceptive selves change and vanish and return with different perceptions. Only God, who isn't real either'—Howard's associations were getting confused—'must think it excessively odd, to see that this tree continues to be. I continue to be. I will continue to write, for any paper that asks me. The poet is asking. The poet disappears, into the tree, since observed by yours faithfully, faithfully . . . '

He got up suddenly and walked to the door, opened it, went out slamming it, strode out of the flat and down the stairs, out into the street, down Campden Hill, into the High Street towards Kensington Gardens, under the fluorescent boxes that mimed the mad full moon, racing wildly in the wispy windy sky of May.

Chapter Eleven

TREES, so many trees accompanying him down Queen's Gate. Plane trees. With the pale street lighting looking up at their hanging hands, numerous, white-palmed. High heels echoed on the pavement and vanished, silent figures moved in the distance, lovers stood clumsily immobile in a portico, and all the porticoes of every house were alike, high columned over the five steps, repeating themselves hypnotically down the road like the grey spines of books. And the traffic lights—the fish-eyed exercises of logic never quite overlapping—blinked overtime, imperceptive that the stone of the wide street now breathed stilly in the traffic-less night.

Howard walked on in a daze, through Onslow Square, across the Fulham Road and into Dovehouse Street, unaware of his fatigue, with thoughts of anger weighing into the latest obsessions of books he was reviewing, articles he was writing, chapters he was planning. You are willing to see yourself in print anywhere. Zoltan's hands, measuring the imponderable distance between each other as an expression of the gulf between his separate selves and the separate selves of other people, floated at him in a threatening embrace, became hands hanging on a cross, leaves on a tree, became very small and white, then hanging on a wooden ledge, gloved in lilac holding a glass, and white again, waving away a joke, a compliment, his mother's white hands fondling him in bed, in the early morning.

The electric bulbs slung across the suspension bridge turned it into a twinkling castle that beckoned him to the river. Small moored rowing boats danced gently on the high tide like drowning lips. Over Battersea Bridge, further upstream, a late bus moved slowly across, lit up, like a distant shrine, reflected shuddering in the black water. Howard walked up the Embankment towards it, trees again on his right, facing, as in a folk dance, the pale globes of gaslights on their slender stalks along the parapet. Tall chimneys beyond the houseboats and the bend of the river poked high into the cloudy moonlit sky. He turned up Old Church Street and into Paultons Square. There was her light, dim and cosy and secure in the drawing room. He couldn't see inside. Was she alone? No, surely not. He leant against the railings of the square and stared vacantly at the house. After a while he turned back towards the river and sat on a bench in a dark corner of the Embankment Gardens, gazing at the bridge lit up through the trees. On the next bench, a pair of lovers sat clenched in the black darkness cast by the bushes, and beyond them the sombre figure of Carlyle, thinking in his chair over that absurd pile of leaden books. The lovers, however, were beyond thinking, Howard peered into the dark corner as the man's hand, just visible against the woman's dress, wandered down from her dimly surmised breasts to her thighs, her knees, and under her skirt. He closed his eyes. A white hand gestured at him in a graceful minuet, small fingers touched his as he bowed over a deeply curtsying satin and lace figure whose powdered wig hid a head bent low over a low cut bodice. The white wig evaporated like mist, to reveal black boy-cut hair, a black fringe and blue mischievous eyes smiling up at him as he looked down into a shadowy cleavage. White hands stretched towards him with a cup, two small breasts peeped from a neckline of wine gold silk, white fingers touched his eyelids and he was dead, lips touched his gently and he lived, breathing scent and skin, and he groped up to a white throat, then down, down, into—Howard fumbled for his cigarettes. The match did not disturb the lovers. Howard puffed furiously, relaxed, then suddenly began to chortle in silence, and the chortling turned to tearless sobs that shook him as they merged with a smoker's cough and hacked his lungs until slowly they subsided, soothed by time and more nicotine. Still the lovers were immobile, gripped in the prolongation of a desire so blissfully unfulfillable on a public path.

Howard finished his cigarette and got up, then sat down again, suddenly conscious of his fatigue, and gazed, miserably at the river. A man walked past beyond the shrubs which at this point sparsely separated the garden from, the Embankment; he stopped by one of the gas lamps on the parapet, looking down into the water. Then a girl approached him. She must have asked for a light, for a flame flickered between them. Howard sat up and stared, the flame went out but he could now see her clearly through the trees in the gaslight. After a moment the man turned his back on her and walked away. The girl threw away her cigarette and crossed the road. She walked along just beyond the bushes and Howard held his breath. She reached the end of the garden-length and he was about to get up and follow her, but saw her silhouette as she hesitated, then walked down the tree-darkened path, slowly, on her high heels. She sat down on his bench, crossed her legs, took out a cigarette case from her bag and a long white holder, and asked him for a light. She wore a clinging dress of black knitted wool, long-sleeved but low cut in front like an evening jumper. He stared at her helplessly.

"Excuse me, can you give me a light?" she said again in a sultry tone.

"Nina... What are you doing here?"

Her large eyes focused on him, puzzled in the dark, blankly as they formulated his small tensed figure, narrowed in vague recognition and wonder, opened again as if dazed.

"Waiting for you ... darling." Her voice was an unreal murmur, with a plum-rich gurgle on the last word.

"Nina, are you drunk?" He moved towards her and took her by the shoulders. "Do you know who I am? Howard. Howard Cutting."

"Howard. Yes. Darling Howard. Kiss me." She dropped her unlit cigarette in its ivory holder. Her hand slid over his arms onto the back of his neck, fondling his fuzz of hair and drawing him towards her. She closed her eyes and parted her lips, and there was not a whiff of alcohol as his moved down into hers, slowly, mouthing her breath, and deep, deep his tongue into her palate as his arm encircled her waist and his other hand wandered from her neck to her shoulder, moulding it under the malleable wool, then down into her breasts, fingering them in the small lace brassiere, and across into her underarm, which was soft and silky.

The Sycamore Tree: Chapter Eleven

She sank to his touch and moved her leg against his, undid his shirt buttons, plunged her hand beneath it, roving into his hair, pinching his nipples and knuckling in under his arms, then almost at once, out again and down, feeling him wanting her. He grew under her hand through the trousers and time grew with him to an eternity.

She sighed with content and moved her lips away from his a fraction.

"Darling... You're nice. Kiss me again."

He kissed her gently and removed his hand from inside her dress, stroking her down from the chin like a cat.

"Nina," he murmured, "what is it?"

"What is what?" she said almost sleepily.

"Why are you like this? I never dreamt—it can't be me you want, tell me, it can't be me."

"You? ... Who are you? Oh yes, you told me. Howard. Nice, nice Howard. Kiss me, Howard."

"Nina!" He sat up and shook her. "Nina, what is this? Are you—do you think—Nina, what do you want?"

"Want? I don't want. You want. You want me, don't you? You picked me up. Don't you know what I am?" She laughed lazily, then giggled, then laughed again, wildly, hysterically, with her fourth finger on the tip of her nose. She rang out metallic sheets of laughter at the metallic moon. Howard looked round in a frenzy. The lovers had gone and not a sound disturbed the late spring night except the breeze. Carlyle loomed in his black chair, thinking black thoughts. The bridge lights had been switched off and only the pale round gas bowls stood sentinel beyond the trees. Still her laughter tumbled out, pebbles on a stone floor, and she rippled with it, uncontrollably laughing. He slapped her cheek, and she stopped, and suddenly she was crying silently, her face in her hands. He bent down to pick up her ivory holder which had fallen at her feet, and played with it nervously.

After an interminable while she looked up and stared ahead of her into the trees, through them at the river, through the darkness into herself, tears rolling out of her eyes unstopped, unblinked, her lashes growing with them. A sob shook her, then silence.

"Give me a handkerchief."

Her voice was completely changed, almost a whisper, but matter-of-fact, distant and yet confidential, small and yet more overwhelming than all the alluring richness it had possessed itself of before.

She blew her nose and wiped her eyes.

"Thank you. I must go home now. Goodnight."

"Nina, you can't go like this." He took her hand but she withdrew it quickly and got up. Then he grabbed her arm and pulled her down on the bench again, almost violently. But she flopped on the bench quite limply, and sat there, staring still ahead of her.

"Nina, what is it?" he asked again very gently, not touching her but bending forward to look anxiously into her face. "Are you in trouble? Tell me. Why did you kiss me like that?"

"Kiss you?" She gazed at him steadily and her eyes shone with tears in the dim light. "Yes, I kissed you, didn't I?" Her hand went up to her eyes and she held it over them, her head bowed down, as if to stop the tears from falling.

"Nina, listen to me. You don't have to assure yourself that I want you! I've wanted you since I first saw you. But I tried not to think about you. I even went on with the case in order to hate you, not to see you. At the trial—"

"The trial? . . . Oh, yes, the trial. You are Howard . . . Cutting," she said slowly. "How very funny."

"What's so funny about that?" he snapped suddenly, tired of her little game and afraid of being mocked and duped.

"Nothing, really." Her voice had gone quite dead.

"Nina, you must explain. Tell me why——" Her troubled eyes met his and he suddenly gripped her again and bent his face close to hers. "Tell me you love me, Nina, tell me . . ." He felt lost and hopeless. "Tell me you wanted me then, at least for a moment, me, not just anyone. Oh, Nina, Nina." His lips fluttered on hers and he was talking into her mouth, but she turned her face and pushed him away gently.

"Howard . . . I'm sorry. I'm sorry it had to be you here. I can't explain. This happens to me sometimes . . . I . . . well, I . . . I don't know, at least I do know, it's happened before. The police found me once, I was soliciting . . . I couldn't believe it, afterwards. I seem to imagine that I'm a . . . I saw a doctor there, and, well, I gave my name, and they were very nice and took me home. I never told Gael . . . I just can't, I don't understand it, I'm terrified of it. I think he knows. I seem to go into a trance, I don't remember afterwards, but then you told me, so I suppose I must have . . . Howard, what did I do? Did I ask for money? Tell me, did I? Or was I just . . ."

"Yes, you were just . . . Nina, it was wonderful."

"You mean . . . ?"

"No. No, unfortunately. Oh, Nina, I love you."

"You mustn't. You, of all people."

"You didn't . . . want me . . . just a little?"

"I don't know, Howard, I don't know. I don't think so. I'm sick. I'm terrified."

"Nina, let me help you. No one will know about this, I promise."

"How can you help me?" She sounded so lost he almost wanted to cry himself and a lump choked his throat. He took two cigarettes and lit them together, then fixed one into the holder and placed it between her lips. Her small white fingers went up to it, holding it like a long lost familiar relic. Her silver nails glimmered in the moonlight and she inhaled deeply. He put his arm round her shoulders; he was small, but she was minute, and fragile.

"By talking to me. If someone knows about this, someone who cares about you and admires you and hasn't for one moment lost his respect for you, doesn't that help a little?"

"Perhaps. You . . . still . . . respect me?"

"Oh, Nina, I lo—— Of course I respect you. And I feel—protective, does that sound silly? You're so very—vulnerable, I don't want you to get hurt. Talk to me, say anything, tell me about yourself."

"It's getting late."

"Is . . . Gael expecting you?"

"No, no. He's in Oxford, That's part of the trouble, he's away during the week. Then after I've put the children to bed I usually work, or read, or sew, listening to the wireless. It's funny. I'm so in love with him, even after seven years of marriage, and we're so happy. Yet I never miss him. I'm always terribly pleased when he comes home, and I snuggle up and feel all . . . protected. But I don't miss him. I like being alone. Only this, this thing . . . It's the third time it's come over me, to my knowledge, I mean. I daren't think how often . . . perhaps . . . without anyone telling me afterwards . . ."

"Have you ever taken . . . anyone home?"

"Not as far as I know. Funny," she said with a suddenly crude laugh, "it's not so easy—must be the wrong beat." Then quietly again: "I don't know whether I'd even remember where I lived in the first place. I suppose if I had I would have come to sooner or later and found him there." She laughed again, ironically. "But it's just possible . . . if he went away first. I don't think so, though. My maid, Frieda, would have heard something and behaved peculiarly, but I watched her, she never did. She is attractive, Frieda, don't you think?"

"Well . . . I hardly noticed, you know. I was looking at you."

"But she is," Nina insisted, "in a Germanic way, blonde and buxom. She is, really."

"All right, she is. Why is it so important?"

She puffed in silence for a moment, then flicked the stub out of the holder with her nails, and a dying ember flew out on the path. She watched it go out slowly and sighed.

"I don't know." Her voice was almost inaudible, then suddenly became a louder echo of itself, like someone else's voice. "I don't know, I don't know anything. I don't understand it. It's not as if I just wanted an affair—even if Gael were that sort of husband."

"Don't you?" said Howard softly, his arm still round her and pressing her towards him. He touched her chin with his forefinger and turned her face up to his, very near his mouth. "Don't you think it might help, darling? Help both of us?"

"No." Nina shook her head and turned her face away. She opened her bag to replace the cigarette holder, her cropped head bent low over it. "Leave me alone, Howard, I'll be all right, please, please, leave me alone." She got up. Howard was slumped on the bench, looking crestfallen.

"I'll try, Nina," he whined, "if that's what you want."

"Yes . . . that's what . . . I want."

She turned away, then stepped back.

"I want to ask you, please, will you . . . I beg you to be discreet."

She seemed completely to evaporate in the undignified pathos of her question, except her eyes, which grew larger than her own anxiety, larger than the night, larger than the sudden, stillness in his heart. He seized her hand and covered its palm with kisses.

"Nina, oh, Nina, of course. Oh, Nina, I do love you."

The palm pressed gratefully on his cheek, then slipped away. Quick steps, lighter and lighter, and she was gone.

Zoltan and Elizabeth had been having a very different kind of conversation in a very different part of London. Elizabeth had caught him up at the street corner and trotted, panting, to his long strides, begging him to listen to her, not to leave her, not to stop loving her.

He stopped, not, perhaps, loving her, but walking.

"Erzsebét, you must not beg for anything," he said sternly as they stood in a small street that sloped down Campden Hill. She was just ahead of him and looked shorter than she really was in relation to him. The warm spring breeze swept her hair in auburn wisps across her eyes, and he unveiled them gently and took her head in his hands, modelling her cheekbones with his broad thumbs soothing her eyes shut and stroking her eyebrows. Then he bent down and kissed her softly on the lips.

"I cannot stop loving you, Erzsebét, Erzsi, Erzsike, but you must not do anything to hurt me."

"Zoltan *drágám*. You know that's the last thing I want. I'm in a difficult position too, you must understand."

"I do understand. The Institute is phoney but that is not your fault. Just be careful, keep out of politics. Such a visit is a political act, Erzsike, you would not be going as a private person. Do not go, Erzi, do not go."

"It's so difficult, Zoltan. I accepted as a matter of course. I was so pleased, and I thought you would be too."

"You are going?" His hands dropped from her face and he stood almost to attention.

"Zoltan. I—I have to go, now."

He said nothing, just looked at her.

"Zoltan, please, try to understand."

"Many of your countrymen, Erzsebét, think of my countrymen as very fierce, splendid and heroic, gallant and very, very romantic, with *Tziganemusik* playing by the Danube as we leap on to the barricades to die for freedom. I am not romantic, Erzsebét —you are more romantic than I, and that is very right in a woman. I liked it and was romantic for you sometimes. But from the East of Hungary, Erzsebét, we are horribly stoical, and melancholy. Oh, yes, we are lighthearted on the surface, quick-witted, in our own tongue, that is, but we have not the sense of romantic tragedy. That is for the solid people of the plains, that is how they compensate for their solidity. We only have a philosophy of resignation, and of revolt in despair." He turned to a front garden where early rosebuds were shyly testing the breezy night air, and bent over the fence to pick one. "I steal my romanticism from you, Erzsebét, from your great, anonymously hospitable, uncommitted country. Take this, and think again while it is flowering, do nothing rash until it has faded. Roses for Saint Elizabeth. Goodbye, Erzsebét. I love you."

She took the bud from him and drew a deep breath to stop herself from crying. Yet even her despair partly revelled in his gesture. The sincerity of her emotion and the reality of her fear expressed themselves in cheapened romantic phraseology, which she felt by some erroneous instinct was suitable to an eternal farewell and a heroic renunciation. She pinned the rose over her heart and said:

"I shall always put roses on your grave, Zoltan."

Chapter Twelve

THE hearse had come from a village graveyard some way outside Oxford, the man said, but it was empty now, the funeral was over.
Nevertheless Nina crossed herself as she stepped into the front seat next to the driver, who wore black but looked otherwise remarkably cheerful and smelt of beer. He had left his colleague, he said, at a pub in Wheatley, where he lived, as they had no more work that day. They had drunk a toast to the dead man, and another to the dying living who would keep them and their successors in happy employment for ever and ever amen.

"Do you like your job?" Nina asked conversationally.

"Oh, it's not too bad, miss. No backseat driving, for one thing. I used to be a chauffeur, you know, before the war. One of them rich ladies, and she didn't 'arf fuss. She was so old, she might as well have been a corpse, for all her furs and jewellery and perfumes. She probably is by now, rest her soul. Still, she was a proper lady, they don't make 'em like that anymore. Oh, no. I tried to go back to it after the war—but I'd got out of the way of it, you know. Started with colonels, then ambulances—I didn't like that, too much hurrying—then ammunition trucks. Ended up in the Service Corps. From the Service Corps to servicing corpses, eh?"

Nina smiled politely.

"But doesn't it get a bit morbid sometimes?"

"Morbid? Oh, no, miss. We all have to die, you know. People get upset of course, but we're used to it. 'Arf the time they ain't mourning the person at all—especially an old one, they're quite relieved really. But they're upset by the paraphernalia, if you know what I mean. The paraphernalia of death." He rolled the words out proudly. "It's a nasty reminder, like, but we're used to it," he repeated. "All in the day's work. Mind you, we have to keep solemn-looking for the show itself, but after, well, we relax a bit. My pal, he's quite an old hand at the game, been in it for years. He's wonderful going in the houses—I never like that bit, always feel like saying something nice to the kith and kin, like, but he goes in poker-faced and quiet, and ever so polite, it sets the tone, if you know what I mean, they don't get so upset if you keep it on a business level. And then there's the slow drive with the coffin and flowers, that's okay, 'cos everyone turns and looks. Still," he leered at her and winked, "it's nice to have different company." Nina didn't know whether he was referring to her sex and self, as opposed to his colleague, or to the fact of her being alive, as opposed to his usual cargo.

She certainly didn't feel very alive. An immense wave of fatigue and depression had engulfed her in the last few days since her meeting with Howard. It was early June now. Gael was in Oxford, invigilating Schools. He was an examiner that year and would have to stay up well into August, until vivas were over. Nina was annoyed at being alone and more annoyed at not missing him. Although she had so far contributed only one month's review of selected books, films and theatres to *Elegance*, she had been invited to several literary parties: one given by Sonya, who was pushing her, another by Charles Fortescue, who was over-attentive, and one party always led to another. She enjoyed them at the time, but they usually left her morose, with unlikely doubts about the purpose of the universe and the salvation of the human soul hovering uneasily on the edge of a black mood—each dispelled by another party, until a huge storm-cloud of unknown causes weighed so heavily upon her she wanted to bury her head in the sand. *There is fatigue deep as the grave.* A line of poetry kept coming into her head as she drove so symbolically into the Headington suburb of Oxford.

Gael had sent her a telegram. An odd thing to do, since he rang up almost every day. An odd telegram, too: "Come if troubled, Gael." How did he know she was troubled, since she hardly knew herself? She was always gay and loving on the telephone, murmuring sweet nothings into the mouthpiece which became his ear, across several counties and across the barriers of unspoken fears. On the spur of a sudden feeling of communication, of gratitude, of love, she had given Frieda an extra pound for taking complete charge of house and children for twenty-four hours, and had set out on the road, with no luggage except a blue cardigan, wearing only a tight yellow cotton dress, hitchhiking to make up for the frittered pound.

At first she had enjoyed the sense of freedom, the lifts in lorries and luxury cars, the flirtatious conversations with different kinds of men, the cup of tea at a wayside café with a truckdriver, the drink in Beaconsfield with a commercial traveller, the business man's hint about spending the night at his grass-widowy house in High Wycombe. But then the novelty had worn off and as she neared Oxford, weariness and depression seized her again. Lifts were harder to get. People stopped on a highroad but not near a town where buses functioned. In Wheatley she thought she would cheat and take a bus, and was waiting alone near the hearse outside a pub when the driver came out and offered to take her into the town. "Go on, miss, it's good luck," he had said by way of encouragement.

"Come if troubled, Gael." He seemed to know her thoughts before she did. Was she troubled? Life was pleasant, she was popular, she had become interested in her new work, had met lots of new people. She had an ideal husband, a saint almost, three children she adored, living-in maid, enough money to live in reasonable comfort, to clothe herself and her children, to feed her family, and to entertain their friends quietly but hospitably. What more could she want? An unideal husband? A sinner, not a saint?

"'What more can we want?' they ask," her companion was saying. "It's all very well, miss, as jobs go, but the pay ain't too good. Not but what the firms don't charge plenty to the customers, mind you, but what with costs going up, and everybody having less money, they cut down on the wages. Well, it ain't fair, is it now? It's a hard job, I keeps saying, all this poker-face stuff, and what with the sadness and all, after a while it sort of gets you under the skin, if you know what I mean, like miners' dirt. Well, we have to keep cheerful, don't we, or we wouldn't be efficient, now. So we got to have a bit more money to keep cheerful on. But the firms say they can't get anything out of the clients—the poor can't afford much and the rich—well, the richer they are the meaner they are, especially about death . . . So we all went on strike."

The monologue ended so abruptly and incongruously Nina was startled out of her half-listening reverie.

"On strike? You mean nobody—" she changed the unfortunately apt word "—no one could get buried for weeks."

"That's right, miss," He grinned. "Two weeks, we came out, and a proper to-do. Things were beginning to stink, if you know what I mean. 'Course, there was a bit of blacklegging—funny, really, as we all wear black—and black market burials. Then the town council had to get some volunteers in and of course they allowed people to do their own. Dug their own graves, if you know what I mean."

"So you were defeated?"

"Oh, no, miss. We walked up and down the streets, all dressed in black and carrying placards, Quite picturesque, we looked, and very lugubrious, if you know what I mean. In the end the Union got a raise—not much, you know, not what we'd asked for, but it was something, and besides, things had got a bit unseemly, if you know what I mean. We're a respectable profession, we are. Couldn't make too much fuss. A gesture, that's what it was, a gesture on both sides. Both sides of the grave, if you know what I mean. Where d'you want to be dropped, miss?"

The man's juxtapositions were a little unnerving. Suddenly Headington stopped and they were crossing Magdalen Bridge. The midday sun was throwing bright coins through tall trees on the stone-gold flanks of colleges. Oxford occurred so abruptly, round the corner from suburbia, she was startled into a shock of smiling recognition, back in the happy, half-conscious days of adolescence, back in the womb of holy-mother-culture.

"Anywhere will do. Which way are you going?"

"I'm turning left here, just beyond Rose Lane and Maud Lane"—for so he pronounced Magdalen—"but I can take you further up."

"This will do fine, thank you very much."

The Sycamore Tree: Chapter Twelve

He stopped the hearse outside Queen's College and she got put, much to the amazement of a long straggle of undergraduates in full examination regalia, emerging from their morning ordeal. They all raised their mortarboards and cheered. She waved to the driver as he drove off, smiled wickedly at the young men and tripped through them sexily in her tight yellow cotton dress.

"*Oh death, where is thy sting?*" one of them sang out, as the group closed in on her.

"*Timor mortis conturbat me,*" shouted another.

"Rigor mortis masturbat me," sniggered a third, very close to her.

"*Odi profanum vulgus et arceo,*" she quipped back, tossing her head, and this was her mistake, for she tried to walk on, but they barred her way. The last young man grabbed her wrist and declaimed: "*Te teneam moriens deficientemanu.*"

"Let me go!"

"Tell me first who you are, angel of death."

A complete change came over Nina. Gone were the talking eyes, the flirtatious smile, the provocative pose. She stood perfectly still, pale and calm, with her head raised, her eyes fixed on St. Mary's steeple, waiting for the recovery of their good manners. Small as she was, she had in one moment reacquired a dignity and adulthood, which was at once apprehended by the students, who all at once felt like small boys shamefaced before their mother. The young man dropped her wrist and muttered, "okay, okay, no offence meant." The shift in atmosphere was endorsed by the sudden disappearance of the sun behind a cloud. The undergraduates shuffled off, quickly forgetful, to talk about the questions they had answered, the questions they had not answered, and the questions they expected to answer that afternoon.

Nina walked on up the High and turned right down a narrow street clustered with colleges. The tide of fatigue and depression was creeping up again, literally up from her feet as if she were wading deeper and deeper, until it reached her neck and she was swallowing bitter salt with every step. She turned into a stone gateway on her right and across a small quad, through another arch into a second, larger quad in the middle of which flourished a solitary sycamore tree. Its thick base divided itself quickly into three main trunks, smooth, pale olive, but flaking off in white and pink patches and darker seams; and it branched straight upwards into the massive foliage. Its flat wide leaves greened freshly, but impenetrably in the re-emerged sunlight, casting a round pool of shade on the lawn, out of which it seemed to grow like a contorted nymph, a Daphne Laureola proudly impervious to the wooing of the sun-god. Beverley College was proud of its sycamore, and firmly encouraged the tradition that the famous limerick had been written in a room overlooking the quad. Nina smiled at it sadly, in familiar but embarrassed recognition of an old friend mysteriously betrayed, a second self who yet bore her no grudge and stood there comfortably, held in existence by the percipient eye of love which had created it, which was always around in the quad.

She went in through a doorway at the far corner and climbed up the worn wooden stairs. Dr G. C. Jackson, said the white painted letters on a shiny black door. She pushed it open gently and poked her head into the room. The walls were lined with the dark and dusty bindings of knowledge and wisdom, which repeated their gold-ringed knuckles over and over again along endless shelves that reached the ceiling. An open book lay in a dilapidated armchair, another among the faded flowers of the well-worn carpet. Examination papers were piled neatly on Gael's table by the window. Nina went and sat in his chair, glanced through the first answer of the topmost paper, smiling with sympathy at the sign of strain and panic in the swift handwriting, and the pompous, uninformative style. *Where is the wisdom we have lost in knowledge, Where is the knowledge we have lost in information?* she quoted again to herself, and gazed blankly out of the window at the security of the sycamore tree's undeniable presence.

Then Gael came in and she leapt at him, was lifted into a hug that creased his invigilator's stiff shirtfront and sent his mortarboard and another wad of papers flying.

"Darling!"

"Nina, you've come! Oh, honey, it's good to see you."

He covered her neck with kisses as she buried her head in the shoulder-ruching of his gown.

"Darling, I'm sorry, I'll pick them up. Are they all out of order? Does it matter? No, it doesn't, nothing matters, does it, if we're together. Oh darling, hold me tight."

Then they picked up the papers together, chatting in their own baby language, the language of adult love that has found the secret of happiness in mingling childhood with maturity and innocence with experience. Gael put the papers next to the first pile, took off his black gown and flung it on the settee. Then he walked over to the row of low cupboards under the shelves and got out a bottle of sherry and two glasses.

"Let's celebrate. I need a drink, anyway, after this morning. No one ever seems to cheat, however hard I watch them walking up and down between the rows. The atmosphere's so oppressive too, the heat, and nothing but pens scratching and bursting brains ticking miserably away. Did you cheat, darling?"

"Of course! I had an entire translation of Plato's Dialogues hidden in my knickers! That's why I looked so much more pregnant than I was, didn't you know?" She laughed, holding up the tip of her nose with her small ringed finger. But the question had struck a discord beneath her laughter and she stopped and sighed, suddenly exhausted again. "Isn't it hot? Funny, there's always a heat wave during Schools. D'you know, I've got nausea out of sheer association." She gulped down her sherry and lit a cigarette.

"Honey, you must be hungry. Didn't you have something on the train? You must have been here ages if you came on the 11.50."

"I hitchhiked. It was enormous fun." And she told him about the truckdriver, the commercial traveller, and the hearse, omitting, somehow, the grass-widow's offer and the taunting of the undergraduates. For Nina was sincere by omission. In an obscure way, she instinctively protected the depth and purity of her love for Gael by crowding out her hidden fears and desires with exuberance, hero-worship, and overwhelming affection. In spite of the tacit admission of her response to his wire —"Come if troubled, Gael"—the telegram was not mentioned, nor was trouble even hinted at. His understanding was silently accepted and camouflaged into a sudden mutual desire to see each other, for no other reason than the expression of happiness.

"We'll have lunch at the Mitre. And I'll fix up a room. You are staying the night, aren't you, honey?" He looked at her with a slight anxiety which was twinkled away as she said, "yes, yes, oh, yes," and curled up to him for a kiss.

"Is three a crowd?" said an amiable voice from the door.

"Phineas, how nice." Gael sprang up and greeted his friend. "What are you doing in the rival place? Everyone seems to have come to Oxford to see me. Or have you just come to—er—Oxford?"

"Two birds, old boy, two birds. Hello, Nina. You're one of them, the other's the Bodleian. Three, I should say. I've just seen old Prof. Bingham. Bad news, bad news. I'm just a one-year-old cowshed."

"What on earth?"

"My name, Nina, my name. I'm heartbroken, but your classical instinct was right, Antrobus doesn't come from *anthropos*. I knew it was a place name in Cheshire, of course, but the Oxford Dictionary said 'origin unknown', and I had always hoped. Thank you." He took a glass of sherry. "The other day I asked the Cambridge Professor of English to trace its etymology for me. Do you know, he gave one look at it and said 'one-year-old cowshed'. Well, of course, I wouldn't believe, it, so I asked old Bingham.' Oxford, I thought, the mother of philology they'll tell me. He worked it out for me and look," Phineas Antrobus sadly produced a piece of paper from his watch-pocket. "Pure Anglo-Saxon—*anwintrigbur*, the w drops out at some remote Primitive Germanic period, so the two n's join up, then the palatal g falls out before the b; final r for some reason best known to itself becomes s. A one-year-old cowshed, that's what I am, not a man at all."

"Poor Phineas! Never mind, I love you just the same." Nina laughed, tapping the tip of her nose.

"Bless you, dear child. Wouldn't you rather I were a bull-shed, at least?"

"That sounds almost rude," she giggled, and leapt across the room. She seized Gael's red and blue doctor's gown, which was hanging on the door, for ceremonial use only, and she faced Phineas, her legs tightly held together and her heels stamping the floor in a *zapatillado*.

"*Toro! Toro!*" she growled, inviting him to plunge into academic honour, which he did, falling at her feet and embracing the tangle of legs and robe. Gael was roaring with laughter.

"Thank God for our pagan subconscious!" Phineas exclaimed when the fun had subsided. "Look at the way we can enjoy even a mock-bullfight, back to the Minos myth. How we love pageantry and everything that harks back to the Old Religion."

"Phin, you're incorrigible!" Gael looked at him with great affection. "Does everything have to go back to the Old Religion, even pageantry?"

"But of course. Look at Shakespeare, he knew all about it. Look at the sheep-shearing episode in *The Winter's Tale*."

"Don't Christians shear sheep?"

"Look at the boar symbolism in *Venus and Adonis*."

"Isn't the boar pretty Universal?" Nina punned. He snorted at her and ruffled her hair playfully. "Stop it, Phinny." She laughed with delight and pretended to fight with him, hammering at his chest with her fists. "You know," she went on breathlessly, "I heard a rumour that a school of psychologists in America have discovered there's no such thing as the subconscious." She evaded his blows. "They daren't make it public because everyone would feel so lost. I hope the twenty-first century will discover that things mentioned in ancient texts aren't symbols for other things but just . . . things." She ducked.

"All right, you minx. But what about Shakespeare's neo-platonism, why, he simply must have read Plotinus and Porphyry."

"I thought you said it was all subconscious?" Gael smiled with mock irony.

"As well. Residue in the memory, my dear chap, telepathically communicated through good old *Anima Mundi*."

"Oh her. You might have brought her in as a witness at my trial. No doubt she could have explained the phenomenon of Howard Cutting."

Without looking at her, he felt Nina's quick glance.

"Oh, forget Howard Cutting," she exclaimed, with a gaiety that was left over from her playful exertions, rather than caused by genuine unconcern. "Let's all go to lunch, I'm starving. I want to hear about your Greek code. How's it coming out?"

"Nicely, nicely, thank you. *Mine own* is, of course *Minoan*, so is *mine eye*, in a different case."

"*So apple of mine eye* would be *Minoan Apollo*?"

"It would indeed, if it occurred. How very bright of you, Nina. I've discovered that every *the* or *this* or *those* or *these*, even *thee* and *thou*, is a pun on some inflection of *Theo*."

"Oh, Phinny, don't be mad."

"But it's true, my dear. You can help me, with your classical training. Moreover, the incidence of definite articles and demonstratives in Shakespeare is remarkably low. Not a very godly man, evidently."

"But he is," Gael put in. "He's been claimed as a Catholic by the Catholics, a fairy by the fairies . . ."

"A Greek scholar by a pseudo-Greek scholar!" Nina said maliciously.

"You monster!" But he was used to being teased and they often wondered how seriously he took his own theories.

"He is all things to all men," Gael said pacifically.

"Phinny-ass?" Nina mooed at him. "*Please* don't turn him into a one-year-old cow."

Chapter Thirteen

"WHAT are the cows and donkeys doing there, Mummy?"
"They're looking at the child Jesus."
"But why is he in the cowshed?"
"Well, because when it was time for him to be born, his parents were travelling on the road and they couldn't find any room at the inn, you know, like the hotel we stayed at last year on the way to Uncle Gino. So they had to go to a stable and he was born there."
"How smelly!" Josephine sniffed. She had just had her bath and herself felt very clean. "You mean a real stable, like at Uncle Gino's?"
"Yes, but smaller. I expect St Joseph cleaned it up a bit first, and got some fresh hay."
"Yes, he must've. It looks pretty, doesn't it, Mummy? Why have they got plates on their heads?"
"They're haloes, darling, made of holy light, because they were all so good."
"Why haven't you got a plate, Mummy?"
"Because I'm not as good as the Virgin Mary and Joseph and Jesus."
"You're not?" Josephine turned incredulous blue eyes on her mother. She was sitting in a red dressing gown on her lap, looking at a picture book Life of Christ before going to bed. Like most firstborn she looked more like her father. She had Gael's blond hair and at six seemed already to have inherited his quiet, studious disposition. Nina was wearing a white linen dress with a blue stole, and sitting together on the red velvet sofa they looked rather like a holy picture themselves, though as far removed from the simplicity of the stable as the Baroque is from primitive Christianity. "Am I good, Mummy? Can't I wear a golden plate?"
"We're none of us good enough to wear a halo, darling. But we have

little ones, our souls, which are invisible. Nobody can see them because we're not good enough. That's why Jesus came, to make us better, so that our souls can be seen, like haloes."

Josephine was silent for some time after this long explanation. She turned over the pages quietly, and when she came to the Crucifixion she quickly turned back to find the stable again, gazing at it intently.

"If he was wearing a plate like this, why did they kill him, Mummy?"

"Because they couldn't see it, darling. Bad people can't see real goodness."

"But it's there in the picture!"

"Yes, of course. We now know it was there all the time. But they didn't, and we often can't see the real goodness of people, even around us."

"Mummy?"

"Yes, darling?"

"Really, really, really."

This was Josephine's customary introduction to a truly enormous question, not to be dismissed with grownup jokes or grownup babytalk.

"Yes, Josephine?"

"Jesus died to make everybody in the world good, didn't he?"

"Yes, Josephine."

Silence.

"Mummy?"

"Yes?"

The child whispered ominously: "It didn't work, did it?"

Nina suddenly felt helpless before this vast theological doubt of a six-year-old. She tried to explain, about prayer, about wrong actions which kill Christ every day, and how every day He rises again in His forgiveness if we are truly sorry. But Josephine was as unconvinced as a humanist suddenly made to hold a rosary. Moreover, having thus questioned the entire doctrine of Salvation through the Incarnation, she suddenly lost interest in the whole affair and demanded, by a process of association that would be gratifying to students of comparative mythology, to be told a fairytale, "a real one."

"Darling, it's long past your bedtime. The twins will be fast asleep."

"Michael and Marisa will be fast asleep," the child repeated, unconsciously correcting her mother's collective reference. Michael and Marisa were so much a double black-fringed echo of Nina's own boy-girl personality that she often thought of them, as she thought of herself, as one person. But to Josephine they were separate persons, however alike they seemed to cooing visitors. "Not a teeny-weeny fairytale? Oh Mummy, let's play at ob-djex." Nina had been teaching her to read for a year, and she loved guessing objects beginning with this or that letter.

"No. Come on, darling, off you go."

"But Mummy! It's daylight!"

The late summer evenings were always difficult. Josephine scrambled down and started to run around the room, hiding behind the sofa and the armchairs, cackling like a hen and shouting her favourite song:

"Mummy is the root of all evil . . ."

Nina played up to her for a moment, pretending not to be able to catch her. Then she went to the door and held it.

"Come on. Finished now."

Josephine knew the tone of command and obeyed at once.

"When's daddy coming back?" she chatted as they walked hand-in-hand down the corridor.

"Not for a little while. Now, darling, keep quiet or you'll wake the others."

They crept into the nursery. When Josephine was eight she would have to have a room of her own, Nina thought. Frieda's room. There would be only a daily help. But then the children would be at school. It would no doubt balance out. She suddenly felt very tired. Her trip to Oxford, two days ago, had only increased her deep sense of insecurity, so completely unwarranted by the basic framework of her life, so deceptively disguised as fatigue and causeless depression that even she was convinced of her own sincerity with herself and with those she loved.

She tucked up Josephine affectionately and kissed her goodnight. Then she tiptoed out, shut the door quietly, and went back to the drawing-room. Frieda, who by now had reached the letter p in the dictionary, had announced that she would "peregrinate to the picture house for the nonce." Nina drew up her sewing table to the sofa and looked into its untidy contents perplexedly—Gael's socks to be darned, a dress begun for Josephine, a blouse for herself. Which should she do? She went to the record-player and put on Brandenburg No. 3. Then she sat down and took the blouse, almost without thinking.

In the middle of the second movement the bell rang. Puzzled, she went downstairs and opened the door. A tall man with black jutting hair and wild black eyes stood there nervously shifting his weight from one foot to the other.

"Yes?"

"Is Mr Jackson in?"

"No, I'm sorry. He's in Oxford."

"Oh, you are Mrs Jackson?"

"Yes. Can I——"

"You are very pretty."

She smiled wearily in acknowledgement.

"Can I give him a message? He'll probably ring me up tomorrow."

"Telephone! No, no. They listen."

"Who?"

"They. My enemies." He looked at her suspiciously.

"Well—" she felt a bit lost "—perhaps if you'll give me your name I'll tell him you called. He can write to you."

"No, no. He must not write." The man was glaring anxiously over his shoulder. "When is he coming back?"

"Not for several weeks, except perhaps an odd weekend. He's examining, you see."

"Several weeks. Can I go to Oxford, to see him?"

"Well, he's rather busy ... Could you tell me who you are?"

"I am his Hungarian friend, you say, he will know. I am ... I am in great trouble," he explained on an impulse of sudden trust, fixing her with a hypnotic gaze of black eyes.

"Oh, Zoltan—what's-his-name—the one who rang up Elizabeth!"

"Shsh." He suddenly clapped his hand on her mouth. She struggled, pushing away his arm with both her hands and he let go, suddenly penitent.

"I am sorry, Mrs Jackson, I should not have done that, not to the wife of my friend, whom I trust. Please forgive me."

"Yes, of course." Nina was completely bewildered.

"Please tell your husband—" his voice dropped to a whisper "—Zoltan called and he is in trouble. Goodbye."

"Goodbye."

In a flash he was gone, into the dusk, round the corner of the square and down a side street. Nina went upstairs to the drawing room. The Brandenburg was drawing to a close and she ferreted nervously among other records for something different, Nina followed the jazz cult, but also liked the stuff. She had just put on a collection of re-recorded King Oliver when the bell rang again. Tears of irritability and exhaustion pricked her eyes as she went down. Darkness had fallen quite suddenly during those ten minutes, winning the race from the gas lamps which were late lighting up. Howard Cutting's small stature was only barely discernible on the doorstep. Uncertainly, Nina stepped back to switch on the hall light and he followed her in.

"Hello, Nina."

His monkey-face blinked at the illumination and they stood for a moment face to face, saying nothing.

"Hello."

"I called the other night, but your maid said you were in Oxford."

"Yes. I went to see Gael. He's examining."

"I know. She told me."

He looked at her anxiously, searchingly. Her lipstick was still smeared by Zoltan's hand and her eyes seemed unnaturally bright.

"I saw a man leave just now. Who was he?" He couldn't disguise the strain of jealousy in his voice.

"Just a friend of Gael's. He only called for a moment," she added, a little defensively, and he pounced on her and gripped her wrists.

"He kissed you, I can see it, don't lie to me."

"No, no, he didn't," she gasped. She knew he wouldn't believe the truth. She knew that five evenings ago she must have been in this man's arms, he must have touched her, goodness knows where. "You're hurting me. Let me go."

He dropped her wrists and stood close to her, lips open, eyes staring hungrily.

"Nina, Nina, don't do this to me. If it must be someone, let it be me, please."

She closed her eyes and the corners of her mouth dropped in fear and dismay. She was trembling violently and stammered, so low he could hardly hear:

"Howard . . . d-d-don't take adv-vantage of what you know about me."

Idiotically he dropped on his knees and took her hands, covering her fingers with kisses.

"Nina, oh Nina, forgive me. I won't . . . I just—"

"I swear this man only came to the door." She was sobbing suddenly, quietly, and tears streamed down her face. Melted by his sudden romantic, sentimental gesture, she yet could not recover her poise sufficiently to stop defending herself. For he had stumbled upon her weakness, her Achilles' heel, and there was shooting his beastly arrows of desire. Dimly aware of his new strength, yet infinitely tender and in all sincerity, he rose to his feet keeping her small white hands in his and kissing their palms gently.

"Come. No tears, now. Relax," he murmured. "I hear clarinet music. Let's go and listen quietly together, shall we?"

She nodded with a sniff and they climbed up the carpeted stairs in silence. A burst of piston-rhythm jazz greeted them and Howard, who had mistaken the clarinet solo of *High Society* for Mozart, looked momentarily disconcerted. Nina flopped on the sofa, her head down, the crook of her elbow over the red velvet arm. He sat down next to her, restraining his hands, and lit two cigarettes; then he put one between her lips, but she shook her head, and he stubbed it out in the ashtray. Johnny Dodds's clarinet began to weave its strains of intolerable tenderness through the gaily throbbing mechanism of *My Sweet Man*. He leant forward and touched her hair, so softly, she didn't move. But she closed her eyes, letting his fingers caress her black fringe and stroke the neatly cropped hair in her neck, as if she were a purring cat. Still the clarinet solo trickled down her spine, piercing to the marrow in the small of her back, climbing up again to flood the nerve-centre and trill into some memory of fingers touching her hair (whose fingers?) as she listened to . . . Mozart. A clarinet. Fingers touching her hair, it was something to do with lawyers, a trial, yes, barristers always liked Mozart, because they wore wigs, daddy said. Fingers touching her hair . . . clarinet . . . barristers . . . daddy . . . Gael studied law once . . . but he lost the case . . . Bach . . . bop . . . Mozart . . . fingers on her hair.

Howard was mesmerised by her immobility. And now the slide whistle was breaking its heart through *Sobbing Blues*, winding its patterns of pathos through their sensuality. His fingers moved down from her neck to her shoulders lightly, slowly, barely touching her white skin, feathered across under the arm where her head was laid, and back, lower, into her breast. She shuddered. He slipped his other arm round her waist and lifted her gently back, his hand still on her breast, and lay her down next to him on the red velvet, her white dress echoing the white walls, her blue stole crumpled under her, echoing the carpet, her hair black as the elegant ebony furniture. She made no resistance, her darkened lids were closed, as if sealed forever by the long black lashes, and her lips, still slightly smeared, were open. She stretched her arms out in abandon, her legs intertwined with his. As his mouth met hers he felt her hands on his neck, then languorously round his open collar and into his shift, moulding his shoulders and sculpturing his small strong muscles. His hand wandered down to her thigh, under her skirt, and the stiff frills of petticoat. One of her legs was stretched to the floor over the edge of the sofa, the other was arched up against the red velvet back. He felt his way up her thigh, under the frills, his tongue still lost in her mouth and his eyes wide open with incredulity at her being really there, soft and pliant in his arms. Then his hand stopped with reflex surprise. She was wearing no pants. He plunged up to explore, gratefully, passionately, and her hair was long and silky.

He took her as *Sweet Baby Doll* ground its wheezy cacophony into the room, like an old disk running down. The piece was short, but it far outlasted him.

She lay completely still, rigid almost, when he got up to dress. The front door clicked shut and quilted steps came up the carpeted stairs. He started and stood paralysed for a moment.

"It's only Frieda," she said without opening her eyes. "She won't come in here. The gramophone's on."

Just then the record came to a stop. Still she didn't move. A bedroom door opened and closed on the top floor.

He dressed quickly. Her silence frightened him. He wanted to get out as soon as possible, but he couldn't go without some word, some little word of commitment. He started chattering, jocularly, crudely.

"I say, what's the idea of not wearing pants? You should have warned me. Quite a shock, not finding the expected amount of barrage. Tell me, does it make you feel more sexy not to wear them?"

Still she said nothing and her eyelids were blue and fringed, her lips pale, the paint kissed away.

"Oh, come off it, Nina, don't pretend I've exhausted you." She opened her eyes at last and stared at him, stonily it seemed, for an age, unnerving him. He went over to the looking glass behind a small ebony table with flowers on it, and adjusted his tie into a reflection that grew weirdly out of a bunch of roses. "Or do you want more?" he continued with a laugh. "I must say you look pretty satisfied. It's amazing the change in a woman. That relaxed look and those clear eyes." He turned and suddenly couldn't face the supposed clarity of her eyes.

"Nina, Nina, darling." He knelt by her and took her hand. "You were wonderful." Still she was silent.

"Nina, tell me, my darling, tell me you love me, a little. Tell me—" He changed his tack, hopelessly. "Was it all right for you?"

She stretched herself, gave a long sigh and her limbs relaxed suddenly on the red velvet. Without moving her head she smoothed out her dress, crossed her ankles and lay there looking at him almost with wonder. Then she smiled and he could hardly bear that either, for it was a mocking, mischievous smile. But she stroked his wrist softly and her voice was very gentle.

"The beginning was nice," she said.

Chapter Fourteen

THE beginning of a love affair is always nice, however unpleasant one or both of the persons concerned may be. At seventeen or at seventy, their life acquires a new and enormous dimension, that juts every object sharply into a focus of relativity, all, all relative to a pair of hands, a pair of eyes, a mouth, a mannerism, a shimmer of laughter, a few words out of context, out of time, out of place. One being floods another with its shape, its gestures and its constant surprises. Crossing a street together, buying cigarettes, tendering a bus fare, all the routine actions normally performed almost unaware, assume a supernatural significance, enhanced, it seems forever, by the awesome aura of memorability. It seems forever but alas, these are the first to be forgotten. Only the moments of mock-romance, only the sentimentality and, in bad cases, the lechery, pervade the memory with nostalgic longing, after the hurting and the colliding of two creatures, who in each other have sought only themselves, is slowly healed and hidden away beneath restoring pride.

As when the Yogis, or the followers of Ouspensky, teach men to become aware of their every action, all other men being asleep, to think about the spoon as it approaches the mouth, the digestive muscles as they expand and contract to send one morsel of food on its long beneficial journey; as when Zen Buddhists sit, comfortably contorted, meditating on a meaningless word—all other men being asleep; as when the Christian in a state of grace, pursues his worldly occupations, fulfils his role, walks abroad among the wickednesses of creation, and finds them all illuminated by a purpose—all other men being asleep; so new lovers for a week, a month, a year perhaps, become aware of every drop of rain that plucks black satin streets, aware of all the windows hiding some happiness, some sorrow, climbing up the high buildings like a film reel to be projected through the chimneys on a heavenly screen; aware of passing faces, asleep, unalive, unloving and unloved.

A complete change came over Howard. He was buoyant, relaxed, care-free, and worked at top speed, full of ideas and energy. He was kind and gentle with Elizabeth, gay with others, and above all, eager to see Nina again, to please her, to shower her with attentions. He stopped wearing his tight jacket of beige checked cloth, and had a new suit made to measure, taking her advice, buying sober shirts and more subtle ties. He kept reiterating, with wonder that he couldn't believe it, that she would get bored with him, find him dull and unsatisfactory. But this was nothing to the change in her. With him, she became vulgar, sensual, knowing. A hard look began to mask her features, tightening her mouth at the corners. She made rude jokes and rippled with laughter at his. She couldn't stop talking about sex, its technique, its positions, and relished his intimate references to parts of her body, to glimpses of her underwear she carefully posed herself to let him see. With others, she was excitable and promiscuously flirtatious if he was there, subdued and dead if he wasn't. At home she was happy and chattery with the children and Frieda, kittenish and loving with Gael on the telephone or at weekends. She had, in fact, become two persons.

After the first time, she insisted that Howard could not visit her at Paultons Square. He had no right to expect her to take all the risk, with three children and a resident maid, and Gael likely to turn up unexpectedly at any moment. So she went to his flat when he was free, in the afternoons. Elizabeth was away all day, busy at the Institute which had organised an English Summer Course for Hungarian students. They would meet in Chelsea or South Kensington for lunch, usually an erotic affair with much knee-juncture and wandering of hands under the table; then they would take a 49 bus to High Street, Kensington, and spend the afternoon, with or without Mozart, on the nobbly leaf-green and grey tweed of his sofa, with the chestnut tree in the backyard casting its ponderous blessing on their sensuality; or, sometimes, in his bedroom.

"It won't last," she kept saying, as if to justify herself, or perhaps to prepare herself for the inevitable pain she dimly apprehended. "Gael will be back in August, till early October. In November you'll be off to Hungary."

"Darling, darling, take a long-term view!"

"You'll be tired of me, soon," she quipped. She too had her turns of uncertainty.

"Want to take a bet?"

They were travelling on a 49 bus, which was going up Queen's Gate, because Gloucester Road was being pulled up for repair.

"It won't last longer than this diversion," she punned merrily. "Only as long as the buses are going up Queen's Gate."

"All right, we'll see."

But July came, the buses resumed their normal route and still their passion was unabated. Partly, perhaps, from lack of opportunity to overdo things: with four people's timetables to consider, it wasn't so easy for them to meet as much as they wanted.

They often went to the same parties now, and although they tried to seem indifferently friendly, they gave themselves away with every look, and with a small but unrestrainable compulsion to mention each other in conversation. Everyone was smoothly, officially oblivious, glad that the unfortunate business of the trial was forgotten, but everyone knew, and the general comment all round was: "Why *him?*"

Why him indeed! Nina would have been the last to produce an explanation, even to herself. She had no illusions about his vulgarity, his pushiness, his clever knowingness, his arrogance in argument; and none about his ugliness. Perhaps it was the very fact that Gael so disliked him, that he had tried to destroy Gael's reputation, that he was, strictly speaking, Gael's enemy. But something basically coarse in her responded to him, as if some puff of diabolical breath had blown away the soft thistle-down from her personality, leaving only a prickly stub. His very vulgarity was like a safety valve, protecting her from her own fears and half-conscious other urges. Yet still she could divide herself, gathering the fluff and wrapping it warmly, protectingly, desperately perhaps, around her home, her children, and her sincere love for Gael. What was it Howard gave her? She didn't know herself. He had never once satisfied her. Indeed, she would joke about it unduly, saying that he made her accumulate such a mountain of pent-up desire she could work it off on Gael. She needed one man for the preliminaries and another for the climax. He would laugh, disbelievingly, to mask his sense of failure. 'Conjures quite a picture. Anyway, you certainly relish the preliminaries,' he would say, and she certainly did, she was obsessed with them, electrified by his mere touch, anywhere, at any time, she wanted it to go on forever, and let the desire as such continue, not be taken by him at all.

Howard, too, was obsessed, as unhealthily, and all the more desperately for his feeling of inadequacy: obsessed in his imagination by a vision of sensuality that no action could assuage, obsessed in action by a self-gratification which masked a hidden, tormenting fear of his incapacity, not to make love, but to satisfy. He lay awake at night imagining her wild unwithheld climax, he dreamt of her small white body and long white thighs, waking as turbulently as in adolescence; her legs dangled from his desk as he worked and even her voice on the telephone churned his loins.

Reality had become for both of them ten times as sharp and ten times as unreal.

Another love affair, cleaner, quieter, but as unreal, had ended. Elizabeth hadn't seen Zoltan since May, and she was experiencing all the nostalgia, the heartache, the intolerable jabs of hurt pride that any woman must suffer who has been left for high-toned but incomprehensible reasons. What had she done but accept an invitation to visit his country, to see for herself, to complete her knowledge of his background? She had dreamt, impossibly, of going one day with him, one day, one day, when the foreign yoke was broken, when his people were free. He would show her round Budapest, he would take her to his village, introduce her to his long-lost parents—no, not his parents, foreigners only did that when they intended marriage. Marriage! It had always been dimly at the back of her mind, somehow, some day, she never particularised just how. And now he had gone in anger. It jabbed her throat as memories overwhelmed her at the oddest moments, so that she could hardly hold back the tears reeling behind her eyes. '*I have swallowed the stone of a lost alphabet?*' a line from the poet Szendrey kept floating through her pain. 'Swallow your pride,' she told herself, 'it's all for the best, anyway. I would have betrayed Howard sooner or later, and there's no future in that. Only more torment, more pain.' But true as these trite phrases were, she was uttering them as lies, as self-deceptions which comforted her little. Elizabeth was naïve, romantic, and not naturally intelligent. She had a flair for languages and so had unduly developed the mechanical side of her brain, leaving both intuition and analytical capacity at a sixteen-year-old level. Emotionally, she would have been happy in the world of women's magazines, had she not forced her intellect through the grammatical mills of multilingualism, which is so often a substitute for thinking. In her own eyes, she had married in her innocent youth, a dull inferior *don manqué* eaten up with journalistic ambitions; her real 'soulmate', a romantic dark foreigner with gallant manners, noble bearing and heroic aspirations, had come just too late in her life, so that they could but love each other from afar, purely, magnificently and eternally. This she naturally felt still held good, and the *idée* was so *fixe* that it considerably helped her to endure their mutual sacrifice. But she missed him like hell. And nagging at the *idée fixe* was the unadmitted knowledge that the sacrifice had not been as mutual as all that. She hadn't wanted it, nor was she certain that it was, for him, such a sacrifice. The one thought she could not bear kept sweeping through, over and over, like a flood: he hated and despised her. Or worse, he was not missing her, he had forgotten her. If she was obsessed by anything it was by this. She had to find out.

He had never come again to the Institute. Twice, in an agony of hesitation and shame, she had called at his rooms in Leather Lane, but he wasn't there, and she had run off, almost thankfully. Now after six weeks, she was more desperate deep down, but calmer on the surface. 'After all,' she apologised to herself with dignity, 'I am still his supervisor. He has no right to disappear without informing me. The Institute must know what

is happening about his book.' If by 'the Institute' she meant herself she was marvellously hypocritical, for she knew perfectly well that Howard, in a fit of guilty enthusiasm, had sent it off with a rave letter, first to his publisher, Geoffrey Brandon, who much regretted that 'his list could not include such an unmarketable, though fascinating proposition'; then, with an equally rave but more cautiously worded letter, to Truelove & Thorne, from which it had not yet returned. 'Nevertheless,' she convinced herself, 'I must get in touch with him. He can't leave the Institute just like that.'
She decided to write.

Dear Zoltan,
As you must know, the term is now over and I shall have to make my report to the Director of the Institute. I wonder what your plans are. I am supposed to enter you as a student for next year, or next term at least, until the final version of your book is accepted. As you have disappeared from my life without leaving a trace of your existence, I don't know what to do, darling, I don't know what to do. You have disappeared, leaving no trace at all of the things which meant so much to us. They flood over me, with every memory of you, and it hurts so I can't bear it. Drágám, please, please let me know where you are, what you are doing. Do you ever think of me?

After a while she tore this up and started again:

Dear Zoltan,
As you must know, the term has now ended, and I have to make a report to the Director of the Institute. Would you be kind enough to let me know whether or not you intend to return next term, and if you have changed your mind about withdrawing your book. I have as yet said nothing to anyone officially, but there will probably be some objections about your grant and the sooner it is cleared up the better.
Yours very sincerely,
Erzsèbet

P.S. I miss you.

Then she copied the second version out again, without the P.S., and signing *"Yours sincerely, Elizabeth."*

Ten days of agonising post-watching went by. Nothing. She called at Leather Lane once more. No, said the tobacconist landlord, the foreign gentleman hadn't left, but he was out all day, and he was away at the moment. Oxford, he thought the foreign gentleman said. Oxford? Well, it may have been Cambridge, the tobacconist wondered vaguely, it was one of the two, but he always confused them, and never knew which side he was on for the boat race. He liked the dark blue rosettes best, but then the others were always winning, weren't they? Now rugger, that was a different matter.

Then a letter came from Mr Truelove. He liked the book very much. His firm had always had a special coverage for the great Russian novels, and had even ventured into translations of Pushkin and Lermontov. Howard chortled at the tone of the letter. "Funny," he said, "how virtuous publishers always feel about volumes of poetry. They treat them as a dead loss, an annual duty, and never bother to distribute them or promote them in any way, even classics. Then they grumble that poetry doesn't sell." "This book," Mr Truelove went on, "will help us to widen our Slavonic list considerably. The English is perhaps a little odd, but it could be edited." Elizabeth was indignant. "That means watered down," she said. "His English is perfect, I saw to that, myself! Why, the man's so ignorant he calls Hungarian Slavonic! Pooh!"

"Darling, don't fuss. This is a very good offer and I'm delighted to have fixed it. Besides, you know what editors are—if you accept all their changes with humility and gratitude, they never look at the final result. He can change it all back in proof and they'll be none the wiser. Then everybody's happy. This is quite a chance for Zoltan, you know."

Howard's conscience was oddly cleared by this visible token of his power and influence. The letter had come by the second post and he was sitting in his swivel chair, typing out his novel column for *The Sunday Supplement*. "Funny how the fashionable phrases in blurbs change," he had said to Elizabeth, who was free that morning and had brought in the post and some coffee. "Last year it was always *its classic simplicity*, these days the characters are always *beautifully realised.*" Now Elizabeth was sitting in one of the green armchairs, holding the letter, thinking of Zoltan's so-called chance.

"Yes, if he accepts it."

"Now, look here, I'm not having any foreign dramatics and sinister politics spoiling this. This is my baby, and I don't want to be made to look a fool, I hope that's understood."

"That is the first thing you make clear in all your machinations. But no one is ever made to look a fool unless he is one already."

"And what might you mean by that?"

"Oh, nothing, darling, I'm sorry. I'm very worried, you see, I haven't seen Zoltan since he came here to dinner. I've no idea what's happened to him."

"Lordy! You don't think he's gone back to Hungary?"

"No, no. He can't do that, he'd be imprisoned at once."

"So he says. These people always make themselves sound so much more important. Who was he, after all? A student, a critic. None of the émigré writers at the International Writers' Association has heard of him. I made quite a few inquiries, you know, before committing myself."

"Why did you push this book then?"

"There's one thing you seem to forget," said Howard in his smoothest tone of hurt integrity, "I'm a professional critic. When I like a book, I like it for its own qualities, irrespective of the author's character, personal circumstances or political background. I remember once," he started reminiscing on a scene which had particularly flattered his sense of importance, "Jim Craig coming up to me at a party and saying, 'You don't like me.' 'My dear chap,' I said, 'I've never even met you.' 'Well,' he replied, 'you gave my book a bad review.'" Howard chuckled with pleasure. "The idea that I should dislike a man because he'd written a bad book was a revelation! As a matter of fact," he added after a pause, "I did dislike him, after that."

"Okay, okay. Nevertheless you checked up on Zoltan."

"Only because I wanted to make sure I hadn't got a maniac on my hands. He did behave rather oddly, you must admit. At least I know that *I'm* pushing him from scratch."

"So he will owe it all to you, is that it?"

Howard refused to be ruffled. "If you want to see it that way, yes. As far as I'm concerned I admired his book and thought it worth publishing, and that's all there is to it."

"Well, let's hope he turns up."

He didn't turn up, but a few days later; towards the end of July, a plain-clothes man from Holborn Police Station called one evening. Elizabeth was completely flustered, but Howard showed him in, with excessive politeness.

"Just a routine inquiry, madam, please don't be alarmed. No thank you, not on duty."

"Sit down, officer, you'll have a cigarette, then?"

"Thank you."

"Somebody been murdered?"

"No, no, sir. I'm just checking up on a rather odd foreigner."

Elizabeth started. The detective looked at her and smiled.

"A Mr Zoltan Torday. You know him, I gather?"

"Yes. He was one of my students. Has . . . has anything happened to him?"

"No, not at all. You know, we get a lot of cranks coming into the station with peculiar manias. We have to humour them, but we just like to know who they are."

"Cranks?"

"Mr er—Torday has been behaving a little oddly, madam, but I assure you he is not in any trouble, as far as we know. He comes in to the station about once a week, to report a theft. But the theft is of a somewhat unusual nature, not, one might say, within our normal line of duty. He reports, for instance, that a poem of his has been stolen, and gives us a detailed description. Last week *they*—it's always *they*—stole two of his—er—metaphors—is that the right word? Yes, metaphors." He looked down at his notes. "You know, I'm not altogether sure what a metaphor is. Some sort of poetic ornament, am I right?"

"Yes." Elizabeth's voice was small and strangled.

"Well, you know, we can't do much about that. At first the sergeant just pretended to make an entry, but when it went on we thought we should find out who he was. He was very cagey about giving his name and address, so we had to explain that stolen property must be returned to the owner when found. I didn't want to call on him direct, but we discovered that he was registered as a student at the—er—Fidler Institute of —er—Danubian Studies. Danubian, that's nice. Strains of Strauss. I waltzed round there, as it were, and they sent me on to you. We just like to know who he is, and whether he's, well, harmless."

"Of course he's harmless!" Elizabeth exclaimed, almost in tears. Then more quietly: "I don't really know much about him, officer. He's a good student, and a fervent patriot. He was very upset, naturally, by the Hungarian Rising. He even went—" she suddenly changed her mind "—he did become a bit odd, I admit. I don't honestly know what his position is in his own country, but he's very right wing, almost reactionary, and he has always told me he is blacklisted there as a fascist. Of course, that's all nonsense, anyone against the regime is a fascist, a counter-revolutionary, a bourgeois and a decadent, you know their terminology. He's an ardent Roman Catholic. He does believe that he's a wanted man, but I don't—I never thought—well, one has to be careful, after all, he *may* be in danger."

"Well, thank you very much, madam, that's all I wanted to know. He's still living at Leather Lane, I take it?"

"I think so. I—I—haven't seen him for some weeks," she faltered.

"We can check up on that. You've been very helpful. Nothing to worry about, madam, you've no idea the people we get. Far worse cases, far worse. Goodnight, madam, good night, sir, I'm sorry to have troubled you."

"Not at all, officer, I'll see you out." Howard took him to the door. Elizabeth sank into her chair, her face in her hands, weeping silently.

"Lordy, lordy, didn't I *tell* you?" Howard chortled as he came back into the room. "I certainly had my suspicions, you must admit. I know *this* one! We've got a maniac on our hands! Stealing his metaphors, I've never heard of anything so cuckoo! Should be in a nuthouse! A straightforward, fully-fledged, clear-as-daylight case of persecution mania!"

Elizabeth did not raise her head. He shrugged his shoulders, muttering, "screwy, that's what it is, screwy," and returned to his swivel chair and his evening's work. After a while, Elizabeth got up silently and went out of the room. Howard was typing fast and hardly noticed.

Chapter Fifteen

"I KNOW, Mr Jackson, I know. But I think that people with a persecution complex really *are* persecuted." Zoltan smiled sadly, aware of the glimpse of his old humour which now seemed almost alien to him. "I think there is an element of truth in every mania."

"That's rather like turning the mania upside down to prove the mania, isn't it? Zoltan, please stop calling me Mr Jackson. My name is Gael. I'm your friend. You must believe that."

"I would not be here if I thought otherwise, Mr Jackson, Gael, I am sorry, it is difficult for us, we continue to use Mr for much longer, even with friends. Gael. It is a strange name, Celtic, yes?"

"Yes. Irish ancestors." Gael smiled pleasantly. "Not too well thought of in Boston society, the Irish."

"I understand. We have, too, our minority groups, Croats, Serbs, Vends, Romanians, Ruthenians, Germans. They show also in names—Török, that meant a Turk, Lengyel, a Pole, Horvath, a Croat, Nemet, a German. Torday, that is a very ordinary Magyar name, very ordinary, Mr—I mean, Gael. That is what I am trying to tell you."

They were sitting by the Cherwell along Addison's Walk, under a willow tree, surrounded with clover, bird's foot trefoil like red speckled yellow butterflies, harebells, hairy pink willow herb and strong-scented yarrow. Behind them the bank rose steeply under the shade of the great elms, feathering the white puffs of cloud in the summer sky, and a few birches bowed like thin white waterfalls against the green. Blue throatwort and nettle-leaved purple bell-flowers jutted spasmodically between the tree trunks, and, hidden among their stalks, the small scarlet petals of bishop's bedfellow peeped and winked. Beyond the stream, a few stumped willows edged a large meadow in which a few sad cows were grazing. They were completely enclosed by trees and flowers. Although Oxford was empty, Gael had chosen the Fellows' Walk in Magdalen grounds, because it was his favourite resort for solitude. He had taken Zoltan past the deer grove, he had shown him the great Lombardy poplar at the western end of Addison's Walk, and the cluster of rhododendrons planted in the vegetable mould that had collected at the top of a pollarded willow overhanging the river. And now they were lying in the grass among the soothing scents of July.

"Zoltan, what *are* you trying to tell me? You have an ordinary name. So have I. Jackson, I ask you, hardly aristocratic. A Civil War general. My father was a Boston lawyer, my grandfather had a drugstore. So what?"

Zoltan chewed a long blade of grass. "But you see," he said at last, "I chose it, because it was ordinary."

"You chose it?"

"I have told this to nobody. Zoltan Torday is not my name."

"Well, I guess you have good reasons for . . . "

"I have. My name is Árpád Szendrey. This will not mean anything to you, but I was once a famous poet, when I was twenty, just before the war broke out in Poland—already I was famous. I do not boast, Mr—er—Gael, I am not proud of it. I hope I was a good poet, I do not know, but my fame came too quick, and for many wrong reasons. I attacked every other poet, I was very arrogant in those days, Mr Gael, but it is a funny thing, I was nearly always right. Very few of those poets I attacked have survived, in reputation, I mean. Many of them were much to the left, before the war, and these were of course the first to be liquidated by the Communists. But even without death and imprisonment, everyone sees now many were no good. Then also I was politically committed, on the other side, and that brought me the wrong kind of fame."

"You mean as a Fascist?"

"Not exactly. I never collaborated with the Germans, on the contrary, they sent me to a concentration camp. I called myself a Nationalist—I was very young, you must remember—and formed a group of—how shall I say —almost mystical nationalists. But I escaped from Germany and worked with the Underground. Then I was betrayed, by a friend, to the Communists. The Underground was full of Communists, you know. I was sent to Kolýma. Do you know about Kolýma, Mr Gael?"

"Gold mines, isn't it?"

"Gold is everywhere, even on the paths and under the moss. It is exploited with the most primitive methods, then transported by air to the South. The journey from Vladivostok to Kolýma in North East Siberia, takes fourteen days, in the most terrible conditions. But these are nothing compared to Kolýma itself. No one survives Kolýma, Mr Gael. It is reserved for the most criminal, and of course political prisoners. There is only frost, reaching eighty degrees below zero—centigrade, you know—and scurvy, and gnawing hunger, then the bayonet or the bullet when you have become useless. It is possible to last a year, at the most two."

"But you survived?" Gael was staring up at the white clouds through the leaves. "I escaped after ten months, it was—I can only call it a miracle. Nobody ever escaped from Kolýma. I was ill, dying almost, and they shot me. But not well, not well. I fell into the snow, and crawled away later. Then more snow fell very heavily, and when they came back to bury me, they must have thought the snow had already done the work for them. Anyway, I was reported dead, many years afterwards when my country made representations to find me. Our Government was then on good terms with the Russians. I have never loved the snow so much, Mr Gael, as on that day. You do not know what real snow is in England. I have thanked the Blessed Virgin for that snow, so many times."

"But how on earth did you get away?"

"It is a very long story, I will not bore you with the details. I managed to hide in a wagon, then somehow I got to Magadan. Some people helped me, in great fear. I had luck, so much luck I was more terrified of the luck than of the hardships. Hardship cannot get harder, but luck can turn, then all the hardship is useless, as if it had not been, and then hardship does get harder, worse than the human mind can bear to imagine. In Magadan I hid for a long time, to get healed and a little stronger. If those kind people have suffered because of me—oh, Mr Gael, the debts I owe, which I can never repay, you cannot know how they torment me. Somehow or other I got to Sakhalin Island, and then to Japan, hiding, always hiding. By then Japan was under the Americans. They were very kind to me, your countrymen, Mr Gael."

"But you didn't tell them who you were?"

"No, I had had much time to think, in the long nights of walking and the long, long days and nights hiding under boxes and crates. I knew I would only be arrested again if I returned to Hungary. I invented a name, I said I had escaped from a prison camp at Bukhta Nakhodka—that is much further South, nearer to Vladivostok, and also more plausibly near Japan, and I said I could not bear to talk about it. It was true, I could not bear to think of the last eighteen months, I asked for their discretion, and not to put anything on my papers. They trusted me. They were very kind, your countrymen." A swan floated by on the water, silently, like something in a dream. "But I did not want to go to America. I thought, if I went to England, it would seem less likely that I came through Japan. I wanted to leave no traces. They sent me in an airplane to a camp in Western Germany, because I was Hungarian. Then I managed to get to England."

"I'm very sorry, very sorry, Zoltan. But why are you telling me all this?"

"Because I have to tell someone. I am in great difficulty. I trust nobody, except you. I do not know why I trust you. I have read both your books, I know that you are a poet—yes, you write prose, but you are a poet. There are very few real poets in the world, Mr Gael. A poet is a man who sees through. A man who is not taken in, by fashions, by factions, by movements, money, fame, power, even by beauty, Mr Gael, even by beauty. He may sometimes be taken in by love, but never for long."

Gael was silent. He turned over and leant on his elbows, picked a flower of clover and chewed the honeyed petals. They were a strangely contrasted pair: Gael blond, long-limbed, but lanky enough to look slight, pale and with blue-grey eyes and delicate hands; Zoltan burly, dark-skinned, with square hands, his near-Mongol face, piercing black eyes and black hair jutting backwards in a wide sweep.

"How can I help you, Zoltan?" he said at last, gently, and gazing fixedly into the trees, with narrowed eyes as if he wanted to snuggle their burning tiredness into the cool, restful green.

"It is like this. When I went to the Institute—this phoney Institute I told you about last time—I did not of course know that it was phoney. I thought it was part of London University. They wanted me to write a study of Árpád Szendrey. A study of myself! I was frightened, I tried to say no, I said he was my friend, but that made it worse."

"No University would have allowed you to do a thesis on anyone so modern, not in this country."

"Oh, yes, I know now, I know now. I was a fool. But they gave me a scholarship. I was starving. Then, you know, I had some sense of humour, though it may not seem like it now, and it is not like the British. I began to think it would be quite funny. The only poet ever to have written a posthumous study of himself."

"It has its element of macabre, I grant you."

"You see, I stopped writing poetry at twenty-five. Just like that. I felt I had done my job well, and should not spoil it. Some poets go on and on, but I do not believe they are any good after thirty. Composers, yes, and painters, they do not begin until they are sixty, but poets, poets die young."

"What about Goethe, and Shakespeare?"

"Goethe I do not admire at all. Shakespeare is the greatest exception that—how you say—proves the rule, I am not an exception, I am just a good poet. Or I was. And it was very strange, very exciting at first, to find all my volumes in the library. After all those years—I am thirty-eight now, it was really like reading someone else. Sometimes—" he grinned "—I did not understand him at all. Sometimes I thought 'what a terrible line, it spoils the whole poem', and I wanted to cross it out."

The breeze announced the lateness of the afternoon through the shimmering elms. Gael sat up and threw a pebble in the river, watching it dial the dark water. Zoltan sighed, lying back with his head on his hands gazing at the branch-swept sky.

"But then," he went on, "something started to happen, very peculiar, in my mind. For a long time I did not notice, I was in love. With Erzsebèt, you saw her photo. The wife of Mr Howard Cutting."

Gael winced at the name, but said nothing. Zoltan had been talking in a monotone, as if none of it mattered, as if reciting a lesson he had to get through before the really difficult question came. Now he too, sat up, and looked at Gael intensely.

"Slowly, Mr Gael, I became a dead man. Can you understand that? I became Árpád Szendrey again, the poet, who was dead. Mr Gael, I was not Zoltan Torday any more, I could not believe in my own existence. I began to have hallucinations. I was a ghost, I was floating, I was invisible, I was talking to myself, to Árpád Szendrey who stood in front of me, then I was in his body and looked at Zoltan Torday and he wasn't there. Mr Gael, I had ceased to exist. I was dead."

Gael put his hand on his shoulder. "I know. I have such sensations of not being there, or losing my identity. I guess we all have at times, but God knows you have more cause. It must be a hundred times more real, more terrible. But you must try not to let it get hold of you. Couldn't you see a doctor?"

"A doctor!" Zoltan almost squeaked. "What can a doctor do? He cannot free my country, he cannot give me a passport in the name of Árpád Szendrey! He cannot unbury me from under the wreaths and monuments of posthumous fame! Many people prefer to forget me, too. I said many uncomfortable things, which have come to pass. And then there was the November Rising. I became mad, Mr Gael, mad and angry. I went to Hungary secretly, and I fought. Some of the men of my generation recognised me, in fact, I was so mad I revealed my identity. They were amazed, they wanted me to stay, they offered to hide me. It was crazy, impossible. But I agreed to write for their Underground paper, under the name of Árpád Szendrey. For months I sent articles and commentaries, by secret channels. My existence shook everybody, it seems. I did not tell anyone here my real name, I would meet an agent by appointment to give him the articles. But somehow, it was discovered. I do not know how. I told Erzsebèt only that I was writing articles, but as Zoltan Torday. I got some unfortunate publicity, as Zoltan Torday, at your trial, Mr Gael, but I cannot see how they equated me. Nevertheless, the Communists know who I am. Perhaps someone at the Institute guessed it, because I was writing about Árpád Szendrey, I do not know. But they are after me."

"How can you be sure?"

"They have printed, in Hungary, about me. I am often followed. Perhaps I am followed to Oxford, perhaps..."

He looked around him nervously. There were only the harebells, the yarrow, nodding in the gentle evening breeze, and the patches of sunlight on the buttercups and pink willow-herb. One of Magdalen's rare black swans passed by on the stagnant water and Zoltan looked at it as if it were an evil spirit.

"You know what this is called in English?" Gael asked, holding up a purple flower he had been twiddling in his fingers. It looked like a large bumblebee, with two thick stalked leaves for wings.

"No. In Hungarian it is, literally, common lizard-grass."

"We call it self-heal. In the old days it was considered one of the best medicines for both inner and outer wounds."

"This is a pretty name. I take it with me to London, yes?"

Gael handed it to him with a smile.

"Zoltan, I'm not much use to you. I know nothing of politics, I never read the papers. I assume that if there was a war, someone would tell me, and if an atom bomb dropped, I would either hear it or be dead. But I understand these things more than many people think. By keeping aloof, one often sees more clearly. I don't know how I can help you, I have no contacts here, and I too have left my country, though voluntarily, and for reasons different from yours. Nevertheless I am at your disposal, and when I say that to anyone I mean it entirely. I have some friends back home who would gladly assist you if I asked them. I shall be in London at the beginning of August and you may use my house whenever you wish, we have a small garret room upstairs. But..."

"Mr Gael, you are very kind." Zoltan's head was bent over his hands, on his knees, and he held the spiky purple flower so that it seemed to be growing out of his black hair, like a tattered plume. He spoke into his chest, without looking up and in a strained voice. "I did not come for that kind of help. But perhaps I will have to use your house one day, later. Thank you. It is not that . . . "

"I was just going to say, none of that really matters. You can take it for granted—and I don't say that to many people, though most do in fact take an intolerable amount for granted. What matters is you, your own personality, what is going on in your mind, and above all your soul."

"My soul, yes," Zoltan muttered.

"The word is almost a joke these days, it's only mentioned in quotes, or with an apologetic laugh. Most people, Zoltan, hide their soul under so many layers of self-protection one sometimes wonders if they have one. I'm not talking about sin, mind you, but about the many people one meets whose spiritual life has remained at the foetus-stage while their body has grown full size. They are perfectly good people, they may even believe in God and pray every night and go to church, and whether they do or not, they enjoy life, work well and use their brains, but they are not alive. The nearest I've come to disbelief is when I have wondered whether some people have a soul."

He paused, and looked intently at the cows in the field beyond the stream, as if to find inspiration from their placidity.

"You see," he went on, "being spiritually alive has nothing to do with being good. One may not have a particularly nice soul. But it does mean having a certain resistance, a hidden strength beyond which others know they cannot go. Again, this has nothing to do with not giving oneself, on the contrary. I don't altogether understand it, but I have met very few people who have this strength, this fundamental identity. Now you have it. My wife—" Gael's voice suddenly faltered "—has it. But such people can get terribly hurt, because others somehow feel that inner resilience, that spiritual life which they know they can't destroy, though they try. Oh, they don't mean to. Nor does the victim mean to get hurt. She doesn't even know——" Gael used the feminine pronoun, unconsciously thinking of Nina, and gazing at the dark river.

Aware of his lapse, he turned to Zoltan and went on more forcibly: "What I am trying to say is that however terrible the crisis may be that you are going through, however deep you may sink, you must at all costs hold on to that inner strength, which I can see in you, which will get hurt, which is your real, true indestructible self, through all the million changes of cell-composition, through all the conflicting, shifting personalities and all the disguises. For practical purposes we may say keep your head, but I say, at all costs keep your soul."

Zoltan looked up and stared at the water. The white swan reappeared from beneath the hanging willows on the river bend, and he smiled at it, then at Gael.

"I understand. Thank you, Gael." He had dropped the 'Mr' at last. There was a long silence, then he got up.

"It is late. I have kept you from your work."

"It's only six, and the fresh air has done me the world of good. Besides, I've grown very fond of you, Zoltan, though I won't pretend I'm not tired out. Your story has given me much to think of."

"It is strange," said Zoltan as they walked slowly back towards Magdalen College gardens, "do you know what set me off on these hallucinations? When I got really bad, I mean—I have been having certain illusions before, but not—well, not like this. It was not the break with Erzsebèt, nor even the Rising, or discovering about the Institute, or being found out in Hungary. It was the Centenary."

"What Centenary?"

"The Communists are holding an International Congress of Writers in November, to celebrate the centenary of Alexander Petöfi's death. He was a Romantic poet. He fought for freedom, in the Insurrection, they should not be proud of him, but they say it was against the Imperialists. It is all phoney. He died in 1849, or rather, he was officially declared dead in 1854, but they did not want an International Congress in 1954 so they are holding it now. It is all a great mockery."

"But why should that upset you so much, apart I mean, from the hypocrisy and uselessness of Congresses?"

"Alexander Petőfi disappeared mysteriously in the War of Independence. He was twenty-six, and married to a poetess, Juliet Szendrey. I am descended from her family, from some country cousin, I think. It was a great love-match and she was later criticised for marrying again so soon, and accused of wanting him to be dead, of obtaining the favour of an official declaration of his death from the military authorities. But then she had to remarry—it wasn't easy for a woman alone in those days, and Petőfi's memory, you see, was in a way under a cloud. He was not a regular officer, but only nominated by the Insurrection, so that if he had returned he would have passed before the Imperial Council, and been put into the disciplinary battalions of the regular army, or gone to prison. They never found his body, and it is possible that he burnt his identity papers, tore off the three stars on his collar or changed his clothes. Then he wouldn't have been identifiable among the dead. But he could have escaped and not dared to return. Some of the Insurgents followed the Russian Army Volunteers, to avoid reprisals at home. After the war the Austro-Hungarian Ministry for Foreign Affairs inquired in St Petersburg but he wasn't among the prisoners. The mystery was never solved. There were many false Petőfis later, even producing some good poems in his style."

"I see. And you think the parallel——"

"It is not so much a parallel as a peculiar identification on my part. I never admired him very much as a poet, but since my own disappearance I have felt sometimes as if I *were* Petőfi. I have been declared dead, my wife remarried a man in the secret police. Now they are celebrating my centenary, me, Árpád Szendrey, and I have been dead a hundred and eight years. It is very strange."

When he came back from the station, having seen Zoltan and his flower on to the London train, Gael walked slowly back to Carfax, then turned down St Aldates, past Christ Church and beyond, unaware of his limbs. He was tired, very tired, examination answers in unfamiliar writings danced before his eyes, yet, in spite of the afternoon's unaccustomed exercise, he felt ready to walk on for ever, to climb up Boar's Hill, to get out, away and over the edge of the world. But he stopped at Folly Bridge and gazed over the parapet at the Isis below, suddenly conscious of fatigue surging up his legs. This same water would be flowing through Chelsea day after day on its interminable journey, replenishing itself all the way, only to be lost in a vastness as unimaginable to its present strength as eternity is to us. Was Nina leaning over the bridge in Chelsea, thinking the same thoughts?

No. He knew she was not. He knew, he knew so well what she was doing, it hurt. There is an element of truth in every mania, Zoltan had said. Yes, if you feel like a doormat someone will treat you like one. If you feel persecuted you will be. Every masochist somehow finds his sadist. A hidden vulgarity will find its projection somewhere. And a jealous man is given cause.

But where did this knowledge, this certainty come from? Gael held his head in his hands and watched its reflection dither. It looked like a football he was about to throw into the water. But it wasn't a football, it was a diabolical wireless set, receiving every wavelength, delicately tuned to every high and low frequency but jammed now, crackling, strangled with atmospherics. It was that early jazz she was so fond of which had come into his mind that evening in June, and the gay mockery of a clarinet had trilled unbearably, and he knew, he saw, he heard. What? On the red velvet sofa. It was preposterous. Then her voice on the telephone the next day, cajoling, caressing, catastrophic. And every day more false, harder, more cajoling, more caressing. He loved her so much he didn't know whether he suffered more for her future suffering or for himself. But no, it couldn't be. He was a maniac, he had telepathy on the brain, he was imagining this persecution on the part of this man who had somehow got into his novel. He took out a bundle of letters. They were from a student, a Miss Tooty. Audrey Tooty. Poor Miss Tooty. Owing to someone's illness last winter she and another girl had come to him for three tutorials, and out of this brief and excessively formal relationship she had built up a harmless but embarrassing little fantasy. She wrote to him every week, telling him of her day-to-day existence which God knows was drab enough. It was like reading a schoolgirl's diary, but with none of the freshness, the giggles or the excitement.

Dear Mr Jackson, she would write,
It's such a beautiful morning that I feel you must be very happy today, and that makes me happy too. I am sitting in the Parks reading Berkeley, and I feel so certain that something nice has happened to you, I feel very much at peace although you do not answer my letters, I understand it of course in your position and I would not wish to annoy you in any way, that is the last thing in the world I would want, you must believe me. I am finding Berkeley very difficult, I don't think I really have a philosophical turn of mind after all and my tutor keeps saying I should read English which is easier, but then it means so much to me that you were the first to open my eyes as it were . . .

She had read both his novels and would send him detailed banal commentaries on her reactions to every character and situation. "A handful of letters from readers, that's what counts," he had once said to Mr Truelove. And it didn't in the least. Nina teased him about her, calling her his Cosy Fan Tooty, with the sudden mania for puns she seemed to have acquired from—to put it charitably—her new literary circles.

He seemed to attract cranks and neurotics, perhaps because he had enough of both in himself. A crank, he felt, was a neurotic who had learnt to live happily with his manias, like Phineas. Why did they get on so well, agreeing on almost nothing? Did he give such people a sense of security, because he was their other side, their balance? And the neurotics? He felt appalled at the way one human creature could build another into his or her life with no more reality of response than a brick wall. He remembered a middle-aged little woman at Harvard, a librarian with whom he had unfortunately allowed himself to be politely conversational. She had a precise, old-maidish voice and a precise, virginal, little-girl walk, and she would tell him long stories about imaginary lovers and complications. The more he avoided her, the more she sought him out, until finally he had to ask her to leave him alone. Then she had become periodically obsessed with calling his attention to her somehow, and would ring up with nonsensical but supposedly ominous questions:

"Mr Jackson? Do you remember asking me where I had worked during the war? No? Are you sure, because my solicitor has asked me to draw up a list of all the people who have ever tried to find out what I did during the war..." "Mr Jackson? Can you tell me when your thesis is due? Because I think your examiners would be very interested in certain information I propose to make available to them..." "Mr Jackson? I assume you are aware of the latest findings by the Un-American Activities Committee? Because..." She was just clever enough to do it rarely—the fit seized her every two months, so that he had come to assume that something was wrong with her left (or right) ovary. Anyway, it wasn't worth complaining to the police, indeed, he completely forgot about her existence in the interval. Once, a week after he had gently suggested on the telephone that she should address herself to a psychiatrist rather than to him, he had received a typed initialled note thanking him for being "so co-operative with the tape recording" as "his reaction had been even better than she had expected". She was so far from his mind that for some days he idly wondered whose initials they could be, and smiled sympathetically when out of nowhere he suddenly remembered. And yet, all this was presumably real enough to her, however nonexistent it was to him.

So Gael kept some of Miss Tooty's letters as a reminder of the intolerable reality in self-delusions, a reality which nobody outside oneself could ever begin to feel. Miss Tooty seemed a clear enough case to him, but her world, what was it like, what did she imagine as she penned these terrifying weekly proofs of unutterable loneliness? His own duty was obvious: he had to ignore them, for her sake. Sooner or later she would tire or turn to someone else; one reply, however formal, even asking her to desist, would create a bigger fantasy—for if she made so much out of no letters at all, what would she not make out of one?

But then, what of his own fantasies? What of Zoltan's? Zoltan, who had been through the prison camps of both Fascists and Communists, who had no illusions left, could yet be called a counter-revolutionary or an unreasonably extreme patriot. And did his own fantasies seem as pathetic to someone else, or as unwarranted by facts? Did he really have a gift of precognition or was he no better than Miss Tooty, "feeling that something nice (or nasty) had happened"? How had he hit on Howard Cutting in his novel, without knowing him? Was he writing in the future? He had brought him into existence out of his own imagination. And now he was being persecuted by him—no, no, not persecution! Howard Cutting had brought him nothing but bad luck, and he himself had created it. And yet he had not really hit on him. For he had to admit, the fact far outshone his portrait. He would never have been able to conceive anyone quite like that, so very unpleasant and yet so very common. There were too many of them to invent one. Was he then inventing his premonitions, his certainties?

Folly Bridge . . .

Chapter Sixteen

NINA had invented a new way of giving up smoking. It's only a question of keeping one hand occupied, she said, and so she took up the yo-yo. It wasn't very practical while writing, which was when she smoked most, but then she didn't write much, only a monthly column. It worked best at parties, where smoking is no more than a social gambit or something to take away the taste of cheap wine and dubious punch mixtures. Her small wrist flicked quietly and gracefully as the rounded red wooden blob danced up and down and over her hand and down again between the gay skirts and the lounge-suited legs. Did she really want to give lip smoking, Howard asked her, or to draw attention to herself? Surely she was Different enough without trying? She laughed, holding the tip of her hose for a moment with her finger, then calmly continued her playing. "Of course I'm drawing attention to myself," she said, "all the attention I can get. Do you mind?" And she struggled through the tops of people's voices to reach Gael, who was standing in a corner talking to Mr Quentin Yellowstone, solicitor.

Nina had also invented, or thought she had invented, a perfect recipe for having it both ways. A lover she despised, a husband she adored. The excitement of intrigue and perpetual stimulation kept her in a state of nervous hilarity and wild energy that charged her affection for Gael with sheer overflow. She was sincere within the very deception. The lies were told in order not to hurt him. The lust was indulged and the invasion of her spirit allowed, in order to infuse her love for Gael with a new strength, a new self, a new kind of desire. She was, she felt, taking from one man to give to another. For so the body thinks, when the mind, possessed by folly, turns life upside down. Little did she suspect that she was in fact taking from Gael to give to Howard. Whatever she had been before marrying Gael, she had become what she now was through him. Seven years of married love cannot be put away as if they had meant nothing, done nothing to one's character. She echoed Gael's views, she saw life through his eyes. She never agreed with anything Howard said, and they quarrelled a good deal, smoothing their bristling personalities down with kisses and caresses. But all the time she thought she was taking only what she wanted, it was she who was giving, giving generously, all that she was and all that Gael had made her, while Howard, on whom her influence was surreptitiously beneficial, was injecting her with all those aspects of himself which she most hated, which she thought she was rejecting.

She had tried to rid herself of her unhealthy need for him. Always during their fluctuations, their sudden vanishing tricks—usually on her part—she had first been relieved, proud of not missing him. But never for long: a few days at most. Then other aspects of him would slowly form a phantom in her mind, acquiring more and more reality—his tenderness, his uncertainty, his veneer of sentimentality and his sensuality. And they would meet again, as if by chance. He would loiter near her house, or worse, she would wait for him in the street when she knew he was bound to come out on his way somewhere. Or she would ring up for some information or other. Then they would overwhelm each other with mutual confessions of agony, delighting in each other's delight at the reunion. But never for long: a few days at most, before the irritation and the hatred stirred once more, hatred of herself, rather than of him, for having given in once again to the essential boredom, the spiritual emptiness of their relationship. Even what there was couldn't be indulged when Gael came back and Elizabeth had finished her summer school. They had nowhere to go, they met in cafés and pubs and restaurants and parks, nor had he the money, the imagination or the courage to make other arrangements. They met, by a complicated system of quick messages, through ostensibly wrong numbers. This was what Gael had thought up in his novel, she had recalled in irony, and now Howard had brought it into existence. But he said Gael deserved it by his damned prescience. They had nothing to talk about, except literary news and views, about which he was intolerably predictable. He was a slot machine of ready-made opinions: mention a name, a book, an -ism, and out came a comic, debunking definition, a rude or knowledgeable story. He was an encyclopaedia of smartness.

Howard was aware, without being able to formulate his awareness, of draining Gael through her. Elizabeth in similar circumstances would no doubt have said to Zoltan: "You're not taking away from him anything he hasn't lost already." But Howard was intelligent enough to know that Nina was one with Gael, in the full religious sense of the phrase, even though he would have been the last to use such terminology. The fact gave him a sense of triumph, but also of great unease. Deception in any marriage always has a slow schizoid effect which sooner or later becomes intolerable, but when, in addition to the usual home-switch, one is imperceptibly absorbing the personality of the mistress's husband, the nerves begin to crack earlier and more violently. He hated Gael and every mention of him, in spite of his apparent affability about him. Any opinion of hers with a spiritual or high moral tone was unconsciously relegated to him and dismissed with facile crudeness of argument and denigrating wit. "Do you think any moral point of view is *ipso facto* ridiculous?" she would ask, and he would merely reply that it depended who held it—coming from her it seemed invalidated by her practice.

Thus his own vanishing tricks were sincere enough, but not easy. At first she had panicked on Gael's return and refused to see him for a fortnight. He had been so tormented by rage and desire, by fits of overwhelming tenderness, and by humiliation at her strength of mind, that he cursed himself for being capable of such suffering. But then she had worked out a system. She would go to all the film previews, instead of only a few. But not really go to them. Seeking him out. Begging him. Seducing him all over again. Over again? Hadn't he seduced her? Yet wasn't it always the woman who did the choosing, unconsciously even, though the man made the first move?

Then he had panicked, once reassured of her desire and satisfied in his, disappearing into the Kensington Library, to the offices of *The Sunday Sup-*

plement, anywhere out of the telephone's insistent reach. He was alarmed at the change in himself, at the depth of his obsession, and its steady undermining of all that he stood for and aimed at in life. To work, to get on, to pursue his interests, not to be entangled, upset, encroached on, involved, committed. With Kitty Lipmann, it had been different. Neither of them really cared, and she had helped him to get on, not taken up his time. Apart from work, the business of getting on was a full-time occupation—people to be lunched, parties to go to, meetings to attend, chairs to be sat in, letters to write to authors of books in the news, controversies to be joined in. It all took time. It was all very important. To be left alone. Not to be split up. Not to let love invade his every action; his every thought.

What *was* it about her? And her body would float between him and the African student opposite him in the library, lying languorously on the desk, her scent pervaded his nostrils, and her laughter rang out of the words with which he was covering the page. Carlyle. Carlyle. Revolution, thought, Revolution. Hungarian Rising. Szendrey. *And who shall shrive what we choose not to do?* Plane trees down Queen's Gate, hanging their pale hands, sycamore trees, Carlyle, the Embankment, Nina. Always back to Nina. Buses not going down Queen's Gate any more. It was over. He had run away. Nina.

And now she was at Truelove's party, in the big oak-panelled reception room, with Gael. With her absurd yo-yo, attracting attention. And now he wanted to beg.

She was wearing the same gold silk dress in which he had first seen her last November. It was a cold, drizzly August and the dress seemed as summery as it had been right for the glow of her drawing room fire, it was cut very low in front and her neck belied the boy-cut of her hair by its grace.

"Nina, I must see you," he whispered, "it's been unbearable."

She grinned lasciviously, but a look of relief relaxed her face.

"Well? You did the vanishing trick this time."

"I know. Did you miss me?"

She played with her yo-yo and didn't answer, giving him her side-long alluring look through those heavily made-up lashes. It was then he teased her about her new toy, and she left him with a laugh.

"Hello, darling." She nestled up to Gael. "I don't like this party."

"You've met my wife, Mr Yellowstone?"

"Ah, the clever lawyer. Do you like Mozart, Mr Yellowstone? I have a theory that all lawyers like Mozart—something to do with the wearing of wigs."

"But we do not wear wigs, Mrs Jackson. I am a solicitor."

"So you are. So you don't like Mozart?"

"I wouldn't say that, indeed I wouldn't, Mrs Jackson."

"My father was a barrister," said Nina in a dreamy voice. "He liked Mozart."

"Really? What was his name?"

"We used to listen to Mozart together when I was very little," she went on, ignoring his question, "but then . . . then he left us and . . ." Her voice trailed away and she watched the yo-yo intently, up and down, up and down as her wrist flicked mechanically.

"Your husband tells me he is planning to rewrite *The Sycamore Tree*, without the—er—unfortunate—er—coincidences."

"Oh, darling, are you? Why didn't you tell me? I knew you would. I knew you would."

"Well, I've been doing some thinking . . ."

"Nina, you can't talk to your husband all evening. Jackson, I'm carrying her off." Gael nodded vaguely as Charles Fortescue, about whose identity he was clueless, took Nina by the arm and drew her into a circle of critics and writers.

Through the smoke and the puffs of conversation she watched Howard, amazed and amused as she saw him hovering anxiously near a group surrounding a famous writer, hoping to be introduced; then being caught by an earnest young man, and talking with his eyes roving, his "who-am-I-missing" look; then losing himself for a moment, flirting with Sonya Dandridge, wearing his grateful spaniel face; then his pussy-cat face; always wearing a look, always playing a role, and the one role he couldn't hide was his edging-on-the-great role; then he saw the editor of a much more important paper than his, and took Sonya over, forgetting to introduce her, lobbying him, his face screwed up with anxiety to please, then smooth again as he said something very knowing. She hated him. She loved him for the very things she hated. What was it about him?

She was standing suddenly in the middle of next year, watching him at a party, analytically, indifferent, wondering how many people might have been a little less frequently embarrassed and inconvenienced or snubbed, how many women in his life a little less unhappy, if Howard Cutting had been two or three inches taller, and his head not quite so prematurely balding. Then the illusion passed and she couldn't bear the way he was preoccupying himself with others. And all the time she herself was showing off, making bright remarks, playing ostentatiously with her yo-yo, flirting with Charles. But even Charles really wanted to talk to his opposite number on one of the Sundays, about the book they were both reviewing. Nina felt lost when she was not the centre of attraction.

Then Sonya joined her.

"Darling, you look adorable." There was always something a little uncomfortable about her relationship with Sonya. Sonya was very elegant, not prettily elegant, like Nina herself, but sternly, boldly elegant, in a casual and almost masculine way, as if she didn't care. Nina felt that Sonya was her older self—that was what she would be like at forty, with greying, cropped hair and glassy, upside-down eyes, drinking just a little too much, talking just a little too crudely, over-familiar and at ease with men and women alike. She sometimes had a curious illusion that Sonya was a man, flirting with her, and felt impelled to flirt back. Sonya was like a mother and father combined, and a lover kept at a distance.

"I'm so dreadfully upset, darling," Sonya almost mooed at her in her deep voice. "I lost one of my gals, yesterday."

"Your girls? I didn't——"

"Dump, my darling Dump."

"You mean one of your, bulldogs?" Nina asked incredulously.

"Yes," Sonya growled. "She had to be put away. I'm heartbroken. She was such, an angel."

Nina's conception of angels was somewhat more anthropomorphic, but she sympathised politely, trying not to laugh. Then Howard came up to them.

"What are you going to say to your fashionable ladies about the new Schutzberg film, Nina?"

"You tell me."

"When I saw the American reviews I said to myself: ha, this will get embarrassed brief notices at the tail-end of every film column. Much too subtle, no one will see the point, or they'll pretend not to. I was dead right, too."

"Could you be otherwise?"

"How do you mean? What did you think of it?" he added anxiously.

"For once I agree with the critics. The satire was so crude it ceased to be satire."

"La, ma'am! That was the whole point. Couldn't you see through that? It was a double satire on crude satire!"

"You can no doubt teach me to see through the many layers of vulgarity and subtlety to the infinite wisdom lurking below."

"Why the high moral tone?" He shifted uneasily, and put on his spaniel face again.

"Now children, no quarrelling," Sonya boomed amicably.

"Oh, there's Jocelyn. I must talk to him. See you later."

"Oh, lordy, I'm tired," said Howard, as if in apology. "I've been working like a machine. Got through nearly ten thou of Carlyle today, not bad going."

"Hello," said a drunken voice, and a complete stranger peered at Howard, who looked at a loss to give him a name.

"I know you." He swayed a little. "Ring me up," he added brightly and tottered away.

"Why do you always say *hun* and *thou*?" Nina asked Howard. "Are you so pressed for time that thousand and hundred take too long?" She spoke harshly, but her eyes were mocking.

He gave her that uncertain quizzical look of people in bus queues, who aren't looking at you at all but at their own reflection.

"Oh, just professional jargon," he said uneasily. "You sometimes seem to forget that I'm a writer."

"I've never heard anyone else say it except engineers, for a thousandth of an inch. I bet you that a phonetic recorder would show that you lengthen the vowel in *thou* when you use it like that, so you might just as well complete the word, and speak English." She was leaning against the wall, playing with her yo-yo, laughing at him, being altogether damnable. He put his hand on the oak panel over her shoulder, and bent over her, turning someone's pushing past him into a public embrace or the nearest he could get to it without actually touching her.

"Nina," he murmured tenderly, "can I see you tomorrow?"

Her eyes clouded as his closeness troubled her veins. She couldn't meet his gaze and lowered her darkened lids.

"Three o'clock," she whispered almost inaudibly.

"Darling, it's been so long."

"Oh, there you are, Cutting," Mr Truelove broke in. "Good evening, Mrs Jackson. I'm delighted your husband could come—he's a rare bird at parties."

"He doesn't like them much," Nina had recovered quickly and laughed. "Real writers never do!"

"Real people never do, Mrs Jackson. I loathe them, myself."

"You know, everybody says that—it seems to be a badge of their reality. But we all give them, and we all go. And we all come back flattened out and empty and disorientated in a state of vile misanthropy, hating the world. And we all go again. I wonder why?"

"There's always that secret hope we may meet somebody really interesting," said Mr Truelove affably, "or important." He looked at Howard with distaste.

"Gael wants to talk to you, Mr Truelove, he's thinking of re-writing *The Sycamore Tree*." Nina had no sense of discretion at all.

"Is he, by God?" Howard muttered, and then: "What a splendid idea.

You must encourage him. You too, Tom. You know, I was damnably sorry about all that business, but what could I do? I *was* in it, you know."

"A case of 'this hurts me more than it hurts you', eh?"

"Well, you're not so far out, Tom." The confidential knowing look smoothed his features again. "I assure you I didn't enjoy it."

"Nor did Gael Jackson. Look, Cutting, I want to talk to you about that manuscript you sent me. Your Hungarian. Do you mind, Mrs Jackson?" Howard looked pleased at being taken off on publishing business, but Nina had pricked up her ears.

"Do you mean Zoltan Torday? Has he written something? He's a friend of Gael's."

"Is he?" The two men spoke together, Howard with surprise and alarm, Mr Truelove with polite interest.

"Perhaps your husband may know something about this. I'll ask him. You see, a very odd thing has happened. The manuscript has disappeared."

"You mean you've lost it?" Howard was always quick to put his opponents in a weak position by implying their blame rather than his, or that of anyone else unknown.

"In a way, yes. It was on my desk all last week, with the readers' reports. Three days ago it vanished. No one else in the firm has seen it, I made extensive enquiries. My secretary is positive that it was there last thing Friday night, Monday morning it had gone."

"Lordy! . . . Perhaps I should have told you." Howard was knowing again. "The fellow's got a persecution complex as big as St Paul's. He thinks everybody's against him, after him. I wouldn't put it past him to steal his own manuscript from your office."

"Well, it's all rather a nuisance. We want to make some minor changes in the style. I was going to send for him."

"My dear chap, it took my wife three weeks to get him to reply to her letter and sign the contract. And he's supposed to be her student. He'd vanished for nearly two months."

"Do you know where he is now?"

"Don't worry, old boy, I'll find him for you. I can cope with *this* sort of thing. Screwy, that's what he is, absolutely screwy. But I know a good book when I see one."

"Most writers are a little odd," said Mr Truelove, smiling at Nina with a conspiratorial twinkle. "Do you know, one of our authors—on our religious list—sent in a completely blank manuscript the other day, with a scrawled note saying he couldn't afford a typewriter ribbon, but if the printers held each page up to the light they'd be able to read it!"

"Screwy!" Nina echoed mockingly, "absolutely screwy!"

"Ought to be in a nuthouse!" said Howard, happy at her imitation and not noticing her tone.

"Come and talk to Gael, Mr Truelove," said Nina, and took him away, dancing her yo-yo up and down, dancing her eyes round the room, dancing her heart over the smoky haloes of self-delusion that surrounded everybody in the room. Each person, she felt, had balloons corning out of their mouths, as in advertisements: "It's all these wild oats one's supposed to sow that worry me," said a long thin balloon. "My son, who is Registrar of Cheltenham and Gloucester," said another wobbly balloon over a dear old lady. "If we quarrel before my book is out, will you still review it nicely, darling?" said a wilting one. "He's a queer, you know, she married him for copy," said a bright, oblong one. "Thinks: thanks to that good write-up I gave him," said a very wiggly balloon.

After Mr Truelove's party, Nina gave up the yo-yo, but not the sex, game. Her resolutions not to smoke lasted no longer than any others.

Chapter Seventeen

THE incense went up like a cloudy balloon, a half-hidden zeppelin shot through by the rays of the sudden sun from the kaleidoscopic stained glass windows, held into fragrant immobility, it seemed, by angelic searchlights, then dissolving into nonexistence as the eye of heaven withdrew.

A burst of alien, almost pagan song in strong male voices poured into the sudden shadows from a gallery behind the great gold fingers of the silent organ. The crowded congregation joined in as chinking coins fell into the moving plates. The priest had been muttering at the altar, first at one end, then at the other, then in the middle. People had got up, knelt, sat down, got up again, bowed their heads, sat down. An acolyte had lifted the big book, carried it down the steps, taken it to the other side. He had folded the priest's chasuble back over his shoulder, folded it *out* again. Now he was lifting it from behind. Others were handing things to each other, bottles and trays. The procession of choirboys had come in, gone out, come in again. Elizabeth tried to find the place in the missal she had bought. *In spiritu humilitatis, el in animo conlrilo suscipiamur a te Domine* ... No, it must be further on. The Hungarian hymns had confused her. *Sicut erat in principio, el nunc, et semper.* Suddenly the *Sanctus*, an ethereal treble voice from the arching roof, knelt with the others, lost, quickly turning over the pages. *Hanc igitur* ... What was she doing here, kneeling to an unknown god, on the feast of an unknown foreign saint? St Stephen, King of Hungary, Confessor, Semi-double. Why was he a semi-double saint? *Where are you, shining star of Hungary?* they had sung earlier, *Where are you, King Stephen, your country needs you and its mourning cloths cry out before you.* The litanies of Saint Stephen. A statue of a young nun near her in rigid cream and brown folds opened its arms to her in stony benignity. Further up, Christ showing his purple heart like a piece of liver. All along the side-altars, expressionless faces and painted plaster gestures. *When the mosaic of bent heads breaks* . . . A line from one of Szendrey's poems . . . She had translated them with Zoltan. But the mosaic broke, cracked in her mind with the shrill sudden jingle of holy grace. No, the mosaic was still there. The priest was elevating the Host. She bent her head into the mosaic.

Agnus Dei. Agnus, agnus, agnus, the word breaking in fugally, numerously, *agnus* after *agnus,* its uniqueness repeated over and over out of time, out of space, in every church, all over the world, at this hour, at other hours, where time was a quarterday ahead, a quarterday behind, where the antipodes stood upside down. . . . Then an interminable queue for Bread. Shuffling feet, dropped missals as people got up to let others struggle past them. Muttering as the priest went along the altar rail from one kneeling figure to another. Zoltan's bent black head, there at the end, Raising his head, eating. Rising, returning. Not thinking of her. *For I the Lord thy God am a jealous God* . . . *As Art jealous, Lord, so I am jealous now* . . .

She had come, not to pray, but hoping to see him, in the Church of St. Edmund, one of the few English saints she had heard of, on this Feast of St Stephen, King of Hungary, Confessor, Semi-double.

She waited at the door as the people streamed out to another burst of deep bass Magyar chant. *The riches in Saint Stephen's heart* . . . *The chivalrous arms of King Ladislas* . . . *Saint Elizabeth and her heroic love* . . .

"Erzsebèt!"

She stood before him, a picture of misery with her scarf tied under her chin, like a peasant girl reproaching a man for her condition. She was so relieved that he wasn't cutting her dead, or sending her away, she nearly burst into tears.

"Come," he said gently, "we are in the way." He took her arm and walked her into Victoria Street, up towards Westminster, saying nothing. Big Ben was booming its long midday into the late August sunflecked drizzle and out along the thin river mist. The silence that followed descanted his silence, all the more frightening for the occasional swish of tyres on the wet road and growling of bus engines from the rare Sunday morning traffic. The rain stopped for a while. In Whitehall they got a 77 bus. Zoltan crossed himself when they passed the War Memorial. In Trafalgar Square pigeons flocked around the stretched-out hands of a few stray tourists clustered away from the white spray of the fountains, near the guardian lions at the foot of Nelson's sky-bound, haughty and sublime indifference. Still Zoltan stared out of the window in silence.

"One thing I don't want to be in afterlife is a pigeon," said Elizabeth, making nervous conversation. "Look at them, fat, greedy, lazy. Lecherous too, I'm told."

Zoltan smiled.

"If you are a Christian, there is no danger. It is only the Hindus who become pigeons and goats, and things."

She laughed with relief at his joke.

"You mean we all get the afterlife we believe in?"

"The afterlife we deserve," he corrected, "within the framework of our beliefs."

"So if I refuse to believe in hell, I won't go there?"

"I do not think it is as easy as that. Nobody can prevent the existence of God by refusing to believe. He can only prevent God existing within him. I know that hell exists, because I have known hell . . . within myself."

Zoltan's voice faltered with painful memories. She misunderstood him, squeezed his arm and murmured: "Me too."

After a while she took up the theme again, frowning with uninformed concentration.

"Perhaps the hells we go through here and now are *instead*. I believe in God, vaguely, but a merciful God. I believe that there is a hell, but that it's empty. Somehow God finds Himself at the last moment incapable of not forgiving."

Zoltan looked at her with great compassion.

"That is a rather heretical view, Erzsebèt, but it is beautiful, like all heresies. It is a tribute to your sense of charity."

They got out in Kingsway, where the old tramlines descended and disappeared into the now closed tunnel. The drizzle had definitely stopped and the pavement was drying quickly in the sun. Elizabeth felt unjustifiably happy as they walked up High Holborn, past Gray's Inn and the bulging Elizabethan houses, and turned down Leather Lane. Zoltan was at her side again. He was taking her home. They were together, and he was friendly. It was like the old days, when she visited him regularly, when they read Petöfi and Arany and Vorosmarty and Kisfaludy, sipping Hungarian wine, and the earlier poetry of Balassi and Zriny. And, of course, Szendrey. Szendrey was their special bond. She had always loved his poetry, with its haunting, unanswered questions and its strange metaphors. Metaphors . . . she remembered the police inspector and his odd report. But Zoltan looked so serene, so calm.

"Where is Howard?" he asked as he led her up the dingy stairs.

"He went to the pub to meet his friends. I never like that literary crowd, so I said I was going to church. He was very surprised."

"You do not go often?"

"No. I haven't been since I was a little girl. And I've never been to a Catholic service."

They went into his room and she looked round in surprise. All the travel posters had gone, and the paper framework of press cuttings above the fireplace, leaving clean blank spaces edged with grey. Red and black curtains replaced the red and green. The ceiling was still red and the thin carpet still green, but he had painted one wall grey and evidently intended to paint the others, for the tins and brushes were on a spread-out newspaper behind the black divan, which was pulled right out into the middle of the room. Her photograph had gone from the chimneypiece.

She said nothing and sat down gingerly on the end of the divan. It felt disturbingly different away from the wall, cold and bare and inhospitable. Yet this was where they had so very nearly made love, on the day she ran off in alarm. He had been so angry. And later so penitent. Then that terrible dinner, and their parting. What did she want from him? Why had she sought him out?

"Why did you come to Mass this morning, then?" he asked gently, from the clipboard near the fireplace. He was getting out two small glasses and

The Sycamore Tree: Chapter Seventeen

a half bottle of Hungarian wine. Her eyes filled with tears at the sight.

"To see you, only to see you," she whispered.

He poured the wine into the glasses and gave her one. Their fingers touched, but he withdrew his at once.

"Here's to . . . Oh, Zoltan, what happened to us?"

"I do not know, Erzsebèt. I do not know. Whatever it was, it has happened."

"Zoltan, what is it? What's wrong? We were so happy. I didn't want much. I'll do anything, anything you say, only please let me see you again. I've been so desperately unhappy. I won't go to Budapest, I'll say I'm ill, anything . . ."

"It is no use saying you are ill, Erzsebèt. A false invitation must be refused with a truthful reason, to show you know it is false. Especially in politics. But your true reason would not be political, Erzsebèt, your true reason would be that you are buying back my love."

She was so stung by his cruelty she couldn't speak for a moment but sat there miserably, her damp scarf still on her head, gazing at her glass of white wine.

"If your love isn't there any more, I can't buy it," she said at last, "even if I wanted something bought. I just thought . . . I had hurt you, by my foolishness, and that I could undo it, and that if you still . . . loved me, then that would——"

She put her glass down suddenly and dropped her face in her hands. The scarf slid away, and her auburn hair caught the pale sunlight from the window. Zoltan sat down next to her and stroked it softly.

"Please do not cry, Erzsebèt."

"I'm not," she said without lifting her head. "I can't cry. I've been crying inside, for so long, and no handkerchief can dry those tears."

"I still love you, Erzsebèt."

She raised her face, now radiant with hope through the carvings of distress. Four little words, it was as easy as that. All would be now as it had been, no, more than it had been, she would give him everything he had wanted, that had been the real cause of the estrangement, he had wanted her so, he couldn't stand the strain, he preferred to have nothing. She fell into his arms, gasping with relief, joyous with expectation, covering his neck with kisses, his high cheekbones, his lips, combing her fingers through his straight black hair, rousing her own deadened desire with the passionate gestures of a film actor's clinch, and with flooding memories of sentimentality and romance.

He took her arms in a firm grip and moved them gently away from him. Her eyes were closed and she let herself be handled, thinking he was going to lay her out on the divan. But he only put his hand on her shoulder like an epaulette and sat very still. She looked at him in amazement and alarm. Fear, then shame, then anger passed through her and her body tensed. She leant her elbow on her knees, and held her fingers over her eyes to stop the tears which didn't come. Despair is often beyond tears.

"Erzsebèt, listen to me. Listen to me quietly. I still love you. But too much has happened, even things you do not know. I cannot explain to you everything. You will think I am exaggerating if I say I am a hunted man. Perhaps you are right. But I am a changed man, Erzsebèt, can you understand that? How a man can go on loving someone, but be such a different person that he cannot love her in the same way, or continue to see her?"

"No, Zoltan, I can't understand it. I have changed, too. First you changed me, so that I could hardly bear to be with my husband, though I thought the world of him when I married him. Then I came to hate him so much I could only go on living as long as I saw you. Oh, I know it was wrong and I was living in a fool's paradise, a doublethink, but it worked. Then you disappeared. I'm not too proud to admit that I became so wretched I ceased to be a human being. You took that other self with you. I had nothing left. You'd given me a sense of superiority which made life possible. It was only by thinking myself superior, that I could stand him around at all. But it was false sense of superiority, Zoltan. I came to realise that I was no better than Howard. I was as hollow and pretentious as he is, only a bit quieter about it. That's how I've changed, but it hasn't affected my love for you, on the contrary, I want it more, and differently, more fully, more honestly."

"I am very sorry, Erzsebèt, I cannot. I have become a different person," he repeated hopelessly. "I have become—the man who is still married to Ilona, my wife."

"But, but . . ." she stammered in surprise. "But you've always been married to her. She has remarried. That doesn't change anything. I'm married, for that matter."

"Yes. And you come to me, when the whole thing is over three months, and try to make love to me, on a Sunday morning, on St Stephen's day, when I have just taken the Sacrament." He spoke harshly all of a sudden, at a loss how to explain without saying too much, and without hurting her. She got up and started walking around wildly.

"You didn't have all these fits of conscience and holiness before! What about the time when *you* tried to seduce me here, on this very bed? What about——"

"Erzsebèt, you must go. I brought you here because I thought you had some business to clear up, and everywhere is shut on Sundays. You must not talk like this, you will regret it and feel terribly ashamed."

"Ashamed! You want me to feel ashamed, don't you, you want to humiliate me, to punish me for your love, your neurotic behaviour, your persecution mania. I know all about your visits to the police station. Stolen metaphors indeed! You're screwy, that's what you are, screwy. You never loved me; you used me. You're just, a patriotic and religious fanatic, you should be in a nuthouse." She heard herself echo Howard's phrases and suddenly collapsed on one of the brown leather armchairs. "Oh, Zoltan, I'm sorry, I love you so. I love you so." And at last she burst into tears.

He stood perfectly still, watching her with a desperate fury in his eyes. He didn't want to touch her, help her or speak to her.

She calmed down at last, blew her nose, powdered her face. In the silence of love's funeral she got up, collected her bag, her gloves, her scarf, and walked to the door.

Chapter Eighteen

THERE was a desperate fury in the eyes of four out of the six people sitting round the dinner table in Howard's flat, but the cause and the quality of the fury in each were different. The other two, Jocelyn Furnivall and Sonya Dandridge, were aware of the tension, and of the fact that they were not supposed to be aware of it. This made them feel very knowing and subtle, yet their knowledge and their subtlety were crude compared to the multiple crosswires of love and hatred that electrocuted the conversation, among the flickering candle flames of imitation oldworld civilisation.

Gael was on Elizabeth Cutting's right, facing Jocelyn Furnivall. Nina sat between Jocelyn and Howard, facing Sonya on Howard's left. The placing was correct. The dinner could hardly have been more wrong.

Howard had insisted on a return invitation to the Jacksons, almost exactly a year later. So much had happened during that year to make the first dinner a mockery, yet he was determined to pretend, if only to himself, that everything was quite normal, that he really liked Gael, that such things should be taken in one's stride, that one could sue a man for libel, destroy his book, seduce his wife and still behave like the best of friends; that one's own wife, having lost her lunatic lover—for Howard was no fool, though he crudely assumed Elizabeth's behaviour must have been like his own—should be made to entertain one's mistress and her husband. All this had a certain pique which tickled his fancy in advance. And since the dinner was ostensibly to celebrate their prospective departure for Hungary, as well as to declare the quarrel with Gael officially over, he laid his plans in high spirits. He was still in high spirits at the beginning of the evening, delighted with the idea of his trip, of Nina missing him— for the one who remains behind is bound to feel the wrench more than the one who goes off to see new sights—but it wasn't going as it should be.

Nina was morose. She was honest enough to hate this kind of double deception. It was one thing to deceive in someone's absence, to behave differently with two people in different places and at different times; it was quite another to put on the casual manner before them both, being watched by both. And she knew Gael well enough to understand that, even if he suspected nothing, he loathed the hypocrisy of chumminess after a serious dispute. She had consequently refused point-blank to fall in with Howard's suggestion.

"It's quite impossible. You know Gael. He won't accept, he doesn't like you. And if he does he'll be miserable. And probably watching us. I'm sure he knows."

"Nonsense darling, don't exaggerate so. He's always polite when we meet. And if he is eaten up with silly old suspicions," he added with a cunning look, "this is an ideal opportunity to dissolve them. Why, I'll hardly look at you."

"That's the oldest trick in the world," she said sadly, "besides, you will. So will I."

"Well, what *do* you want? Can't we behave naturally? We do at other parties. Of course I'll look at you. He should be proud to have men look at you."

"Howard, I want to stop all this."

"What, again?"

"I mean it, this time. It's—I don't know—it's making me more unhappy than it's worth, I feel I'm being dragged down and down..."

"Down to what, I'd like to know." He spoke flippantly, but the anxiety beneath his boisterousness emerged in unexpected cruelty. "You could hardly go any lower than where I found you."

They were sitting in a coffee bar in High Street Kensington, after making love in his flat one afternoon in late September. She put her face in her hands and started crying silently, with no sobs, just tears burning her eyes and trickling through her fingers as the glands swelled unbearably in her throat, producing more tears. Howard shifted uncomfortably. He couldn't stand a scene in public. The little bitch, she seemed to have no pride, no dignity left at all. Oh, for Hungary, that would do it, that would get her out of his system. But he wasn't going to be dropped by her first.

"Come on, hun, pull yourself together."

He slipped her a large handkerchief and she merely substituted it for her fingers, still hiding her face. Then she blew her nose quietly. Her eyes were swollen and her face was red, but she kept them down, and suddenly the line of her neck melted him and drew his lips, hungry all over again. It was always like this, he went on and on wanting her. How long, oh lord, how long could one go on wanting one mere female?

"I know," she said, so low he could hardly hear, "but you're the personification of all the rest. I turned to you because you seemed safer, because you knew, because you said I was so vulnerable, and you'd help me." Reproaches, he couldn't take that. "But it's as if you *were* all the rest, don't you see? Please help me, Howard, please leave me alone. I can free myself if you help me."

"All right. That goes for me too." His casual tone was half genuine, due to his coming journey, and half defensive. He knew it was the one thing she couldn't bear.

He knew her well. Suddenly she was lighthearted too, as he liked her to be. She powdered her nose, kissed him gently on the lips, her hand wandering over his thighs under the table, unselfconscious in front of the bearded men and ponytailed girls in jeans and sweaters who were sitting opposite.

"Oh, well, we might as well see each other till you go," she said gaily, "distance will cure us, after all, a whole month." She agreed to the dinner and promised to persuade Gael.

And here they were on a Saturday night in late October. Gael had been back in Oxford for three weeks, coming home only at weekends. After the grotesque parade of ignorance about the geography of the house, after the pretence of admiring the sitting room and looking at his index card system, Howard and Nina were sitting at dinner, quite unable to prevent their knees from touching and their ankles from intertwining. Sometimes even his hand wandered.

Gael watched her face out of the corner of his eye as he talked to Elizabeth. It was pale and shadowed, but flushed every now and again, not only with the wine but with the spasms of physical desire that ran through her body like electric shocks. He knew those expressions so well. Once she shut her eyes and parted her lips, suddenly white as paper, uncontrolled. Then it passed, and she turned to Jocelyn over-deliberately, shifting a little in her chair to talk to him.

"Are you looking forward to your trip, Mrs Cutting?" Gael asked conversationally. He always found it curiously easy to make small talk when in a state of cold fury, much easier than normally. It was a kind of protection, another self one could listen to, a companion in one's complete and devastating loneliness. Gael had long accepted the loneliness of the man in sex, the essential loneliness of the man with no illusions, stripped of all pretence, and the loneliness of the man who could turn a running away from his real self into something static, all-enveloping and ruthlessly isolating. He could live with all this and be happy with it. But he found the more superficial loneliness of man, the social animal, much harder to bear, while it lasted. Tonight, however, he was beyond the usual awareness of such distinctions, and only his quiet social self was dancing over his dark, ice-cold rage, as the froth dances over the black sea, not daring to be aware of its depth and destructive power.

"No," Elizabeth answered, unable to disguise her misery at the idea. "Not at all."

Their eyes met and held each other's, hypnotised with cross-currents of half understandings. Although Elizabeth did not know of Gael's friendship with Zoltan, she seemed to surmise his instinctive knowledge and infinite compassion. She might have worked it out—after all, Gael knew about Zoltan from the trial and she knew Zoltan had been to Oxford. But the moment of sympathy between them was not one born of reason. She for her part had followed his anxious looks at Howard and Nina, and known in a flash that he was right. Her knowledge came without shock and without bitterness. She wondered idly how she could have been so blind for so long, as minor incidents in the last six months surged in her mind and made sense. The answer came as idly—that she had been too engrossed in her own misery. And she didn't care. But her own pain went out to mingle with Gael's in that long look, and he knew that she knew too. Her fury was embalmed, so that her eyes looked glazed and dead. His was quiet and cold, but alive. Nina's fury, on the other hand, was hysterical. She said nothing for minutes on end; abstracted into an artificial calm of absolute indifference to everyone in the room, the calm induced by total loss of belief in all values once held. She wanted to leave Gael, to live with Howard, it was agonising, to know one could enslave a man, given full scope, yet have to withhold so much and be enslaved instead. The last three weeks, with Gael away again, had been easier, and she had come to believe it wasn't so much the lovemaking she wanted, but the many times one doesn't make love, the little things in a home together, to go home together, to live together. But no, she didn't want Howard, not for long. She only wanted to be free from Gael's goodness, from the incessant reproach of her children's presence, to be free to do as she pleased, to be irresponsible. Then her abstracted mood would suddenly break into loud argument, voluble disagreement, sarcasm following anger and rudeness, shrieking laughter following her own sarcasms.

And Howard's fury? Howard's was the smouldering fury of humiliation, as always in Gael's presence, but hidden away, so far, very successfully, by the unruffled geniality he always put on when afraid. His role as host and the genuine excitement caused by both his Hungarian holiday and what he felt was the dramatic irony of the present scene, made it easier for him to switch on the charm. His closeness to Nina in such circumstances of untouchability heightened his elation. Since the scene in the coffee bar, they had been curiously as one, tacitly agreeing to enjoy what they never referred to as their last few weeks, each silently hoping that his departure would miraculously solve everything, or at least (for there was always a secret reserve clause) help them to get each other in perspective and continue the affair more quietly, less destructively. In the meantime, all decision was suspended. Much as he resented the depth to which his love for her had gone, he now admitted that it was love, and allowed his better feelings full play, overwhelming her with tenderness and understanding. And if there was an element of fear in his kindness—fear that her diagnosis of her own need for him was true, fear of Gael's essential superiority to him, with which she could not help but be identified—nevertheless he was sincerely happy to have her here in a different role, seeing him as host in his home surroundings, yet bound to him by her helplessness, and near him. He also enjoyed flirting openly with Sonya, to annoy Nina, and revelled in the counterpoint of stimulation—bass and descant—which was going on under and over the table.

Sonya, feeling the strain, decided to launch the two philosophers on an argument, choosing, for some no doubt deeply significant reason, the perfectability of man.

"Of course we've progressed." Howard leapt gratefully to the bait. "And I don't mean just medicine and telephones and the Welfare State. We've progressed morally, too. Bestiality goes on, of course, but many more people protest and have the right ideas, whereas before those bestialities were taken for granted. People thought it quite natural for small children to work fifteen hours a day, or for thousands to die in a religious war. We've acquired new moral values which didn't exist before."

"Can you honestly look at the twentieth-century record of wars, mass murders, deportations and labour camps and say that?" Jocelyn put in, smoothing back his hair and in a languid tone, as if his question was a mere move in a game of chess.

"Bestiality persists, yes." Howard loved an argument. "But it's only localised, it's caused by a handful of maniacs. At least the rest of the world doesn't approve."

"I wonder," Gael murmured, "they don't do much to stop it."

"What can they do, hey, short of war?" Howard gave his friendliest I've-got-you-cornered look.

"You say it's only localised. But there's no difference really, except that the units of evil, bestiality, warring nations and so on, have been getting steadily bigger and bigger. Tribe against tribe, city against city, country against country, now it's hemisphere against hemisphere. Later it'll be interplanetary. That's a Wellsian truism, of course, but I maintain it has always been a handful of maniacs, they merely have more power now. They were always there, but much more scattered, and we didn't always know about all of them, say, outside Europe. Now the world is in easy communication and the units can grow bigger by drawing all minor evils into their orbit, into one huge over-simplification."

"That's the most utter——"

Nina clattered her knife and fork down on her plate of half-touched hors-d'oeuvre.

"Sorry . . I believe," she went on in a very quiet voice, "that the proportion of good and evil in the world remains exactly constant. We've progressed in many ways, of course, especially material ones, and we have, as you say, acquired new moral values. We've also lost some of the old moral values, for instance, humility and real spirituality, just as we've got rid of some of the old evils. The balance remains exactly the same, though it doesn't seem so if you look at only some things." She sipped some wine and no one said anything, her voice was so unusually calm it created a hypnotising silence. "Take Greece, for instance. No, the dice are too loaded on the side of the glory that was. Take the Middle Ages. Some people see only darkness, religious wars, royal murders, ignorance encouraged by the Church, fear bred by superstition, witchcraft, poverty, famines, plagues. Others see only bright courts with knights and ladies and troubadour poetry, the chivalric ideals, the gay tournaments, the spirit that built the cathedrals, the revival of learning, the monastic life, the scholastics. But all of it is true, and a good deal more we can never know because we weren't there. Today we can look at some things only and smugly declare we have progressed morally, or at others, and condemn the whole century. But even some of the things in which we have progressed have their bad side. Has the ideal of equality, for instance, proved so good as when it was first thought up? It all depends on how you look at it, but the absolute balance, beyond our own varying visions of it, stays the same, for the simple reason that man isn't perfectable as a race, only individually, and with divine help. If he were, we would be better morally than we used to be, and nearly perfect by now. But we're not. Moreover, if the balance weren't constant, we wouldn't be here."

Everyone was astounded at Nina's long discourse, for she seldom aired her philosophical training, or indeed, used it at all. But Gael smiled approvingly, for they had often discussed this very subject and she was only echoing his own views. He approved, not because they were his own views, or because she had stopped Howard's rude outburst and come to his rescue, but because he knew Nina was trying to tell him something, 'I am with you really,' her whole being had called out beneath the unnatural calm of her voice, 'but I'm lost, here on the other side of the table, I've been lost for a long time but I know that if I repeat my lesson, like a prayer, mechanically, even when I've stopped believing, eventually the words will bring back peace of mind, and grace. Just the words by themselves.'

Howard knew from their arguments that Nina had a good mind, trained in logic, and he too smiled at the memory of similar arguments, quarrels in which the same echoes of her past happiness had always irritated him. But she was his now, she had given and would continue to give all this to him, it was part of him. There wouldn't be any more quarrels, they would just love each other, stimulate each other by their differences, without complications, accepting the situation gratefully while it lasted, as most people had to and did in these modern times.

Elizabeth cleared the plates and went out to fetch the next course, while Howard started disputing Nina's points, more gently than usual. But Sonya, whose position on Howard's left gave her a sense of rivalry towards Nina (more especially since she was aware that only one of his knees was nudging hers) weighed in with more and more specific examples—for her mind was not trained in logic—of terrors and persecutions in the Dark Ages, the Inquisition, fears sown already in children's minds by the Church's teachings even to this day, resulting in dreadful breakdowns, unhappiness and even madness. This produced more counter-arguments, all irrelevant, and the discussion became an excuse for everyone to air their pet topics. But Nina merely replied: "You're only substantiating my point," and reiterated it in a daze. "The proportion of good and evil remains constant."

Elizabeth's re-entry and the usual interchange of courtesies over plates and dishes provided a pause which redirected the mood towards more abstract generalisation.

"Surely moral values are essentially aesthetic ones," Jocelyn contributed with a graceful wave of his hand after putting down his wine glass. "Something is good because it is harmonious."

"If you like," said Gael, "but the desire for a different kind of harmony can be evil because it destroys another harmony one already possesses, or makes it less harmonious."

This, though spoken at Jocelyn, was intended very specially for Nina, and she knew it. So often, in company, she had sparkled in an argument she would have been lost in were she facing the opponent alone: she took life from the things he said, adding to them and developing them. But it wasn't that kind of support now, it was an answer to her appeal. She gazed fixedly at her dessert spoon, toying with her food.

"Dear me," Sonya exclaimed, "what big words, good and evil. I was just talking about progress. Didn't realise you'd get all theological."

"Seems more like philosophy to me," said Howard glibly. "Our old friend the problem of reality. The sycamore tree, eh, dear boy?" He raised his eyebrows conspiratorially at Gael, as if they alone had been responsible for the problem of universals, the tree in the quad, even the limerick itself.

"Sometimes, and to some people, philosophy is closer to theology than philosophers like to think," said Jocelyn sharply. He was vaguely and lazily attracted to Gael's lanky grace and intense blue eyes, so that it pleased him to come in on his side without any formulated beliefs of his own, knowing that any other kind of advance was pointless and not all that desirable. He was rewarded enough by Gael's smile of polite acknowledgement.

"I believe that is so." Gael's Americanism sometimes emerged in careful phrasing. "I have even come close to concluding that the perceiving self—that basic identity which philosophers have defined as a mere sequence of impressions accumulated by memory—is in fact the human soul, not the mind."

"Lordy! I wouldn't have taken you for a Cartesian!" Howard exclaimed. "You mean that faculty with physical location in the body, his little kidney-shaped thing?"

Everyone laughed, except Nina.

"He didn't quite say that, you know. And I don't belong to any school, I merely teach young people to think. Indeed, if I had my way, I would teach philosophy without any names or labels. All the same, I find it hard to explain why our perceptions change so radically, not only with emotions, moods and physical well-being, but with spiritual strength, grace if you like, acquired by certain disciplines which conquer the emotional and the physical. A man in a state of grace sees the world in a completely different dimension."

"But that's emotional, too," said Howard and Sonya together.

The argument ambled on, with everyone at the usual cross-purposes. Nina remained in a daze, her early hysteria stilled to despair, helpless in Howard's proximity under Gael's observant eye, Elizabeth hadn't spoken at all. She was busy passing dishes, offering bread, salt, second helpings, but she had listened attentively, unable to take in more of the argument than what she could relate directly to her own experience. Now she asked for the guests' empty plates to be passed up, and took advantage of the momentary shift of attention towards her end of the table.

"Look at the way even one human being thinks of another," she exclaimed unexpectedly as she piled up the plates. "Take a woman in love, say after a quarrel. She hates everything about the man, she genuinely never wants to see him again. But after all the anger has gone round and round in her head, after countless imaginary scenes and reproaches, gradually a different figure emerges, not quite so bad. After a while, hours, days, weeks maybe, he's positively idealised and she longs to see him. Yet neither of these versions is true, nor, probably, any of her ideas of him." She was aware of speaking too intensely and generalised lamely:

"I don't know how we dare to think the entire world is as we see it when we can't even see one fact straight."

"Yes, dear, that's just what we've all been saying," Howard said in a patronising tone which was meant to convey his complete knowledge of what she was really thinking.

Nina's head was down, her eyes still fixed on her dessert spoon. She started fiddling with it. The discussion—if this kind of dinner table opium of the intellectuals could be called a discussion—languished after the embarrassed silence following Howard's unkindness to his wife.

"Come, Liz," he said genially, "don't pull such a face. It's a truism of philosophy that what we think is reality doesn't exist. But we have to accept some sort of norm, based on the majority's perceptions, on common sense, in fact, otherwise we'd all go mad, and things like science, mechanics, the practical business of living couldn't go on." She shrugged her shoulders, and he couldn't resist further taunting. "After all, look at the people who can't accept the norm, the minority who see white as black and green as red. They end up screwy, like your Hungarian." Elizabeth flinched and Gael clenched his teeth. "The nuthouses are full of them, in fact the emphasis on individualism's been pushed so far psychiatrists are kept pretty busy."

"Yes," said Elizabeth angrily, "and look at the reverse side of the coin. The emphasis on individualism's been pushed so far everyone's just longing to be like everyone else, to see like everyone else, to join the Church, the Communist Party, a sect, a club, a clique." She was trying to lash back, attacking where she could.

"Darling," Howard replied in his smoothest tone of assumed marital patience, "I was speaking philosophically, I was talking of individual perceptions. You confuse the issue so."

"I'm sorry." Elizabeth got up, very nearly in tears, taking the pile of plates. Gael went to the door and opened it for her. Nina, in the same moment, leapt to her feet and offered Elizabeth her help in bringing the last course. As she passed through the door she tried to smile at Gael—a wild desperate smile—then lowered her eyes as they met his, horribly understanding.

"Sorry about that, chums," said Howard to the remaining three, then added mysteriously—for psychoanalysis was still rather fashionable: "she's got rather a thing about psychiatrists at the moment. I should have remembered."

"For heaven's sake let's talk of something trivial!" Sonya exclaimed. "Watercress, for instance."

And they did. Or the literary equivalent.

Chapter Nineteen

"'AVE you 'ad your catharsis yet, dearie?" said the woman next to Nina in the outpatients' waiting room.

"I beg your pardon?"

"Oh, you 'aven't." She sounded disappointed. "That's when all the fun begins, you know. The things what comes up! This Dr Grobel's ever so good—none of this Freudian stuff, oh no. I don't 'old with Freud. I'm an Adlerian, I am, like 'im. Well, I mean it's common sense, ain't it? Power complex, that's me, nothing sexy about me, now is there?" She was broad and angular, and cackled like a hen. "Mind you, I don't dream much, you know, I can never remember me dreams. But Orrie—that's me 'ubby, 'e's called 'Grace but 'e don't like that much so I calls 'im Orrie—my Orrie 'e dreams ever so much. So I brings 'is dreams along, what 'e tells me at breakfast, they're ever so funny some of them. Well, I don't like to come empty-'anded, like, it kind of disappoints the doctor, don't it? 'E says I got a power-complex, does the doctor, that's what I 'ave, a power-complex. That's why me womb keeps dropping," she ended with a note of triumph.

Nina looked at her in alarm and nearly left the queue. If this was psychiatry on the Health Service it was rather more than she had bargained for. She wanted to run away, to burst into tears, to crash into the doctor's room, to run away. Miles and miles away, on a desert island, the top of a mountain, a hermitage, a nunnery, anywhere, away, alone with herself, away from herself, away from Gael, from her children, from Howard. With Howard. No, away from Howard. Alone. But the world was not planned for women solitaries. There had surely never been any such thing as an anchoress: always in congregations, in convents, in hospitals, in colleges, in henhouses. And at the moment, Nina loathed herself in the whole of womankind.

"I'm at the end of my tether," she had said to Howard when she had seen him last, in despair and hardly able to hold back her tears. "Which one?" he had replied, shunning an emotional scene. Yet always he could get round her with a gentle word, a confidence, a touch. She seemed to love him for his very faults, as opposed to Gael, who in her eyes had none. For that was all it was really: a suicidal blend of hatred, sentimentality and lechery. Not love, she knew it wasn't love. For love, however painfully, creates, illuminates, love does not destroy and darken. It was far worse than love.

And now Howard had gone off to Hungary with Elizabeth. He was reporting on the Congress for *The Sunday Supplement,* in clever, amusing articles in which he carefully showed how he was not taken in by anything; yet saying, according to Gael, precisely what the present regime wanted him to say. Elizabeth had written also, as naïvely but, oddly enough, less harmfully.

They were combining the free trip with a late holiday in Austria and wouldn't be back till the beginning of December. At first she hadn't cared, then she missed him as a hungry lioness rages for her ration of raw meat. And she couldn't bear the idea that he was having a good time without her, probably not giving her a thought. She became irritable with Frieda and the children, quarrelsome with Gael, criticising everything he said and did. She sought the company of Howard's literary friends to hear him talked about, and what she heard was none too flattering. He was evidently a joke, as a climber and a meddler. "Oh, you mean Press-Cutting! Old press-on-Cutting." In the competitive world of journalistic ambition everyone was on the make, but it had to be done subtly, and people were only too glad to denigrate a more bungling rival as a fool, even if he was not. Any rope was good to hang one with, especially if the victim provided it himself. Soon she felt ashamed of her double role as mistress and listener to gossip. Not to mention her treble, quadruple, quintuple role as loving wife, model mother, fashion reviewer, sophisticated glamour-girl, kittenish charmer ... imaginary prostitute ...

"How many are you, madam, one?" a waiter had asked her in a restaurant that morning, and she wanted to say, "there are at least a hundred of me today." Indeed, she thought, a woman without an escort is automatically schizophrenic, providing her own escort. She smiled grimly: reading Greats, which was supposed to produce the Complete Man, had produced a very Incomplete Woman.

After Howard had gone, she threw herself into a frenzy of new domestic arrangements. She insisted on redecorating the bedroom, from pale blue to a blend of fiery reds. She painted the walls and ceiling for a week, made new curtains, cushion covers, counterpane and dressing table frill in bright cyclamen, tangerine and purple. She bought pink sheets and a red carpet. The result was a mixture which American colour scientists, unbeknown to her, had proved from experiments in small rooms would send a man mad in a few hours, or produce nausea within minutes. But a bedroom was seldom seen open-eyed for long. The matrimonial sanctum looked like a bridal suite for Satan in Hell Hotel, lit up by a fine view over the Inferno, and with constant hot water from Flegeton. Indeed, she, installed a large electric radiator: winter's back, she said, and English bedrooms are so freezing—forgetting that she was only half English and that if she had really cared *she* would have seen to the heating years ago. Passion was heat enough at first and then...

Gael had watched all these activities of smitten conscience with an understanding she found unendurable. In fact he was very touched by them, and alarmed for her, apprehending the coming crisis.

And it came: the sudden overwhelming fatigue, the migraines that split her head with an icy bar of fire behind the left eye; the inexplicable tears at a word of tenderness, silent, sobless tears that burnt her brain and slashed into her in throat; waking up in tears, falling asleep in tears, silently, soblessly; the tearing period pains, the tension of muscles holding back the relieving flow of blood, the fainting and the vomiting; the sudden flaring anger and again the tears; the weird, ambivalent sincerity of the talk they had had two nights ago, on free love.

"Of course it's fine in theory," Gael said. "But are those who advocate it any happier? Look at Phineas: he has this woman tucked away in the background, he refuses on principle to marry her, in order to stay free. Yet he's more married than any man I know. In marriage one can always divorce, but apart from a genuine fondness he's tied to her by moral obligation. What does he do? He carries on with his university job, pretending she doesn't exist. He has affairs on the quiet. He plunges himself into his cranky studies, his psychic phenomena, refusing to face facts, and gets further and further away from reality."

"Oh, he'd be a crank anyway."

"All right, maybe it works for some people. People who have no sense of their own fundamental reality, their own continuous personality, their own spiritual strength, their own soul. But not for people like us. Why do you think religion is so down on adultery, as 'opposed to' unmarried lust? Not for puritanical reasons, but for spiritual ones: because of its disintegrating splitting effect on the inner personality, that personality which has become what it is through the oneness of marital love. A stormy love affair or a sudden brief romance perhaps doesn't do quite so much harm, I don't know. But the quiet arrangement, the silent gnawing away at grace, at singleness of mind and purity of heart, that's what corrupts. It may not even be the man himself—or the mistress—they may be well-meaning enough. It's the situation. Because one knows all the time that it's incomplete, impossible, unwanted even, yes, even if one were free one wouldn't want it whole. It's more corrupting because one accepts it as apparently harmless, compared to something more overwhelming. One drifts, fluctuates, hardens. Standards go overboard, one begins to hate, quarrel, lust after and beg."

She was sitting at the empty dining room table and looked drawn and sick even in the soft candlelight. She lit another cigarette, nervously, and her tone was harsh and brittle.

"All that is true, but only because it's kept secret. If both sides admitted it, openly, understandingly, there would be no torment."

"As I've said, it may work for some people. But it's not feasible in a true marriage. There is no acceptable system of organising it without hurting, so that secrecy and deception become essential and are bound to affect the relationship, even if the ... deceived person never knows. If both sides accept it openly, the affairs never coincide. It's impossible with people like us, who live fully at every level. You can't give a secondary passion, because a lighthearted affair is not enough, you have too much to give and you can't help getting deeply and personally involved."

Suddenly the impersonal tone of "ones" and "theys" had become urgently direct. Gael was looking straight at her, and his voice was steady but charged with emotion. "And if you don't give a secondary passion," he went on, "you're bound in the very nature of things to be duped and to give more than you get. You must recognise your own character. We all have our failings and those are yours. You have too much and you can't hold back." He got up and pushed his chair into the table, gripping its curved back as he spoke, suddenly ironical. "But if you do it, do it properly. Impress me. Don't choose some poor type with no place to take you to and no money. Don't cuddle in parks and espresso bars. Go by plane to Morocco, to Greece, to Mexico. Do it grandly, not sordidly."

He went out. She put her head down on her arms to shut out the aching light. But the light was still in her head, as if entering from behind and surrounding the back of her eyes inside, burning them coldly.

And now she was sitting miserably on a hospital bench, listening to a cheerfully batty neurotic with a power complex and a dropped womb. I must get a grip on my mind. I must ... my mind ... I dropped it ... somewhere ... slipping ... my mind is a slipped disc, a dropped womb ... I must ... get a grip ... I lost something ... I dropped it outside ... in the street ... walking ... on the Embankment ... I dropped it in the river—flowing ... flowing back ... under the bridge ... the bar ... daddy ... he's gone ... he's in disgrace, debarred. Debarred from the Bar ... no ... debarred from a barmaid ... mummy ... he's gone ... he lost something ... the judge said it was a disgrace, contempt of court, contempt of Nina, he awarded costs and a farthing's damages to Mr Howard Cutting ... I lost it. I must get a grip ... on daddy ...

The nurses took her in, struggling, screaming. The doctor pricked her arm. She started sobbing quietly. Then the ambulance. The nurse was very nice. Blonde, like Gael. But she had Sonya's voice. "I lost one of my gals," said Nina, "she was a bulldog angel, with hairy wings."

"Hello, are you new?" said the girl in the hall. She was and buxom and comforting. "It's horrid waiting here, we call it Agony Hall. They always keep us waiting before every session, just to unnerve us. But don't worry, they're all right, really."

The doctor was dark and small and smug. He hardly talked at all, and she didn't know what to say. After half-an-hour of incoherence, he smirked knowingly.

"You don't get on with women, do you?"

"I ... er ... yes, I do."

"I don't think so." He evidently fancied himself as a man of few words, enjoying his power as diagnostician of her helplessness, miracle-worker, speaker of cryptic, parabolic wisdom, teacher, healer and restorer of faith, father figure and dispenser of the understanding that passeth all love. He was Jewish, too, but a very little man.

"You are going to join a group session, with five other women."

"Oh no! I can't."

"Oh yes, you can. They have not your—er—education or your social position. But it will help you to listen to their problems, to get you out of yourself, to help them to express themselves, to draw them, out. We believe in group therapy here. But it is slow work. I have taken this group for three weeks and so far they have made very little progress. You are the very person to—— "

"Three weeks! But ... but ... how long will it take?"

"Four or five months. You will live in, and be very well looked——"

"It's impossible."

"Don't you want to get well?"

"I want to be alone, for a while, that's all," said Nina miserably.

"You want to have private, personal attention." His voice was smooth, oily. "You want a father-lover relationship with your own personal psychiatrist, with me, in fact. My dear child, what do you think such sessions would turn into? Intellectual flirtations around philosophy and literature, intense and emotionally involved for you, boring for me. It would do you a great deal of harm."

Nina meekly let herself be led out by a cheerful sister who took her to the psychologist. There she saw witches dancing, mountains breaking, crosses turning into sycamore trees and rivers of blood, hands meeting and wombs opening, for two hours through a series of large ink-blobs. She was taken to the canteen and met two of her companion victims to her room which she shared with three others. They were kind, unhappy, bewildered and utterly uninformed. One of them asked her what did 'neurotic' mean? She just had these terrible headaches. She didn't know why she was here. No, she wasn't in any trouble, she just got these terrible headaches. They all hated Dr Funk.

The sessions were a masterpiece of unguided, clueless conversation between five terrorised, shy, incoherent women whose powers of communication and level of intelligence Nina had never even imagined as a possibility among human beings. Dr Funk sat in complete silence, watching them and smiling. Nina attended two, for two days. Group therapy was indeed a miraculous cure. It shocked her into sanity. She was appalled by the helplessness of these poor creatures. No doubt she could help them, no doubt at all. She wanted to, her heart went out to them. But they couldn't help her. She needed far more than good-works therapy how. If she had to be a neurotic let it be among her own kind. Her own world was mad anyway, yes, even Gael's sanity was a kind of madness in the mad world he had to inhabit. 'Among my own kind,' she kept muttering, 'if I must go mad.' In the afternoon of the third day, she ran away. But at least she ran away home.

Chapter Twenty

SHE ran all the way over the common and into the country lane to the bus stop, with nervous glances over her shoulder and straining her impatience as if it could give the bus more speed; all the way across the high street that looked so much like any other suburban high street, with its fussily gowned and bloused windows and its repetitive ironmongery and kitchenware, to the tube station and into the red train that seemed to wait so long to take its bloodstream thundering into the subcutaneous heart of London that London, she felt, would surely be dead before she arrived. She ran all the way up the Knightsbridge escalator, and past the smart shops with their models made of basketwork, blank skeleton faces and skeleton bodies striding forward, holding skeleton dogs on leads, standing akimbo or holding up some invisible tray with invisible nectar glasses to the gods, all wearing the latest fashions over their fleshless, passionless, mindless frames. Oh, to be made of osier, woman, unthinking reedy trembling with a secret whispered to her by the barbers of civilisation, by a king with asses' ears, whose touch turned food and flesh to useless gold, or by a king with a serpent's tongue. Her chain of associations went wild as she leapt on to another bus, trying again to hurry it on with her own urgency. She ran all the way home, all the way upstairs—flinging off her coat on the landing—and into Gael's arms. He sitting on the red velvet sofa, staring at nothing. She couldn't speak, she couldn't cry, she could only gasp out: "Darling, hold me, hold me tight." He held her and gradually her panting became breathing, and her breathing slowed down to normal. Suddenly she was fast asleep.

He held her for an hour, without moving. The ticking of the clock would vault upon his awareness for interminable seconds, then sink away into nonexistence as thoughts flooded over it. The shifting of reality, the nonexistence of its tangible, visible, audible symbols. Even one's own personality offered no anchorage. One day everything looked fine, drenched with optimism, wisdom or at least tinged with resignation. Another day, with the objects unchanged, the circumstances exactly the same, perhaps even with the sun streaming down upon them, the birds twittering in the fragrant trees and the air as light as a dancing heart, things seemed to signalise only black despair. The darkness of the winter evening fell suddenly, yet he was unaware of it.

Her lashes fluttered his neck. She had woken up, but didn't move. He pressed her to him gently and stroked her hair. She gave a small sigh and her arm climbed to his other shoulder. Still she didn't speak, and didn't move her body, which might have been drained of life. His arm was getting cramped and he tried to move it slightly. Then Nina sat up, very slowly, helping herself by pushing her hands into him, like a blind man feeling his way.

"Gael," she murmured. "I'm sorry. I'm very sorry. You must be exhausted." The words seemed to carry all possible meanings.

"So are you, honey. You slept for an hour."

"Did I?"

"The hospital rang me up."

"Oh, darling, it was dreadful. I ran away. It was enough to send anyone mad. But it made me sane, Gael, horribly sane."

"There, darling, you're home now."

"Yes."

Her voice was so small, so quiet, the still small voice of despair. He knew she was beyond even asking for his help. For everyone is ultimately alone, when God has been abandoned and no husband, lover, friend, least of all friend, can do for us what sooner or later even the best of us must do, on this or that side of eternity, the painful and near-suicidal business of facing our own selves. He knew he had to talk now, say anything, cover her with a warm blanket of words, knitting itself as he spoke.

"There is some force in all of us, beyond despair, which drives us towards drama. We want to precipitate drama, we continue unaware, but destructively, so to arrange things that drama will occur, apparently from outside. We manoeuvre the other partner into breaking up a marriage, the lover into a duel, a murder, ourselves into a desperate illness. Anything, as long as it happens, as long as our real problems are apparently solved by it, without our having really to face them, or to make a choice. Unfortunately, the wanted drama is often quite different, quite unexpected, and solves nothing at all, producing only new problems that mask the old. It might be an accident, one might lose one's legs or go blind. Instead of the drama we had envisaged, out of which we come out rather better than the other chap, a tense farewell scene, a family broken up, a new illicit ménage after a romantic elopement abroad, something else happens, quite unendurable. Or something really quite dull. You see, the future is usually much simpler and much more unexpectedly complicated than we think. We always vulgarise the future with our imagination."

"I don't want to lose my legs," Nina murmured, "please God don't let me lose my legs."

Gael smiled at her tenderly.

"When we can bear to imagine being maimed suddenly, we most fear to lose what we most value, basically. I am most terrified of losing my eyes. You think first of your legs. That's how it should be."

"I always run everywhere, up and downstairs, and dance, and walk fast, and walk... and make love."

The doorbell interrupted his gentle kiss.

Two men in white mackintoshes and trilby hats stood on the steps.

"Yes?" Gael said.

"Oh, er, I apologise for troubling you, sir. We're detectives, and we'd like to ask you a few questions. Has Mr Zoltan Torday been here, at all? Have you got a spare room?"

"Could I see your police card, please?"

"Well, we're not from Scotland Yard, we're private detectives. I never said——"

"I'm sorry. I don't answer questions from strangers. Goodnight."

"Oh, look here, sir, we know——"

Gael shut the door quickly. He frowned as he went upstairs. The second man, who hadn't spoken, had been short and dark, un-English-looking. But the other one spoke perfectly natural English. Almost too perfect. No, he was imagining things. All the same, he was worried for Zoltan.

Nina was lying curled up on the sofa, but she sat up when he came in.

"What was it?"

He told her.

"That's odd, isn't it?"

"No, not really." He explained briefly about Zoltan's fears, without telling her of his double identity. A confidence was a confidence, even from one's wife. She took a sudden interest in Zoltan's danger, eager for some subject other than herself, him, them, it, on which to fix her mind.

"Let's go for a short walk," she said. "I feel so fugged and sleepy."

On the Embankment she held his arm closely in both of hers, hanging on to it like a pillar of strength. The tide was high and dancing in the winter wind and the moon raced like a lunatic through the wild blown clouds. Like that other time, in the breeze of May, the moon had been mad then too. But it was December now, a mild December but still much colder than then. Compulsively, she led Gael along the same route, up to the same pale globes of gas that stood like sentinels along the parapet, back along the bushy length of garden towards Chelsea Old Church and then into the darkened path, and the black empty bench where she had first found herself in Howard's arms. She sat quietly, her head on his shoulder, talking about Zoltan, silently exorcising the place with their presence. She still wanted it to be Howard sitting there with her, Howard or whoever else he had come to represent, and she couldn't help closing her eyes as Howard's hand touched her in her imagination, opening her lips as his came down to meet them. Not even Gael's infinite understanding could restore her peace of mind yet, but she knew it would come, with time, if she clung to the emptied formalities of love and prayer. Time would fill them again.

"Look," said Gael suddenly, "isn't that Zoltan over there?"

He was standing a few yards away, at the foot of the Carlyle monument, looking up at it like a tourist. Carlyle's dark figure was thinking his black thoughts in a black shade, sitting absurdly in his Victorian chair, oblivious of the alien counter-revolutionary figure below. Nina followed Gael as he walked up to greet his friend.

Zoltan swung round with a start, his back to the statue, his arms out as if to protect it. A strange foreboding flooded Gael's mind: Carlyle had brought him nothing but bad luck. But he swept it aside, physically, with his hand before his eyes, like so many flies. Zoltan was looking at him wildly, then seemed to formulate his shape in the dark, but he called out:

"Friend or foe?"

"Zoltan! It's Gael. I'm your friend."

Zoltan moved away, backwards, watching the statue stupidly.

"My friend. Come, come quickly, over there, it's safer."

He led them further up the path, still walking backwards, glaring at them with his black eyes shining in the dim gaslight from the river parapet, his head outlined against the bare trees and the fairy castle of the illuminated bridge, his hair spiking out, his teeth clenched.

"Zoltan! It's all right, I'm your friend."

Gael's calm voice stopped his retrogressive steps. He stood irresolutely, but tensed again, as Gael touched his arm. Then his muscles relaxed a little when Gael said again: "I'm your friend. This is my wife, Nina. She's your friend, too."

"Your wife. Yes, I remember. She called me by another name once, so I had to stop her mouth. Stop her mouth. She has a very pretty mouth, your wife. Your wife is very pretty. Very small." He looked at her with sudden tenderness, as if in recognition of kindred helplessness.

"Zoltan Torday," said Nina gently, "I remember you too. Don't be frightened, Zoltan." She put out her hand to him.

"Árpád Szendrey," he replied formally, shaking hands and bowing. "Árpád Szendrey, poet and prisoner. Árpád Szendrey, a dead man. They are celebrating my centenary in Budapest. I am very important. Everyone has gone to celebrate my centenary, all the most important handshakers, speech-makers, chair-holders, boot-lickers, peace-makers, all-is-well-with-the-world-reporters, all, all, have gone to my city to celebrate my centenary. It is very important. *When the mosaic of bent head breaks, When the subcutaneous blood of anger splits The little, little atoms that make up the world Behind the world behind the world behind* . . . Erzsebèt, she translated me, with me . . . *subcutaneous*, she found that, I would not have known such a word, although I am a great poet in my own country, Árpád Szendrey, poet, prisoner, and dead man. How do you do?"

A shooing rustle in the bushes, swift steps on the pavement beyond them, and he was gone, racing along the path, bent double like a four-minute miler at the starting point, like a Red Indian in a Western film.

"What on earth . . ." Nina was terrified and clung to Gael as if she had seen a ghost, the ghost of her own fears. He took her to another bench and explained quickly, in a low voice, who Zoltan really was, why he was in danger. He was not only officially dead but erased from all reference books, all encyclopaedias, all histories, of literature. They had found out about his existence and they wanted him to disappear. They wanted his book to disappear, now that they knew who he was. The strain of fear had proved too much for him. He must go after him, to his home, try and find him, soothe him.

"Will you be all right, darling? Go straight home to bed, and take a sleeping pill and a hot drink. I'll be back as soon as I can."

"Yes of course. Hurry . . . Good luck," she called out after him as he streaked off in long strides, breaking into a run.

She didn't go straight home but sat down on the first bench again, beyond the statue, and lit a cigarette. Her bench, Howard's bench, their bench now exorcised by Gael's presence upon it. She wanted to make sure of it, to make sure of herself. As when the coward, aware for the first time of an alien but infinitesimal grain of courage, tests it too soon and performs some grotesque, useless act of bravery, so Nina sat alone on that malevolent bench, tantalising her newfound fragile calm with memories, urges brought about, almost automatically, by sudden solitude and opportunity. The moon had sailed further up the sky and the clouds were clearing, dropping away beyond the tall factory chimneys at the river-bend. The wind had fallen and the moon was perfectly still.

Suddenly, Howard was next to her.

"Hello, Nina. I'm back."

She gasped and drew away, then dropped her cigarette and fumbled for her bag as she got up.

"Nina, don't go. I got back this afternoon. I rang you up but there was no reply, so I assumed Gael was still in Oxford and you were out. Term's nearly over, isn't it, and I had to see you. I came round, hoping to catch you on your way in but after a while I came round here for old times' sake. So you had the same idea, eh?"

"Leave me alone, Howard." There was a catch in her voice but she turned to go. He grabbed her arm and pulled her down on the bench.

"That's not much of a welcome, Nina," he whined. "I've had a fine old time, I want to tell you all about it. Oh, darling, I missed you so. I wanted you to be with me, to enjoy it all. God, those nightclubs without you! That gypsy-music! Sentimental old bastard, that's me, kitsch gets me every time."

"Let me go, Howard, please." Her whisper was almost inaudible. "I don't want to see you any more," she added, a little more firmly. But her tone was dead and low.

"La, ma'am! Someone new?" he added jocularly, though his voice was pitched anxiously. "Or are you on the prowl again?"

She swung around and slapped his face. Then, as remorse and weakness stupidly, mechanically follow anger in emotionally exhausted women, she most untactically burst into tears.

"There, there," he murmured, "come to uncle Howard."

"You mustn't say things like that," she sobbed. "I'm trying, I'm desperately trying, I'm not what you think, really I'm not. I know I've seemed like it, with you, but I'm not, I'm not." She could hardly sink any lower than defend herself to him. Yet there she was, defending herself. She wanted, irrationally, compulsively, wanted at all costs to raise herself so high in his estimation as to make him feel there had never been anything, that she had never cared, had only played with him, uninvolved. But she was too bewildered to know how, and instead, humiliated herself.

"There, there," he said again. "I'm here. Me, sycamore tree. I'm always around."

She smiled through her tears.

"Haven't you got it wrong? It's God who's always around in the quad."

"But the sycamore tree will continue to be. Oh, darling, I've missed you like hell. I love you so."

He was fondling her again, touching her everywhere. Her blood seemed to drain from her as quickly as her tears. She sat paralysed, unable to get up, unable to stop his roving fingers, and she started talking, quickly, breathlessly, about her walk with Gael, about exorcising the bench, about meeting Zoltan, who was really Szendrey, about his extraordinary behaviour, his flight, Gael's chase, talking, talking, saying anything to show that she hadn't been out in the street, alone, to show that she was at one with Gael, to stop her blood from racing round, to stop his deadly, poisonous touch.

She stopped the latter all right. His hand dropped away and he sat up with a jerk.

"You mean this man's an impostor, a fraud? That he's written a book on himself?" The knowing look came over his face even in the darkness. "I *thought* there was *something* phoney about him. Oh, lordy! So he thought he was going to make a fool of me, did he! Well, he's very much mistaken. Very much mistaken."

"Oh, Howard, but——"

"You remember Tom Truelove telling me the book had disappeared? No wonder, by God! This madman must have really got the wind-up. By Jove, I'd like to lay my hands on that manuscript. I'd show him up for the phoney he is. Why, and he had the nerve to call me a potential collaborator..."

He went on talking, almost to himself. Nina was utterly alone, with his voice, with his hand on her knee, not roving any more, not loving any more, nothing loving, nobody loving. The moon stared into her mind, blankly, unloving, and there deposited the sperm of a mad idea, filling out slowly, enormously, dislodging, pushing away all else that was not itself, growing into a big full moon of calm, white conviction, a vast power for earning back his attention, and his respect. His attention and his respect, at all cost.

"I know where it is," she said quietly.

"Where what is?"

"The manuscript."

"Good heavens, girl, tell me."

"Come."

She got up and walked slowly up the path towards the illuminated bridge. There seemed not a doubt in her mind. She remembered Zoltan's wild, protective gesture. How he had thought of it she didn't even wonder. She knew. She put her foot on the pedestal and her hand on Howard's shoulder. She reached up to the little pile of leaden books underneath Carlyle's black chair. There on the top of it was a small rectangular parcel in dark grey paper. She stepped down with it and handed it to Howard.

"Well, bless my soul! How on earth did you——"

Suddenly a shot rang out. He was so startled his heart missed a beat and he stood stock-still with Nina suddenly in his arms, and he was horribly aware of the scurrying in the bushes and the swiftly running steps, but unable to move. Then she slumped at his feet.

Chapter Twenty-One

HIS feet were leaden books as he tried to run towards the bridge. There was a taxi hut there, but no taxis. He banged on the door. It was locked. The place was empty. Oh, God! Where? How? The police telephone box by the bridge. Across the road. Red lights. Not a car in sight. Quick. She had moaned. She was still alive. He didn't even know where she was shot. His feet were leaden books as he struggled back, through thick webs of terror and barbed wire entanglements of love and hate. That madman, that murderer. She was still there. Nobody had stirred, not a window had opened. People could be shot and nobody would know. A car backfiring, they would think. Carry her to the bench. No, mustn't move her. The police. Murder. Oh, God, make her alive, make her live. But it wasn't murder, she was alive. Must make her comfortable. No, mustn't move her, it might hurt. Carry her, lift her gently, so light she is, so pale. Her blood warm on my arm, through the sleeve. There, her head on my lap. Would they never come? God you can't allow this. God if you allow this you don't exist, oh God, why am I praying when you've never existed. Please, please let her live. I'll do anything you say. Why don't you make them come. Jingling, jingling, jingling, what the hell's all that jingling, why don't they stop it, they'll wake her up, she's ill, very ill, who the hell's making all that noise?

They arrived, they surrounded him, they put her on a stretcher, they took her away. Questions. A police car. The station. More questions. A cup of terrible tea, which he couldn't drink. He knew he was talking clearly, coherently, but he couldn't hear himself, he couldn't remember later.

"You must ring up her husband. He went off earlier, after the Hungarian. I don't know when he'll be back. You must go on ringing up all night.

He must get to her. He must know. Promise me you will ring up."

"Of course, sir, we'll do all we can."

They washed his sleeve for him. They were very kind, and utterly useless to Nina. He rang up Elizabeth. He was going to the hospital, he didn't know when he'd be back.

At one o'clock Gael came into the anteroom. The place was like a prison hospital, a workhouse hospital with long stone corridors and green tiles and screeching wardroom doors. Outside it had looked like a church, a nineteenth-century monstrosity with a black square tower and a Gothic porch. Opposite, Howard had caught a morbid glimpse of the inevitable undertaker's shop, with a large marble cross in the window and an electric clock, pointing at five to twelve.

Gael started when he saw Howard, but shock and anxiety united them.

"They're operating. The bullet hit her in the back, on the right side, but near the heart. There's absolutely nothing we can do but wait."

Gael sat down, his hands clenched together, touching his brow. His eyes were shut, as if he were praying.

"Tell me what happened," he said quietly after a long silence.

"I'd been to see a friend round here. I was walking along the path in the Embankment Gardens and saw Nina sitting on the bench, smoking a cigarette. I said hello, and sat down. She seemed—very far away in her thoughts, not particularly pleased to see me." Howard wanted so much to comfort Gael, and this was the only way he knew. Under the stress of emotion, with so much understood and left unsaid, he could be gentle enough. "I just chatted of this and that, and happened to mention Zoltan's manuscript, which disappeared some time ago from Truelove's office. They were going to publish it. To my astonishment Nina suddenly said she knew where it was. She got up, with such conviction, and almost as in a trance. I followed her and she went up to the statue of Carlyle. She climbed on the pedestal and there it was, on top of the pile of leaden books under his chair. Zoltan must have put it there, earlier. Then suddenly there was a shot, and Nina . . . fell at my feet." Howard began to sob silently, tearlessly, his face in his hands. After a while he fumbled for a cigarette and offered one to Gael. Gael shook his head.

"I thought he'd gone home. He was in a terrible state. I looked all over Holborn for him. He needed me. But oh God, Nina needed me more. Why did I leave her? Why did I leave her?"

The surgeon came in at last. They leapt up, anxiety tearing the moment of silence into worse silence, shreds of silence that strangled their queries.

"I think she's going to be all right, Mr Jackson. But she's still on the danger list. I've done my very best, I assure you."

"Can I see her, please?"

"She will be unconscious for many hours, Mr Jackson. Go home and get some sleep, if you can. Come back tomorrow at noon and we may allow you to see her for a few seconds, if she shows signs of pulling out of it. But ring up the office earlier, they'll give you news of her progress. Goodnight."

"Thank you, sir."

They went out miserably together, all hatred and suspicion drowned in a new bond of guilt and fear.

"If only I hadn't left her," Gael kept repeating. "If only I could understand. What made me leave her? What made me go after that... that... Why did he do it? If only I could understand."

"I hope they get him," Howard muttered.

"I expect they will. Poor Zoltan."

Howard was left speechless by the unnaturalness of Gael's charity. A wave of indignation swept over him physically, like something knocking him down, preventing him from acknowledging or even recognising Gael's uncanny charity towards him. How easily Gael could have ignored him, told him to clear out, to leave him in peace at last, in this their mutual terror.

"Would you like to come home and have some coffee?" Gael asked instead. "I can't sleep, I shall sit up, and I ... it's not that I want to talk ... and I don't expect ... I mean, if you would like to ... stay up with me."

They did talk, on and off, between long silences. Much was half-said, much more was understood. Nothing was forgiven, but suspended only, in a moment of disbelief. At six o'clock Gael rang the hospital. No change. At seven: no change. The cigarettes Howard had smoked were piled high in the ashtray. Children's voices twittered upstairs, counterpointed by Frieda's scolding and much banging and thumping. Gael went out and up to the second floor. The noise quietened a little.

"You didn't tell them?" Howard asked anxiously.

"No, I just said she was ill in hospital, and asked Frieda to take over."

After half an hour, Frieda brought them some breakfast. She knew from their faces and the visitor's presence that it was more serious than Gael had implied, and went out without a word, though by now she had reached the letter *t* and had a considerable vocabulary at her disposal. They couldn't eat much, but the coffee revived them.

"I must see Zoltan," said Gael, "I must find him. He must know what he's done. He must come and see what he's done."

"But how——"

"I think I know where he is." Howard looked at him with terror. The same tone, the same quiet, mad conviction was in his voice as there had been in Nina's, when she had uttered almost the same sentence. "Come," he added gently.

It was the early rush hour and they were separated on the crowded bus journey to Holborn. Two police cars had pulled up outside Ely Place, waiting, doing nothing. The winter morning was brisk and tactlessly bright. A few people came out of the church in the cul-de-sac, and gazed curiously at the cars, then went on their various ways to work and home. A policeman got out of the second car and walked over to them.

"Mr Jackson?"

"Yes." He had waited for Gael on his doorstep the night before and broken the news.

"I thought I recognised you, sir. Good morning, Mr Cutting. One of our cars spotted the man early this morning. He hadn't been to his home, but we were scouring the area. He skipped in there. Clever bastard. The police aren't allowed in there unless called. There's nobody around yet, except the priest, and he's holding a service. Our man's inside."

"In the church, you mean?"

"Yes."

"Can't you get hold of the priest?"

"We did, earlier on. We rang him up and he said he can't turn anyone out of the church."

"Sanctuary," Gael murmured.

"I beg your pardon, sir?"

"Nothing. An old medieval custom. Durham Cathedral, you know, was a famous sanctuary for criminals and outlaws. Once they touched the great knocker on the door, they couldn't be harmed."

"Well, this isn't quite the same, sir. We're not allowed in that street at all, unless called in by one of the inhabitants. The church just happens to be in there and the priest can't force him out. I see that. But if he came out, then anyone could call us in, and even now the priest could call us in if he wanted to. But the man hasn't done anything yet to warrant that."

"He may, though," said Howard. "He's mad."

"Quite so. And we should prevent it. The question is how."

"One of us could go in and talk to him," Howard suggested.

"It might be dangerous, sir."

"Mass should be over in a minute," said Gael, looking at his watch. It was nearly nine, "did it start at eight-thirty?"

"Yes, sir."

"We'd better wait till the people are out: I don't think he'll do anything rash now."

"Well, he may, sir."

"I don't think so," Gael repeated firmly. "We'll have to risk it. I can talk to him more easily if the church is empty."

"All right, sir. Thank you, sir."

The policeman went back to the car. He spoke to someone inside and a plainclothes man got out, looked at Gael for a moment and walked over to the gate, where they were standing. He nodded at them, and Howard recognised him as the man from the Holborn police, who had come to see him.

"Morning, Mr Cutting. You'll be careful, won't you, Mr Jackson?"

"Yes. He's my . . . friend."

The plainclothes man nodded and stood with them, smoking, waiting. . . .

"Hello, Jackson, what's all this?" Mr Quentin Yellowstone, whose office was in Ely Place, toddled up to him as a nearby clock clanged its nine strokes into their fears. "Why, Mr Cutting!"

"You tell him, Gael, I'll go and ring up the hospital again."

Gael explained what had happened, in a dry toneless voice.

"I want to talk to him, Yellowstone. I must tell him she may be all right. He must know, he's probably desperate."

"That's all very well, Jackson, but you're running a terrible risk." Yellowstone looked grave. "You should be at your wife's bedside. She can't afford to lose you now. And what about your children, if anything should __"

"The hospital told me I couldn't see her till twelve. I've been ringing every hour and there's no change. Howard's gone to telephone again now. Of course I'll go if I can see her. But if not I might as well stay here. This man may kill someone, or himself."

"He may kill you. Look, Jackson, I can call the police in, officially. They can wait outside the door of the church, after all he can't stay there for ever. In fact, they can go into the church if the priest will let them. Wouldn't that be wiser?"

"He might kill one of them, just as easily. I must talk to him. Look, they're coming out."

A little troop of people clustered into the light. Some talked to the curate outside the door, some filed past him and up the steps into the street, walking towards the gate. The policemen were still inside the two cars and attracted little attention. The sight of three men talking at the gate was not particularly remarkable. Behind them London life continued apace, girls trotted to work on their high heels, men strode past quickly, buses and cars rumbled by, oblivious of any drama.

Howard returned from the telephone box panting. "No change."

Gael walked slowly up towards the church. Meanwhile, Mr Yellowstone talked to the inspector, and the inspector walked with him towards the police car. Headquarters were called up by radio.

"Is the church empty, father?"

"You are Mr—er—Jackson?"

"Yes."

"Your friend is in there, Mr Jackson. He is praying."

"Thank you, father."

"God bless you, my son."

Gael was wearing rubber soles and entered the church silently.

The lights were still on after the service, and candles blazed before every statue. Gael slipped behind a pillar. Zoltan was in a back pew, alone, to the right of the pillar, his head bowed in his hands.

"Zoltan, this is Gael Jackson, your friend." His voice was calm, very quiet. Zoltan raised his head and stared at the altar, without moving.

"I killed him, Gael, I shot him. The husband of Erzsebèt. When the girl got my book and gave it to him. The communist agents stole it, from that office where they were going to print it. I knew who it was. I stole it back. But I had to hide it somewhere nobody would think of looking. I came to your house, Gael, but I knew they would come. They did come. I saw them. Then I found the statue. But the girl took it, she was a spy, she was with the husband of Erzsebèt, who is a fool. I killed him."

"But you missed him, Zoltan."

There was a silence. Still he didn't move, his eyes were fixed on the dead altar against the rough stone wall. He was talking to the altar, not to Gael.

"You mean he is not dead?"

"It was my wife you shot, Zoltan. She——"

His head dropped down again and his hands covered his ears. The silence so choked Gael's throat he couldn't speak. Five hours, five years, five centuries passed in those five minutes. Then Zoltan sat back on the bench, struggled to his feet holding on to the rail. He didn't even look for Gael, hidden behind his pillar. He assumed invisibility to be the most natural of phenomena, as if the altar itself had spoken.

"I will pay the penalty," he muttered and stumbled out of the pew towards the door.

"Zoltan, the police are out there." Gael suddenly appeared from behind the pillar, but Zoltan was staring at the rectangle of light through the door, and seemed entirely unaware of his physical presence.

"I know, I know. I heard the cars drive in. They must have broken the law. The police always break the law. But I have broken the sixth commandment, and more. I have broken, I have broken, I have broken ... the bonds of love ... friendship ... I have broken ... my soul ..."

"Zoltan, she is alive, she will be all right, she ... Zoltan, she will want to see you. I have forgiven you ... she will ... "

He wouldn't hear, the voice of love that passeth all understanding had sunk away into nonexistence as disintegration and death flooded his brain. He walked into the square of the light, out of the house of sanity and there at the foot of the steps leading up to the street and the waiting black hearses, he shot himself. Both his selves. His aim was dead accurate.

Chapter Twenty-Two

THE house of physical sanity looked like a ghastly parody of a church, with its tall black tower and its hideous Gothic porch, outside which the faithful, the visitors of the sick and old and dying, crowded at a quarter to seven every evening, carrying flowers, baskets of fruit, bottles and boxes, bundles of laundry, and all the shrouding, comforting, feeding, blessing paraphernalia that accompanies the dead on their long journey through the ancient pyramids of timelessness. Opposite, the hopeful clock of the undertaker ticked away its mockery of life behind the white marble cross.

The newspapers had blared its gruesome headlines for two days, increasing their vulgar familiarity: AUTHOR'S WIFE SHOT BY MAD HUNGARIAN... WHERE IS THE MAD HUNGARIAN?... MAD HUNGARIAN SHOOTS HIMSELF IN CHURCH PORCH... NINA: DOCTORS STILL HOPE... NINA HAS LAST SACRAMENT... NINA: IMPROVEMENT. NINA, NINA, NINA.

Gael had sent the children away with Frieda and had shut down the house, which was becoming intolerable with telephone calls and enquiring journalists. The telephone's insistent ringing turned his stomach every time. To think he had originally planned *The Sycamore Tree* as a collection of telephone conversations. He could look only at its white receiver in horror and it looked like a bone, his own arm, through which the ringing shrilled along his veins from the devilish communication system of his nerves. He had taken refuge with Mr Truelove, in his smart Kensington house, and Mr Truelove was the soul of tact. Phineas Antrobus had offered to put up the children and Frieda in his country cottage outside Cambridge, where his unmarried wife was looking after them. Phineas himself was in London, rallying round Gael and bringing Nina books which she couldn't read, fruit which she couldn't eat. He was the only person, apart from Gael, whom she did not refuse to see. Charles and Sonya had come, and Mr Truelove, Jocelyn and Mr Yellowstone, even Dr Grobel from the hospital and Dr Funk from the clinic had called. And of course Howard.

Howard almost lived in the waiting room, in cafés and pubs outside in the drab Fulham Road, on the porch. But she refused to see him, she refused to see them all, but him especially. He came every day from High Street, Kensington, from staring at his damnable chestnut tree in the backyard. Its branches were bare of leaves, bare of blessing hands. And Gloucester Road was being pulled up once more; the 49 bus was going down Queen's Gate, empty of Nina, empty of her laughter and her love. It was over, she had won her bet: the buses would still be going down Queen's Gate when it was over. Queen's Gate, with its green-palmed plane-trees. The common sycamore tree: *acer pseudo-platanus* or bastard plane tree maple. He was drinking heavily, double whiskies in the pubs, black coffees by the dozen in the coffee bars. Intolerable thoughts crowded through the whisky fumes, he couldn't stand the sight of the ambulant flower stall outside the hospital. Chrysanthemums and dahlias, in garish colours, shouted the smell of death every time he passed, death, flowers, coffins, and if you think you're going to turn that son of mine into a ruddy intellectual you're very much mistaken. That terrible white cross, he wanted to throw bricks into the undertaker's window, to pile up barrel-loads of bulbs, and cartloads of manure over that malevolent white cross.

On the third day Elizabeth came, pale, dishevelled. Nina allowed her in. Gael was sitting by her bedside, holding her hand. She was so white, and so still, her chest thickly bandaged, and unable to move. Her eyes looked enormous under the straight black fringe.

"Elizabeth," she whispered, "I asked you once to come and see me. You never did . . . Only that . . . awful dinner . . . You could have . . . helped me."

"I've come now. Nina, I'm so very sorry."

"No, don't be, Elizabeth . . ." She could hardly speak, she breathed words almost as God must have breathed our reality into existence. "It's me . . . I am sorry . . . I took . . . him . . . How . . ." She closed her eyes and made a tremendous effort. "Howard . . . away . . . from you . . . not all of him . . . only the worst part . . . and now Zoltan . . . Forgive me."

Elizabeth couldn't bear it and started to cry softly, her head on Nina's left hand.

"Don't cry, Elizabeth. Tell him . . . he must . . . get it back . . . that worst part . . . he gave away . . . get it back into . . . himself . . . and contain it . . . live with it . . . accept it . . . not . . . project it . . . outside . . . on to others . . . who can't . . . who haven't the strength to . . . cope with it. Tell him that . . . from me."

"I will, I will."

"You're pretty, Elizabeth." Her large blue eyes gazed at her with wonder. "You must remember that . . . have your clothes made to measure . . . it makes all the difference . . . then you feel . . . made to measure . . . inside." She suddenly fell asleep, breathing irregularly, with difficulty, her right hand in Gael's.

The next day she was much better, and talked a little more easily. But she was still as white as the hospital wall behind her.

"Gael."

"Yes, darling?"

"Did they . . . did they give me the Sacrament?"

"Honey . . . yes, I'm afraid I—it was touch and go, my darling, at one point, the doctor gave you an hour. You were unconscious, but I—oh, honey, but you came through."

He buried his face in her hand, which was in his, and her fingers moved slightly to touch his hair.

"I wasn't unconscious, all the time. I remember something vaguely . . . words, and incense and ether. But I couldn't open my eyes, and I kept going out. I couldn't speak, Gael, it's no use if I didn't confess."

"It would have been, my darling, but you're all right now, don't tire yourself, you must keep very still."

"Yes."

She closed her eyes, still holding his hand.

"Gael."

"Yes?"

She spoke with her eyes still closed.

"Your having had a vocation wouldn't do, would it?"

There was a long pause as he painfully took in the question's implications: he was still the *pretre manque* in her eyes, symbol of the authority one had, to bend under or break.

"No, darling, I'm afraid it wouldn't."

"I want you to hear my confession."

Her blue eyes were wide open upon him, unafraid, undeceived by the folly of her sentence, and he knew then that she was speaking to him, her husband, at last truly her husband. He bent his head down again and wept, not the mere tears of stress and strain, but the tears of a man moved beyond endurance.

"Don't. Darling, my own sweet Nina, I know, I know."

"Yes." She was very calm, and still had to speak slowly. "But not everything. I met ... him ... on the Embankment. In May. I was ... soliciting. I didn't want ... it ... only, somehow, the situation, the excitement. He ... used, me, he destroyed me, but he also helped me. I was so afraid, I couldn't under——"

"Darling, stop. I know. I've known all along. I couldn't reach you, help you, oh, Nina, Nina, I was paralysed, it was my fault, I put up such a barrier ..."

"Don't cry, Gael. Your tears, perhaps they are my absolution. But they make me want to cry, and I can't. Ouch, it hurts when I swallow the lump of tears."

"Nina, my sweet, don't talk, rest. I'm here, I'll always be by your side. You don't have to say anything."

But she wanted to talk, to bathe in their renewed understanding, which was still so young it needed words.

"You said, didn't you, about accidents. How we push towards drama, push the other person till he has to initiate the drama, the break ... the unmasking . . . something from outside, anything not to choose." She was panting and stopped for a moment. "Then something quite different happens. And it wouldn't have happened if one hadn't . . . pushed . . . to the very end, if only one had . . . got well before. If I had gone straight home like you said . . . If I hadn't, in the end . . . betrayed . . . to impress him . . . betrayed, not just you, us, but myself, your confidence in me, and that Hungarian's . . . confidence in you. It was right that he should have . . . I mean, that the thing from outside, should be him. But I didn't lose my legs, did I? I lost . . . my heart. Do you think it stopped, and they did one of those deep-freeze things? I always wondered what Lazarus felt like when he came back."

"Honey, *please* don't talk so much."

"No."

She was silent for a long time and the clock ticked loudly into the silence, much faster than her heartbeat. Then she spoke again, her eyes still shut.

"Gael, I want you to tell Josephine, later, that it doesn't work, the Crucifixion, unless one wants it to. She was asking one day, and she said it didn't work. When she's a little older, tell her, won't you, that I said that, though I couldn't wear a plate on my head. That's what she called haloes, plates. She was so sweet. . . . I didn't want it to work. Perhaps even now I don't want it to. It's frightening, sickening. But don't say I said that. And tell Marisa and Michael . . ."

She stopped, suddenly exhausted.

"But darling, darling, you will tell them yourself. You're so much better. You'll get strong, very slowly, but you will. I'll take care of you, my darling, my honey."

"Yes. You will, won't you?"

She smiled, without opening her eyes.

"Of course I will. We'll start all over—oh, darling, we never stopped."

"No. We never stopped."

Her hand moved gently in his, her wrist was so small he couldn't take his eyes off it, as if seeing it for the first time. That's what marriage is, he thought, suddenly seeing things for the first time, things you have seen for the first time over and over again. A new person in front of you, at breakfast or at dinner or in bed, a person you know so well, new every day, the same person, the same essence freshly seen.

"He will ... encapsulate it," she murmured unexpectedly. Through her smile flickered the shadow of her special irony, her special gaiety even, her special self. "Like a bullet you can't take out, and it stays there, forming its own protection of skin, and doesn't hurt any more ... He will harden over it ... he'll be all right. He'll go very far."

Phineas Antrobus came in and kissed her left hand. Her right hand was permanently in Gael's, her left was free for her few and only true friends.

"Nina, my sweet, you look much better."

"Yes. I feel better."

"Marjorie rang up. The children are doing fine. They're very happy in the country."

"Yes. Is it a farm? Is there a stable, with cows and donkeys?"

"No, Nina, I'm afraid not, It's just a typical English village, with pretty houses and secluded cottages for rich townsfolk."

"Phinny, how can you not have a stable? You, a one-year-old cowshed?"

"Perhaps because I'm only one-year-old, Nina. An ancient, primitive Germanic cowshed who's only one-year-old."

"I think . . . the sonnets of Shakespeare are written in some sort of Greek, Phinny."

"Psychic Greek."

"Yes. Psychic pseudo-Greek." She smiled at him happily. "Everything is pseudo, Phinny, life is only a pseudo-heaven, a pseudo-hell. But a little pseudo-madness is often nearer to the truth, and often the saner ones seem mad to others, but they are pseudo-mad, Phinny . . . It's the sane ones who are really mad. Even the sycamore tree is only a pseudo-plane tree. Not like the one in the Bible, that's a real sycamore."

"Darling, darling," said Gael, "don't tire yourself."

"I'm so happy, Gael."

"I'm so happy, too. Darling, I'm going to rewrite *The Sycamore Tree*. With a new character."

"He may exist."

"But he'll be nice. Very nice. I've got a new beginning, darling, isn't that a good omen? A new opening sentence, quite different, not like the opening sentence which I lost and found again. That was a bad omen. I shan't lose this one. It's real, it's much better. *The Sycamore Tree* will come into existence again."

"You do that, Gael . . . Please do it . . . please write it . . . always . . . remember . . . I love you." She closed her eyes.

And she wasn't there anymore. She was dead.

www.ingramcontent.com/pod-product-compliance
Ingram Content Group UK Ltd.
Pitfield, Milton Keynes, MK11 3LW, UK
UKHW021300180426
11947UKWH00015B/942